This Limited Edition of
*McCone and Friends*
by Marcia Muller
is one of 350 clothbound copies
signed and numbered by the author.

Accompanying each copy
is a separately printed pamphlet,
*The Time of the Wolves*
by Marcia Muller.

Number

# McCone and Friends

# M^cCONE
## and Friends

# MARCIA MULLER

Crippen & Landru Publishers
Norfolk, Virginia
2000

Cover painting by Carol Heyer; cover design by Deborah Miller

Crippen & Landru logo by Eric D. Greene

ISBN (limited edition): 1-885941-37-4
ISBN (trade edition): 1-885941-38-2

FIRST EDITION

10 9 8 7 6 5 4 3 2 1

Crippen & Landru Publishers
P. O. Box 9315
Norfolk, VA 23505
USA

Email: CrippenL@Pilot.Infi.Net
Web: www.crippenlandru.com

For Sandi and Doug Greene,

Good People,

Good Publishers

# CONTENTS

*Introduction*                                                      11

If You Can't Take the Heat (*Sharon McCone*)                       15

The Holes in the System (*Rae Kelleher*)                           25

One Final Arrangement (*Mick Savage*)                              49

Up at the Riverside (*Ted Smalley*)                                65

Knives at Midnight (*Sharon McCone*)                               84

The Wall (*Rae Kelleher*)                                          108

Recycle (*Hy Ripinsky*)                                            180

Solo (*Sharon McCone*)                                             188

# INTRODUCTION

Sharon McCone was conceived in 1971, when an insistent and sometimes annoying woman's voice inside my head began demanding I pay attention to her. For months I'd been toying with the idea of creating a female counterpart to the male private investigators whose adventures I so loved reading about; now, it seemed, she wanted to be heard. But as insistent as she sounded, at first she gave me few clues as to her identity. In fact, she seemed more intent upon impressing on me who and what she was *not*.

She was not the kind of private detective who has a bottle stashed in the desk drawer. She was not emotionally immune to the depressing and often tragic events she encountered on San Francisco's mean streets. She did not operate out of a shabby, one-woman down-town office. She was not a loner.

Well, fine. But who and what *was* she?

Some of the specifics proved surprisingly easy to pin down, for I sensed a close kinship between us from the start. She was the kind of woman who liked her wine but didn't let it interfere with business. She was an emotional, caring woman who fully inter-acted with the world and those around her. She worked for an organization whose philosophy and goals reflected her humani-tarian sentiments—All Souls Legal Cooperative, a poverty-law firm. And she had family, friends, love interests.

The family, friends, and love interests developed slowly over five years of writing manuscripts that can only be described as learning experiences. When the first McCone novel, *Edwin of the Iron Shoes*, finally saw publication in 1977, Sharon possessed a large, mostly dysfunctional clan based in San Diego; a boss who had been her closest male friend at University of California at Berkeley; another friend who provided information that enabled her to crack this first case; and a potential lover. Over the ensuing 21 years she has acquired a large (and somewhat confusing, even to the author) circle of friends and associates.

In 1993 I began to experiment with the voice of some of these friends in a number of short stories in which McCone would be viewed through their eyes and sometimes upstaged by their detecting abilities—my way of keeping her fresh and multi-faceted in my own mind, while trying to entertain the reader in a different way than in the novels. These tales, along with three stories from Sharon's point of view, are collected for the first time in *McCone and Friends*.

Rae Kelleher, who narrates two of the stories, initially appeared as McCone's new assistant in *There's Something in a Sunday* (1989), and was the first employee Sharon hired when she moved her new agency from All Souls Legal Cooperative to their present offices in Pier 24 ½. Rae also narrated sections of *The Broken Promise Land* (1996); the events set in motion there will culminate when she marries McCone's former brother-in-law (*Listen to the Silence*, 2000). Both of Rae's tales, "The Wall" and "The Holes in the System," date from the period while she and McCone were still employed at All Souls.

Mick Savage, McCone's nephew, first appeared in the 1990 short story, "Silent Night" (collected in *The McCone Files*, 1995), in which he ran away from his southern California home and his aunt was forced to track him down on Christmas Eve. Still a troubled young man, he was sent to work for her in *Till the Butchers Cut Him Down* (1992), and soon revolutionized her operations with his computer expertise. In "One Final Arrangement," he and another McCone operative, Charlotte Keim, work along with her to prevent a killer from inheriting his missing wife's fortune.

Ted Smalley, originally secretary and later office manager at All Souls, also accompanied McCone Investigations to their new headquarters, and has emerged from a crossword-solver who didn't even possess a last name to one of the most significant characters in the series. He represents San Francisco's gay community, and his personal problems formed a major plot element of *While Other People Sleep* (1998). In "Up at the Riverside," Ted's membership in this community allows him to give McCone insights into a decades-old crime.

Hy Ripinsky, McCone's long-term lover, seldom interferes with her investigations. Although he himself is an expert on hostage-negotiation and a partner in an international corporate security firm, he keeps his distance while she's working—having learned from "long and sometimes hellacious experience" that this is the wisest course. However, in "Recycle," Ripinsky is prompted to depart from his "hands-off attitude."

One of the McCone stories, "Knives at Midnight," is another case she reluctantly shares—this time with older brother John, who first intruded onto her investigative turf in *Wolf in the Shadows* (1993). The other two, "If You Can't Take the Heat" and "Solo," reflect her growing love of flight and understanding of the world of aviation.

I hope the stories collected here will display new aspects of Sharon McCone's character, as well as better acquaint you, the reader, with other ongoing series characters. More important, I hope that when McCone soars into the air on the last page, you'll have enjoyed these glimpses into the world she and her friends inhabit!

Marcia Muller
Petaluma, California
September 30, 1999

# IF YOU CAN'T TAKE THE HEAT
## (Sharon McCone)

The private investigation business has been glamorized to death by writers and filmmakers, but I can tell you firsthand that more often than not it's downright tedious. Even though I own a small agency and have three operatives to take on the scut work, I still conduct a fair number of surveillances while twisted into unnatural positions in the front seat of my car, or standing in the rain when any fool would go inside. Last month I leaped at the chance to take on a job with a little more pizzazz—and even then ended up to my neck in mud. Quite literally.

The job came to me from a contact at a small air-charter company—Wide Horizons—located at Oakland Airport's North Field. I fly in and out of there frequently, both in the passenger's and pilot's seat of my friend Hy Ripinsky's Citabria, and when you're around an airport a lot, you get to know people. When Wide Horizons' owner, Gordon Tillis, became nervous about a pair of regular customers, he called me into his office.

"Here's the problem," he told me. "For three months now, Sam Delaney's been flying what he calls 'a couple of babes' to Calistoga, in the Napa Valley. Always on the same day—the last Wednesday. On the flight there they're tense, clutch at their briefcases, don't talk much. A limo picks them up, they're gone a few hours. And when they come back, it's a whole different story."

"How so?"

"Well, I heard this from this airport manager up there, and Sam confirms it. They're excited, giddy with relief. Once it was obvious they'd been drinking too much; another time they had new hairdos and new clothes. They call a lot of attention to themselves."

"Sounds to me like a couple of rich women who like to fly, shop and do some wine tasting—and who don't hold their alcohol too well."

"It would sound that way to me too except for two things: the initial nervousness and the fact that they come back flush with cash."

"How do you know?"

"They pay cash for the charter, and one time I got a look into their briefcases. Even after the plane rental and a big tip for Sam, there was plenty left."

The cash did put a different spin on it. "I assume you think they might be carrying some illegal substance?"

Gordon nodded.

"So why don't you tell Sam to search their cases? The FAA gives him the authority to, as pilot in command."

Gordon got up and went to the window, opened the blinds and motioned at the field. "You see all those aircraft sitting idle? There're pilots sitting idle, too. Sam doesn't get paid when he doesn't fly; my overhead doesn't get paid while those planes are tied down. In this economy, neither of us can afford to lose paying customers."

"Security at the main terminal X-rays bags—"

"That's the main terminal; people expect it there. If Sam suddenly demands to go through those women's personal effects and word gets out, people might take their business elsewhere. If he does it in a way that embarrasses them—and, face it, Sam's not your most tactful guy—we're opening the door for a lawsuit."

"But you also don't want your planes used for illegal purposes. I see your problem."

In the end, Gordon and I worked out a plan where I would ride in the fourth seat of the Cessna that Sam would fly to Calistoga the next Wednesday. My cover story was that I was a new hire learning the ropes. I found myself looking forward to the job; it sounded a whole lot more interesting than the stakeout at a deadbeat dad's apartment that I had planned for the evening.

❖ ❖ ❖

"They're babes, all right," Sam Delaney said, "but I'll let you judge for yourself." He grunted as he stowed his bag of take-out cartons in the back of the plane—his lunch, he'd informed me earlier. Business had been so bad recently that he couldn't even afford the relatively inexpensive airport diners. Eating bad take-out food, I thought, probably accounted for the weight Sam had gained in the year or so that I'd known him. He'd always had a round face under his mop of brown curls, but now it resembled a chipmunk's, and his body was growing round to match. Poor guy had probably hired on with Wide Horizons thinking to build up enough hours for a lucrative job with the airlines; now he wasn't flying enough to go to a decent restaurant.

"Here they come," he whispered to me. "Look at them—they make heads turn, especially when they've had a few pops of that Napa Valley vino."

The women were attractive, and a number of heads did turn as they crossed from the charter service. But people take notice of any woman tripping across the tarmac in high heels, her brightly colored silk dress blowing in the breeze. We women pilots are pretty much confined to athletic shoes, shirts and pants in cotton and denim—and the darker the color, the less the gas and oil and grease stains will show.

The woman Sam introduced as Melissa Wells had shoulder-length red hair and looked as though she could have used a few more hours' sleep; Angie Holbrook wore her dark hair close-cropped and spoke in a clipped manner that betrayed her tension. Neither had more to say than basic greetings, and they settled into the back seats quickly, refusing headsets. During the thirty-minute flight, Melissa sipped at a large container of coffee she'd brought along and Angie tapped her manicured fingernails against her expensive leather briefcase. Sam insisted on keeping up the fiction that I was a new Wide Horizons pilot by chattering at me—even though over the noise of the engine the women couldn't hear a word we said through our linked headsets.

"Gordon's real strict about the paperwork. Plan's got to be on file, and complete.  Weight-and-balance calculation, too.  It's not difficult, though; each of us has got his own routes.  Mine're the Napa and Sonoma Valleys.  I'd like to get some of the longer trips, build up more hours that way, but I don't have enough seniority with the company.  At least I get to look at some pretty scenery."

He certainly did.   It was springtime, and the length of California's prime wine-growing valley was in its splendor.  Gentle hills, looking as if someone had shaped bolt after bolt of green velvet to their contours; brilliant slashes of yellow where the wild mustard bloomed; orchards in pink and white flower.  It made me want to snatch Sam's takeout and go on a picnic.

We touched down at Calistoga shortly before ten.  The limo was there for Melissa and Angie, as was the rental car Wide Horizons had arranged for me.  I waited till the limo cleared the parking lot, then jumped into the rental and followed, noting the other car's license number.  It took the main road south for several miles, past wineries offering tours and tasting, then turned off onto a secondary road and drove into the hills to the west. I held back, allowing a sports car to get between us; the sports car put on its brakes abruptly as it whipped around a curve, and by the time I'd avoided a collision, the limo had turned through a pair of stone pillars flanking a steep driveway.  The security gates closed, and the car snaked uphill and disappeared into the trees.

I pulled my rental into the shade of a scrub oak on the far side of the road and got out.  It was very quiet there; I could hear only birds in a grove of acacia trees on the other side of the high stone wall.   I walked its length, looking for something that would identify the owner of the heavily wooded property, but saw nothing and no way to gain access.  Finally I went back to the car to wait it out.

Why did everything always seem to boil down to another stakeout?

And three hours later was when I found myself up to my neck in mud.

❖  ❖  ❖

The limo had departed the estate in the hills and, after a few wine-tasting stops, deposited Melissa and Angie at the Serenata Spa in Calistoga. Calistoga is famed for its hot springs, and initially I'd fancied myself eavesdropping on the pair while floating in a tub of mineral water. But Calistoga is also famed for its mud baths, and in order to get close enough, I'd had to opt for my own private wallow. As I sunk into the gritty stuff—stifling a cry of disgust—I could clearly hear Angie's voice through the flimsy pink partition. In spite of the wine they'd sampled, she sounded as tense as before.

"Well, what do you think? Honestly?"

"They're high on it."

"But are they high enough?"

"They paid us, didn't they?"

"Yes, but . . ."

"Angie, it was the best we could come up with. And I thought it was damn good."

"It's getting more difficult to come up with the stuff without making it too obvious what we're doing. And this idea of yours about image—the charter flight cuts into our profits."

"So I'll pay for it out of my share from now on. I love to fly. Besides, it's good for Carlos's people to see us getting off a private plane. It establishes us a cut above the competition."

Silence from Angie.

I couldn't believe what I was hearing—people getting high; difficulty coming up with the stuff; Carlos . . . In the eighties, nine out of ten fictional arch villains dealing in terrorism and drugs had been named Carlos. Was I to assume that one had materialized in the Napa Valley?

"Angie," Melissa said impatiently, "what is with you this week?"

"I don't know. I'm really spooked about getting caught. Maybe it was the way Sarge looked at me last night when I told him we wouldn't be in to HQ today."

"He can't possibly suspect. He thinks we're out in the field, that's all."

"But all day, every fourth Wednesday? We're going to have to shift the deliveries around among our clients. If Sarge finds out we've been stealing—"

"Stop, already!"

Now what I couldn't believe was that they'd discuss such things in a public place. A sergeant, headquarters, being out in the field, deliveries, stealing . . . Was it possible that Angie and Melissa were a couple of undercover narcs who were selling the drugs they confiscated?

After a while one of them sighed. Melissa's voice said, "It's time."

"Yeah. Back to the ghetto."

"Listen, if you can't take the heat . . ."

"Funny. Very funny."

❖ ❖ ❖

When we got back to Oakland I hung around Wide Horizons while Melissa paid for the flight in cash and gave Sam a two hundred dollar tip. Then I went to Gordon's office and made a verbal report, asking him to keep the information confidential until I'd collected concrete evidence. I'd have that for him, I said, before the women's next scheduled flight.

As I drove across the Bay Bridge to my offices at Pier 24 ½, one of the renovated structures along San Francisco's Embarcadero, I thought over what I'd heard at the mud baths. Something was wrong with the picture I'd formed. No specific detail, just the nagging sense that I'd overlooked an item of importance. I wanted to get my computer researcher, Mick Savage, started on the case as soon as possible.

The next morning, Mick began by accessing the Napa County property-tax assessor's records; he found that the estate in the hills belonged to Carlos Robles, a prominent vintner, whose wines even I—whose budget had only recently expanded to accommodate varieties with corks—had heard of. While Mick began tracking information on Robles in the periodicals indexes, I asked a contact on the SFPD to check with the National Crime Information Center for criminal histories on the vintner, Angie Holbrook, and Melissa Wells. They all came up clean.

Mick started downloading news stories and magazine articles on

Robles and his winery, and soon they formed an imposing stack on my desk. I had other work to do, so I called in Rae Kelleher, my field investigator, and asked her to check with our contacts at Bay Area police departments for detectives answering to the women's names or matching their descriptions. At six o'clock I hauled the stack of information on Robles home to my brown-shingled cottage near the Glen Park district, curled up on the couch with my cats, and spent the evening reading.

If you believed Robles's press, he was a pillar of the Napa Valley community. His wines were considered excellent and frequently took gold metals at the various national competitions. Robles Vineyards hosted an elegant monthly wine, food, and music event at their St. Helena Cellars, which was attended by prominent social and political figures, many of whom Carlos Robles counted among his close friends. I couldn't detect the slightest breath of scandal about his personal life; he'd been married to the same woman for thirty-three years, had four children and six grand-children, and by all accounts was devoted to his family.

A paragon, if you believed his press . . .

As the next week passed, I dug deeper into the winemaker's life, but uncovered nothing significant, and I finally concluded that to get at the truth of the matter, I'd have to concentrate on the two women. Rae had turned up nothing though our PD contacts, so I asked Mick to do an area-wide search for their addresses—a lengthy and tedious process, as far as I was concerned, but he didn't seem to mind. Mick, who is also my nephew, has a relationship with his PowerBook that I, no fan of the infernal devices, sometimes find unnatural.

The search paid off, however: He turned up two Melissa Wellses and three Angela Holbrooks in various East Bay locations, from Berkeley to Danville. I narrowed it down by the usual method—surveillance.

The building I tailed Angie Holbrook to from her Berkeley apartment was vine-covered brick, set well back from the sidewalk on Shattuck Avenue, only two blocks from the famous Chez

Panisse restaurant in the heart of what's come to be known as the Gourmet Ghetto. Polished brass lettering beside the front door said HQ Magazine. By the time I went inside and asked for Angie, I was putting it all together. And when she started to cry at the sight of my I.D., I knew I had it right.

But even after Angie, Melissa Wells and I sat down over a cappuccino at Chez Panisse and discussed the situation, something still nagged at me. It wasn't till the Monday before their next flight to Calistoga that I figured out what it was, and then I had to scramble fast to come up with the evidence.

☘ ☘ ☘

"Open their briefcases," I said to Sam Delaney. We were gathered in the office at Wide Horizons—Sam, Gordon Tillis, Melissa, Angie, and me.

Sam hesitated, glancing at Gordon.

"Go ahead," he prompted. "You're pilot in command; you've got the FAA in your corner,"

He hesitated some more, then flipped the catch of Melissa's case and raised its lid. Staring down into it, he said to me, "But . . . you told Gordon we had big trouble. This is . . . just papers."

"Right. Recipes and pictures of food."

"I don't get it. I thought the babes were into drugs."

Unfortunate word choice; the "babes" and I glared at him.

"Ms. Wells and Ms. Holbrook," I said, "are chefs and food writers for a very prestigious magazine *HQ*—short for *Home Quarterly*. Unfortunately, like many prestigious publications, it doesn't pay very well. About a year ago Melissa and Angie started moonlighting—which is strictly against the policy set by the publisher, Sarge Greenfield."

"What's this got to do with—"

"I'm getting to that. For the past six months Melissa and Angie have been creating the menus for Robles Vineyards' wine, food, and music events, using recipes they originally developed for *HQ*. Recipes that Sarge Greenfield would consider stolen. Since they didn't want to risk their jobs by leaving a paper trail, they arranged for Robles and their other clients to pay them in cash, upon acceptance of the proposed menus. Naturally they're always somewhat tense before their presentations to the clients, but afterward they're relieved. Relieved enough to indulge in wine tasting and spending."

Sam's eyes narrowed. "You say these recipes are stolen?"

"I suppose Greenfield could make a case for that."

"Then why don't you have them arrested?"

"Actually, the matter's already been settled." Angie and Melissa had decided to admit what they'd been doing to their employer, who had promptly fired them. They had now established their own catering firm and, in my opinion, would eventually be better off.

Gordon Tillis cleared his throat. "This strikes me as a good example of how we all rely too heavily on appearances in forming our opinions of people. Not a good practice; it's too easy to jump to the wrong conclusion."

Sam looked down, shuffling his feet. "Uh, I hope you ladies won't hold this against me," he said after a moment. "I'd still like to fly you up to the valley."

"Fine with us," Angie replied.

"Speaking of that—" I glanced at my watch "—isn't it time you got going?"

❧ ❧ ❧

Gordon and I walked out onto the field with them. The two men preflighting the Piper next to Sam's plane cast admiring glances at Angie and Melissa, and I was surprised when one of them winked at me. When we got to the Cessna, I snapped my fingers and said, "Oh, there's something I want to check, just out of curiosity. May I see the paperwork Sam gave you for this flight, Gordon?"

Sam frowned, but Gordon, as prearranged, handed the folder to me. I opened it to the weight-and-balance calculation that a pilot always works up in order to know the best way to arrange the passengers and their baggage.

"Uh-huh," I said, "fuel, pilot . . . Sam, you've really got to stop eating that junk food! Passengers one and two, plus purses and briefcases. Additional baggage stowed aft. Hmmm."

"Just get to the point," Sam said, glancing around nervously.

"In a minute." I slipped inside the Cessna and checked the rear compartment. One bag of takeout. One large bag of takeout.

Sam was leaning in, reaching for my arm.

"Golden Arches?" I asked.

"KFC. Leave it!"

I picked it up. Heavy KFC.

"Sam," I said, "you really ought to go on a diet."

After the DEA agents who had been hanging around the Piper with their warrant had opened the take-out containers full of cocaine and placed Sam under arrest, Gordon, Angie, Melissa and I slowly walked back to Wide Horizons in subdued silence.

"What I don't understand," Gordon finally said, "is why he always entered the stuff he was carrying on the weight-and-balance."

"To cover himself. He knew if you caught him stowing any package he hadn't entered, you'd start watching him. But why he put down the accurate weight for the bag is beyond me. Nobody would believe he could eat that much for lunch—even with his weight problem."

Gordon sighed. "And here I thought Sam was just getting fat because of bad eating habits, when all the while he was eating too well on his profits from drug running."

I grinned at him. "Widening his horizons at the expense of Wide Horizons," I said.

# THE HOLES IN THE SYSTEM
## (Rae Kelleher)

There are some days that just ought to be called off. Mondays are always hideous: The trouble starts when I dribble tooth-paste all over my clothes or lock my keys in the car and doesn't let up till I stub my toe on the bedstand at night. Tuesdays are usually when the morning paper doesn't get delivered. Wednesdays are better, but if I get to feeling optimistic and go to aerobics class at the Y, chances are ten to one that I'll wrench my back. Thursdays—forget it. And by five on Friday, all I want to do is crawl under the covers and hide.

You can see why I love weekends.

The day I got assigned to the Boydston case was a Tuesday.

Cautious optimism, that was what I was nursing. The paper lay folded tidily on the front steps of All Souls Legal Cooperative—where I both live and work as a private investigator. I read it and drank my coffee, not even burning my tongue. Nobody I knew had died, and there was even a cheerful story below the fold in the Metro section. By the time I'd looked at the comics and found all five strips that I bother to read were funny, I was feeling downright perky.

Well why not? I wasn't making a lot of money, but my job was secure. The attic room I occupied was snug and comfy. I had a boyfriend, and even if the relationship was about as deep as a desert stream on the Fourth of July, he could be taken most anyplace. And to top it off, this wasn't a bad hair day.

All that smug reflection made me feel charitable toward my fellow humans—or at least my coworkers and their clients—so I refolded the paper and carried it from the kitchen of our big Victorian to the front parlor and waiting-room so others could partake. A man was sitting on the shabby maroon sofa: bald and chubby, dressed in lime green polyester pants and a strangely patterned green, blue, and yellow shirt that reminded me of drawings of sperm cells. One thing for sure, he'd never get run over by a bus while he was wearing that getup.

He looked at me as I set the paper on the coffee table and said, "How ya doin', little lady?"

Now, there's some contention that the word "lady" is demeaning. Frankly, it doesn't bother me: when I hear it I know I'm looking halfway presentable and haven't got something disgusting caught between my front teeth. No, what rankled was the word "little." When you're five foot three the word reminds you of things you'd just as soon not dwell on—like being unable to see over people's heads at parades, or the little-girly clothes that designers of petite sizes are always trying to foist on you. "Little," especially at nine in the morning, doesn't cut it.

I glared at the guy. Unfortunately, he'd gotten to his feet and I had to look up.

He didn't notice I was annoyed; maybe he was nearsighted. "Sure looks like it's gonna be a fine day," he said.

Now I identified his accent—pure Texas. Another strike against him, because of Uncle Roy, but that's another story.

"It *would've* been a nice day," I muttered.

"Ma'am?"

That did it! The first—and last—time somebody had gotten away with calling me "Ma'am" was on my twenty-eighth birthday two weeks before, when a bag boy tried to help me out of Safeway with my two feather-light sacks of groceries. It was not a precedent I wanted followed.

Speaking more clearly, I said, "It would've been a nice day, except for you."

He frowned. "What'd I do?"

"Try 'little,' a Texas accent, and 'ma'am'!"

"Ma'am are you all right?"

"Aaargh!" I fled the parlor and ran up the stairs to the office of my boss, Sharon McCone.

❖ ❖ ❖

Sharon is my friend, mentor, and sometimes—heaven help me—
custodian of my honesty. She's been all those things since she hired
me a few years ago to assist her at the co-op. Not that our asso-
ciation is always smooth sailing: She can be a stern taskmaster and
she harbors a devilish sense of humor that surfaces at inconvenient
times. But she is always been there for me, even during the death
throes of my marriage to my pig-selfish, perpetual-student husband,
Doug Grayson. And ever since I've stopped referring to him as
"that bastard Doug," she's decided I'm a grown-up who can be
trusted to manage her own life—within limits.

That morning she was sitting behind her desk with her chair
swiveled around so she could look out the bay window at the front
of the Victorian. I've found her in that pose hundreds of times:
sunk low on her spine, long legs crossed, dark eyes brooding. The
view is of dowdy houses across the triangular park that divides the
street, and usually hazed by San Francisco fog, but it doesn't
matter; whatever she's seeing is strictly inside her head, and she says
she gets her best insights into her cases that way.

I stepped into the office and cleared my throat. Slowly Shar
turned, looking at me as if I were a stranger. Then her eyes cleared.
"Rae, hi. Nice work on closing the Anderson file so soon."

"Thanks. I found the others you left on my desk; they're pretty
routine. You have anything else for me?"

"As a matter of fact, yes." She smiled slyly and slid a manila
folder across the desk. "Why don't you take this client?"

I opened the folder and studied the information sheet stapled
inside. All it gave was a name—Darrin Boydston—and an address
on Mission Street. Under the job description Shar had noted "background check."

"Another one?" I asked, letting my voice telegraph my
disappointment.

"Uh-huh. I think you'll find it interesting."

"Why?"

She waved a slender hand at me. "Go! It'll be a challenge."

Now, that *did* make me suspicious. "If it's such a challenge, how come you're not handling it?"

For an instant her eyes sparked. She doesn't like it when I hint that she skims the best cases for herself—although that's exactly what she does, and I don't blame her. "Just go see him."

"He'll be at this address?"

"No. He's downstairs. I got done talking with him ten minutes ago."

"Downstairs? *Where* downstairs?"

"In the parlor."

Oh, God!

She smiled again. "Lime green, with a Texas accent."

"So," Darrin Boydston said, "Did y'all come back down to chew me out some more?"

"I'm sorry about that." I handed him my card. "Ms. McCone has assigned me to your case."

He studied it and looked me up and down. "You promise to keep a civil tongue in your head?"

"I said I was sorry."

"Well, you damn near ruint my morning."

How many more times was I going to have to apologize?

"Let's get goin', little lady." He started for the door.

I winced and asked, "Where?"

"My place. I got somebody I want you to meet."

Boydston's car was a white Lincoln Continental—beautiful machine, except for the bull's horns mounted on the front grille. I stared at them in horror.

"Pretty, aren't they?" he said, opening the passenger's door.

"I'll follow you in my car," I told him.

He shrugged. "Suit yourself."

As I got into the Ramblin' Wreck—my ancient, exhaust-belching Rambler American—I looked back and saw Boydston staring at *it* in horror.

Boydston's place was a storefront on Mission a few blocks down from my Safeway—an area that could do with some urban renewal and just might get it, if the upwardly mobile ethnic groups that're moving in to the neighborhood get their way.  It shared the building with a Thai restaurant and a Filipino travel agency.  In its front window red neon tubing spelled out THE CASH COW, but the bucking outline letters was a bull.  I imagined Boydston trying to reach a decision: call it the Cash Cow and have a good name but a dumb graphic; call it the Cash Bull and have a dumb name and a good graphic; or just say the hell with it and mix genders.

But what kind of establishment was this?

My client took the first available parking space, leaving me to fend for myself.  When I finally found another and walked back two blocks he'd already gone inside.

Chivalry is dead.  Sometimes I think common courtesy's obit is about to be published too.

When I went into the store, the first thing I noticed was a huge potted barrel cactus, and the second was dozens of guitars hanging from the ceiling.  A rack of worn cowboy boots completed the picture.

Texas again.  The state that spawned the likes of Uncle Roy was going to keep getting in my face all day long.

The room was full of glass showcases that displayed an amazing assortment of stuff: rings, watches, guns, cameras, fishing reels, kitchen gadgets, small tools, knickknacks, silverware, even a metronome.  There was a whole section of electronic equipment like TVs and VCRs, a jumble of probably obsolete computer gear, a fleet of vacuum cleaners poised to roar to life and tidy the world, enough exercise equipment to trim down half the population, and a jukebox that just then was playing a country song by Shar's brother-in-law, Ricky Savage.  Delicacy prevents me from describing what his voice does to my libido.

Darrin Boydston stood behind a high counter, tapping on a keyboard.  On the wall behind him a sign warned CUSTOMERS MUST PRESENT TICKET TO CLAIM MERCHANDISE.  I'm not too quick most mornings, but I did manage to figure out that the Cash Cow was a pawnshop.

"Y'all took long enough," my client said. "You gonna charge me for the time you spent parking?"

I sighed. "Your billable hours start now." Then I looked at my watch and made a mental note of the time.

He turned the computer off, motioned for me to come around the counter, and led me through a door into a warehouse area. Its shelves were crammed with more of the kind of stuff he had out front. Halfway down the center aisle he made a right turn and took me past small appliances: blenders, food processors, toasters, electric woks, pasta makers, even an ancient pressure cooker. It reminded me of the one the grandmother who raised me used to have, and I wrinkled my nose at it, thinking of those sweltering late-summer days when she'd make me help her with the yearly canning. No wonder I resist the womanly household arts!

Boydston said, "They buy these gizmos 'cause they think they need 'em. Then they find out they don't need and can't afford 'em. And then it all ends up in my lap." He sounded exceptionally cheerful about this particular brand of human folly, and I supposed he had good reason.

He led me at a fast clip toward the back of the warehouse—so fast that I had to trot to keep up with him. One of the other problems with being short is that you're forever running along behind taller people. Since I'd already decided to hate Darrin Boydston, I also decided he was walking fast to spite me.

At the end of the next-to-last aisle we came upon a thin man in a white T-shirt and black work pants who was moving boxes from the shelves to a dolly. Although Boydston and I were making plenty of noise, he didn't hear us come up. My client put his hand on the man's shoulder, and he stiffened. When he turned I saw he was only a boy, no more than twelve or thirteen, with the fine features and thick black hair of a Eurasian. The look in his eyes reminded me of an abused kitten my boyfriend Willie had taken in: afraid and resigned to further terrible experiences. He glanced from me to Boydston, and when my client nodded reassuringly, the fear faded to remoteness.

Boydston said to me, "Meet Daniel."

"Hello, Daniel." I held out my hand. He looked at it, then at Boydston. He nodded again, and Daniel touched my fingers, moving back quickly as if they were hot.

"Daniel," Boydston said, "doesn't speak or hear. Speech therapist I know met him, says he's prob'ly been deaf and mute since he was born."

The boy was watching his face intently. I said, "He reads lips or understands signing, though."

"Does some lip reading, yeah. But no signing. For that you gotta have schooling. Far as I can tell, Daniel hasn't. But him and me, we worked out a personal kind of language to get by."

Daniel tugged at Boyston's sleeve and motioned at the shelves, eyebrows raised. Boydston nodded, then pointed to his watch, held up five fingers, and pointed to the front of the building. Daniel nodded and turned back to his work. Boydston said, "You see?"

"Uh-huh. You two communicate pretty well. How'd he come to work for you?"

My client began leading me back to the store—walking slower now. "The way it went, I found him all huddled up in the back doorway one morning 'bout six weeks ago when I opened up. He was damn near froze but dressed in clean clothes and a new jacket. Was in good shape, 'cept for some healed-over cuts on his face. And he had this laminated card . . . wait, I'll show you." He held the door for me, then rummaged through a drawer below the counter.

The card was a blue three-by-five—encased in clear plastic; on it somebody had typed I WILL WORK FOR FOOD AND A PLACE TO SLEEP. I DO NOT SPEAK OR HEAR, BUT I AM A GOOD WORKER. PLEASE HELP ME.

"So you gave him a job?"

Boydston sat down on a stool. "Yeah. He sleeps in a little room off the warehouse and cooks on a hotplate. Mostly stuff outta cans. Every week I give him cash; he brings back the change—won't take any more than what his food costs, and that's not much."

I turned the card over. Turned over my opinion of Darrin

Boydston, too. "How d'you know his name's Daniel?"

"I don't. That's just what I call him."

"Why Daniel?"

He looked embarrassed and brushed at a speck of lint on the leg of his pants. "Had a best buddy in high school down in Amarillo. Daniel Atkins. Got killed in 'Nam." He paused. "Funny, me giving his name to a slope kid when they were the ones that killed him." Another pause. "Of course, this Daniel wasn't even born then, none of that business was his fault. And there's something about him . . . I don't know, he must reminds me of my buddy. Don't suppose old Danny would mind none."

"I'm sure he wouldn't." Damn, it was getting harder and harder to hate Boydston! I decided to let go of it. "Okay," I said, "my casefile calls for a background check. I take it you want me to find out who Daniel is."

"Yeah. Right now he doesn't exist—officially, I mean. He hasn't got a birth certificate, can't get a social security number. That means I can't put him on the payroll, and he can't get government help. No classes where he can learn the stuff I can't teach him. No SSI payments or Medicare, either. My therapist friend says he's one of the people that slip through the cracks in the system."

The cracks are more like yawning holes, if you ask me. I said, "I've got to warn you, Mr. Boydston: Daniel may be in the country illegally."

"You think I haven't thought of that? Hell, I'm one of the people that voted for Prop One-eighty-seven. Keep those foreigners from coming here and taking jobs from decent citizens. Don't give 'em nothin' and maybe they'll go home and quit using up my tax dollar. That was before I met Daniel." He scowled. "*Damn*, I hate moral dilemmas! I'll tell you one thing, though: This is a good kid, he deserves a chance. If he's here illegally . . . well, I'll deal with it somehow."

I liked his approach to his moral dilemma; I'd used it myself a time or ten. "Okay," I said, "tell me everything you know about him."

"Well, there're the clothes he had on when I found him. They're in this sack; take a look." He hauled a grocery bag from under the counter and handed it to me.

I pulled the clothing out: rugby shirt in white, green, and navy; navy cords; navy-and-tan down jacket. They were practically new, but the labels had been cut out.

"Lands' End?" I said. "Eddie Bauer?"

"One of those, but who can tell which?"

I couldn't, but I had a friend who could, "Can I take these?"

"Sure, but don't let Daniel see you got them. He's real attached to 'em, cried when I took 'em away to be cleaned the first time."

"Somebody cared about him, to dress him well and have this card made up. Laminating like that is a simple process, though; you can get it done in print shops."

"Hell, you could get it done *here.* I got in one of those laminating gizmos a week ago; belongs to a printer who's having a hard time of it, checks his shop equipment in and out like this was a lending library."

"What else can you tell me about Daniel? What's he like?"

Boydston considered. "Well, he's proud—the way he brings back the change from the money I give him tells me that. He's smart; he picked up on the warehouse routine easy, and he already knew how to cook. Whoever his people are, they don't have much; he knew what a hotplate was, but when I showed him a microwave it scared him. And he's got a tic about labels—cuts 'em out of the clothes I give him. There's more, too." He looked toward the door; Daniel was peeking hesitantly around its jamb. Boydston waved for him to come in and added, "I'll let Daniel do the telling."

The boy came into the room, eyes lowered shyly—or fearfully. Boydston looked at him till he looked back. Speaking very slowly and mouthing the words carefully, he asked, "Where are you from?

❖ ❖ ❖

Daniel pointed at the floor.

"San Francisco?"

Nod.

"This district?"

Frown.

"Mission district? Mis-sion?"

Nod.

"Your momma, where is she?"

Daniel bit his lip.

"Your momma?"

He raised his hand and waved.

"Gone away?" I asked Boydston.

"Gone away or dead. How long, Daniel?" When the boy didn't respond, he repeated, "How long?"

Shrug.

"Time confuses him." Boydston said. "Daniel, your daddy—where is he?"

The boy's eyes narrowed and he made a sudden violent gesture toward the door.

"Gone away?"

Curt nod.

"How long?"

Shrug.

"How long, Daniel?"

After a moment he held up two fingers.

"Days?"

Headshake.

"Weeks?"

Frown.

"Months?"

Another frown.

"Years?"

Nod.

"Thanks, Daniel." Boydston smiled at him and motioned to the door. "You can go back to work now." He watched the boy leave, eyes troubled, then asked me, "So what d'you think?"

"Well—he's got good linguistic abilities; somebody bothered to teach him—probably the mother. His recollections seem scrambled. He's fairly sure when the father left, less sure about the mother. That could mean she went away or died recently and he hasn't found a way to mesh it with the rest of his personal history. Whatever happened, he was left to fend for himself."

"Can you do anything for him?"

"I'm sure going to try."

❖ ❖ ❖

My best lead on Daniel's identity was the clothing. There had to be a reason for the labels being cut out—and I didn't think it was because of a tic on the boy's part. No, somebody had wanted to conceal the origins of the duds, and when I found out where they'd come from I could pursue my investigation from that angle. I left the Cash Cow, got in the Ramblin' Wreck, and when it finally stopped coughing, drove to the six-story building on Brannan Street south of Market where my friend Janie labors in what she calls the rag trade. Right now she works for a T-shirt manufacturer—and there've been years when I would've gone naked without her gifts of overruns—but during her career she's touched on every area of the business; if anybody could steer me toward the manufacturer of Daniel's clothes, she was the one. I gave them to her and she told me to call later. Then I set out on the trail of a Mission district printer who had a laminating machine.

Print and copy shops were in abundant supply there. A fair number of them did laminating work, but none recognized—or would own up to recognizing—Daniel's three-by-five card. It took me nearly all day to canvass them, except for the half-hour when I had a beer and a burrito at La Tacqueria, and by four o'clock I was totally discouraged. So I stopped at my favorite ice cream shop, called Janie and found she was in a meeting, and to ease my frustration had a double-scoop caramel swirl in a chocolate chip cookie cone.

No wonder I'm usually carrying five spare pounds!

The shop had a section of little plastic tables and chairs, and I rested my weary feet there, planning to check in at the office and then call it a day. If turning the facts of the case over and over in my mind all evening could be considered calling it a day . . .

Shar warned me about that right off the bat. "If you like this business and stick with it," she'd said, "you'll work twenty-four hours a day, seven days a week. You'll think you're not working because you'll be at a party or watching TV or even in bed with your husband. And then all of a sudden you'll realize that half your mind's thinking about your current case and searching for a solution. Frankly, it doesn't make for much of a life."

Actually it makes for more than one life. Sometimes I think the time I spend on stakeouts or questioning people or prowling the city belongs to another Rae, one who has no connection to the Rae who goes to parties and watches TV and—now—sleeps with her boyfriend. I'm divided, but I don't mind it. And if Rae-the-investigator intrudes on the off-duty Rae's time, that's okay. Because the off-duty Rae gets to watch Rae-the-investigator make her moves—fascinated and a little envious.

Schizoid? Maybe. But I can't help but live and breathe the business. By now that's as natural as breathing air.

So I sat on the little plastic chair savoring my caramel swirl and chocolate chips and realized that the half of my mind that wasn't on sweets had come up with a weird little coincidence. Licking ice cream dribbles off my fingers, I went back to the phone and called Darrin Boydston. The printer who had hocked his laminating machine was named Jason Hill, he told me, and his shop was Quik Prints, on Mission near Geneva.

I'd gone there earlier this afternoon. When I showed Jason Hill the laminated card he'd looked kind of funny but claimed he didn't do that kind of work, and there hadn't been any equipment in evidence to brand him a liar. Actually, he wasn't a liar; he didn't do that kind of work *anymore*.

❖ ❖ ❖

Hill was closing up when I got to Quik Prints, and he looked damned unhappy to see me again. I took the laminated card from my pocket and slapped it into his hand. "The machine you made this on is living at the Cash Cow right now," I said. "You want to tell me about it?"

Hill—one of those bony-thin guys that you want to take home and fatten up—sighed. "You from Child Welfare or what?"

"I'm working for your pawn broker, Darrin Boydston." I showed him the ID he hadn't bothered to look at earlier. "Who had the card made up?"

"I did."

"Why?"

"For the kid's sake." He switched the Open sign in the window to Closed and came out onto the sidewalk. "Mind if we walk to my bus stop while we talk?"

I shook my head and fell in next to him. The famous San Francisco fog was in, gray and dirty, making the gray and dirty Outer Mission even more depressing than usual. As we headed toward the intersection of Mission and Geneva, Hill told me about his story.

"I found the kid on the sidewalk about seven weeks ago. It was five in the morning—I'd come in early for a rush job—and he was dazed and banged up and bleeding. Looked like he'd been mugged. I took him into the shop and was going to call the cops, but he started crying—upset about the blood on his down jacket. I sponged it off, and by the time I got back from the restroom, he was sweeping the print-room floor. I really didn't have time to deal with the cops, so I just let him sweep. He kind of made himself indispensable."

"And then?"

"He cried when I tried to put him outside that night, so I got him some food and let him sleep in the shop. He had coffee ready the next morning and helped me take out the trash. I still thought I should call the cops, but I was worried: He couldn't tell them who he was or where he lived; he'd end up in some detention center or a foster home and his folks might never find him. I grew up in foster homes myself; I know all about the system. He was a sweet kid and deserved better than that. You know?"

"I know."

"Well, I couldn't figure *what* to do with him. I couldn't keep him at the shop much longer—the landlord's nosy and always on the premises. And I couldn't take him home—I live in a tiny studio with my girlfriend and three dogs. So after a week I got an idea: I'd park him someplace with a laminated card asking for a job; I knew he wouldn't lose it or throw it away because he loved the laminated stuff and saved all of the discards."

"Why'd you leave him at the Cash Cow?"

"Mr. Boydston has a reputation for taking care of people. He's helped me out plenty of times."

"How?"

"Well, when he sends out the sixty-day notices saying you should claim your stuff or it'll be sold, as long as you go in and make a token payment, he'll hang onto it. He sees you're hurting, he'll give you more than the stuff's worth. He bends over backward to make a loan." We got to the bus stop and Hill joined the rush-hour line. "And I was right about Mr. Boydston helping the kid, too. When I took the machine in last week, there he was, sweeping the sidewalk."

"He recognize you?"

"Didn't see me. Before I crossed the street, Mr. Boydston sent him on some errand. The kid's in good hands."

Funny how every now and then when you think the whole city's gone to hell, you discover there're a few good people left . . .

❖ ❖ ❖

Wednesday morning: cautious optimism again, but I wasn't going to push my luck by attending an aerobics class. Today I'd put all my energy into the Boydston case.

First, a call to Janie, whom I hadn't been able to reach at home the night before.

"The clothes were manufactured by a company called Casuals, Incorporated," she told me. "They only sell by catalogue, and their offices and factory are on Third Street."

"Any idea why the labels were cut out?"

"Well, at first I thought they might've been overstocks that were sold through one of the discounters like Ross, but that doesn't happen often with the catalogue outfits. So I took a close look at the garments and saw they've got defects—nothing major, but they wouldn't want to pass them off as first quality."

"Where would somebody get hold of them?"

"A factory store, if the company has one. I didn't have time to check."

It wasn't much of a lead, but even a little lead's better than nothing at all. I promised Janie I'd buy her a beer sometime soon and headed for the industrial corridor along Third Street.

♣ ♣ ♣

Casuals, Inc. didn't have an on-site factory store, so I went into the front office to ask if there was one in another location. No, the receptionist told me, they didn't sell garments found to be defective.

"What happens to them?"

"Usually they're offered at a discount to employees and their families."

That gave me an idea, and five minutes later I was talking with a Mr. Fong in personnel. "A single mother with a deaf-mute son? That would be Mae Jones. She worked here as a seamstress for . . . let's see . . . a little under a year."

"But she's not employed here anymore?"

"No. We had to lay off a number of people, and those with the least seniority are the first to go."

"Do you know where she's working now?"

"Sorry, I don't."

"Mr. Fong, is Mae Jones a documented worker?"

"Green card was in order. We don't hire illegals."

"And you have an address for her?"

"Yes, but I'm afraid I can't give that out."

"I understand, but I think you'll want to make an exception in this case. You see, Mae's son was found wandering the Mission seven weeks ago, the victim of a mugging. I'm trying to reunite them."

Mr. Fong didn't hesitate to fetch Mae's file and give me the address, on Lucky Street in the Mission. Maybe, I thought, this was my lucky break.

♣ ♣ ♣

The house was a Victorian that had been sided with concrete block and painted a weird shade of purple. Sagging steps led to a porch where six mailboxes hung. None of the names on them was Jones. I rang all the bells and got no answer. Now what?

"Can I help you?" An Asian-accented voice said behind me. It belonged to a stooped old woman carrying a fishnet bag full of vegetables. Her eyes, surrounded by deep wrinkles, were kind.

"I'm looking for Mae Jones." The woman had been taking out a keyring. Now she jammed it into the pocket of her loose-fitting trousers and backed up against the porch railing. Fear made her nostrils flare.

"What?" I asked. "What's wrong?

"You are from them!"

"Them? Who?"

"I know nothing."

"Please don't be scared. I'm trying to help Mrs. Jones's son."

"Tommy? Where is Tommy?"

I explained about Jason Hill finding him and Darrin Boydston taking him in.

When I finished the woman had relaxed a little. "I am so happy one of them is safe."

"Please, tell me about the Joneses."

She hesitated, looking me over. Then she nodded as if I'd passed some kind of test and took me inside to a small apartment furnished with things that made the thrift-shop junk in my nest at All Souls look like Chippendale. Although I would've rather she tell her story quickly, she insisted on making tea. When we were finally settled with little cups like the ones I'd bought years ago at Bargain Bazaar in Chinatown, she began.

"Mae went away eight weeks ago today. I thought Tommy was with her. When she did not pay her rent, the landlord went inside the apartment. He said they left everything."

"Has the apartment been rented to someone else?"

She nodded. "Mae and Tommy's things are stored in the garage. Did you say it was seven weeks ago that Tommy was found?"

"Give or take a few days."

"Poor boy. He must have stayed in the apartment waiting for

his mother. He is so quiet and can take care of himself."

"What d'you suppose he was doing on Mission Street near Geneva, then?"

"Maybe looking for her." The woman's face was frightened again.

"Why there?" I asked.

She stared down into her teacup. After a bit she said, "You know Mae lost her job at the sewing factory?"

I nodded.

"It was a good job, and she is a good seamstress, but times are bad and she could not find another job."

"And then?"

". . . There is a place on Geneva Avenue. It looks like an apartment house, but it is really a sewing factory. The owners advertise by word of mouth among the Asian immigrants. They say they pay high wages, give employees meals and a place to live, and do not ask questions. They hire many who are here illegally."

"Is Mae an illegal?"

"No. She was married to an American serviceman and has her permanent green card. Tommy was born in San Francisco. But a few years ago her husband divorced her and she lost her medical benefits. She is in poor health, she has tuberculosis. Her money was running out, and she was desperate. I warned her, but she wouldn't listen."

"Warned her against what?"

"There is talk about that factory. The building is fenced and the fences are topped with razor wire. The windows are boarded and barred. They say that once a worker enters she is not allowed to leave. They say workers are forced to sew eighteen hours a day for very low wages. They say that the cost of food is taken out of their pay, and that ten people sleep in a room large enough for two."

"That's slavery! Why doesn't the city do something?"

The old woman shrugged. "The city has no proof and does not care. The workers are only immigrants. They are not important."

I felt a real rant coming on and fought to control it. I've lived in San Francisco for seven years, since I graduated from Berkeley, a few miles and light years across the Bay, and I'm getting sick and tired of the so-called important people. The city is beautiful and lively and tolerant, but there's a core of citizens who think nobody and nothing counts but them and their concerns. Someday when I'm in charge of the world (an event I fully expect to happen, especially when I've had a few beers), they'll have to answer to *me* for their high-handed behavior.

"Okay," I said, "tell me exactly where this place is, and we'll see what we can do about it."

❖ ❖ ❖

"Slavery, plain and simple," Shar said.

"Right."

"Something's got to be done about it."

"Right."

We were sitting in a booth at the Remedy Lounge, our favorite tavern down the hill from All Souls on Mission Street. She was drinking white wine, I was drinking beer, and it wasn't but three in the afternoon. But McCone and I have found that some of our best ideas come to us when we tilt a couple. I'd spent the last four hours casing—oops, I'm not supposed to call it that—conducting a surveillance on the building on Geneva Avenue. Sure looked suspicious—trucks coming and going, but no workers leaving at lunchtime.

"But what can be done?" I asked. "Who do we contact?"

She considered. "Illegals? U.S. Immigration and Naturalization Service. False imprisonment? City police and district attorney's office. Substandard working conditions? OSHA, Department of Labor, State Employment Development Division. Take your pick."

"Which is best to start with?"

"None—yet. You've got no proof of what's going on there."

"Then we'll just have to get proof, won't we?"

"Uh-huh."

"You and I both used to work in security. Ought to be a snap to get into that building."

"Maybe."

"All we need is access. Take some pictures. Tape a statement from one of the workers. Are you with me?"

She nodded. "I'm with you. And as backup, why don't we take Willie?"

"*My* Willie? The diamond king of northern California? Shar, this is an investigation, not a date!"

"Before he opened those discount jewelry stores Willie was a professional fence, as you may recall. And although he won't admit it, I happen to know he personally stole a lot of the items he moved. Willie has talents we can use."

"My tennis elbow hurts! Why're you making me do this?"

I glared at Willie. "Shh! You've never played tennis in your life."

"The doc told me most people who've got it have never played."

"Just be quiet and cut the wire."

"How d'you know there isn't an alarm?"

"Shar and I have checked. Trust us."

"I trust you two, I'll probably end up in San Quentin."

"Cut!"

Willie snipped a fair segment out of the razor wire topping the chain-link fence. I climbed over first, nearly doing myself grievous personal injury as I swung over the top. Shar followed, and then the diamond king—making unseemly grunting noises. His tall frame was encased in dark sweats tonight, and they accentuated the beginnings of a beer belly.

As we each dropped to the ground, we quickly moved into the shadow of the three-story frame building and flattened against its wall. Willie wheezed and pushed his longish hair out of his eyes. I gave Shar a look that said, *Some asset you invited along.* She shrugged apologetically.

According to plan we began inching around the building, searching for a point of entry. We didn't see any guards. If the factory employed them, it would be for keeping people in; it had probably never occurred to the owners that someone might actually *want* in.

After about three minutes Shar came to a stop and I bumped into her. She steadied me and pointed down. A foot off the ground was an opening that had been boarded up; the plywood was splintered and coming loose. I squatted and took a look at it. Some kind of duct—maybe people-size. Together we pulled the board off.

❖ ❖ ❖

Yep. A duct. But not very big. Willie wouldn't fit through it— which was fine by me, because I didn't want him alerting everybody in the place with his groaning. I'd fit, but Shar would fit better still.

I motioned for her to go first.

She made an after-you gesture.

I shook my head.

*It's your case,* she mouthed.

I sighed, handed her the camera loaded with infrared film that I carried, and started squeezing through.

I've got to admit that I have all sorts of mild phobias. I get twitchy in crowds, and I'm not fond of heights, and I hate to fly, and small places make my skin crawl. This duct was a *very* small space. I pushed onward, trying to keep my mind on other things— such as Tommy and Mae Jones.

When my hands reached the end of the duct I pulled hard, then moved them around till I felt a concrete floor about two feet below. I wriggled forward, felt my foot kick something, and heard Shar grunt. *Sorry.* The room I slid down into was pitch black. I waited till Shar was crouched beside me, then whispered, "D'you have your flashlight?"

She handed me the camera, fumbled in her pocket, and then I saw streaks of light bleeding around the fingers she placed around its bulb. We waited, listening. No one stirred, no one spoke. After a moment, Shar took her hand away from the flash and began shining its beam around. A storage room full of sealed cardboard boxes, with a door at the far side. We exchanged glances and began moving through the stacked cartons.

When we got to the door I put my ear to it and listened. No

sound. I turned the knob slowly. Unlocked. I eased the door open. A dimly lighted hallway. There was another door with a lighted window set into it at the far end. Shar and I moved along opposite walls and stopped on either side of the door. I went up on tiptoe and peeked through the corner of the glass.

Inside was a factory: row after row of sewing machines, all making jittery up-and-down motions and clacking away. Each was operated by an Asian woman. Each woman slumped wearily as she fed the fabric through.

It was twelve-thirty in the morning, and they still had them sewing!

I drew back and motioned for Shar to have a look. She did, then turned to me, lips tight, eyes ablaze.

*Pictures?* she mouthed.

I shook my head. *Can't risk being seen.*

*Now what?*

I shrugged.

She frowned and started back the other way, slipping from door to door and trying each knob. Finally she stopped and pointed to one with a placard that said STAIRWAY. I followed her through it and we started up. The next floor was offices—locked up and dark. We went back to the stairwell, climbed another flight. On the landing I almost tripped over a small, huddled figure.

It was a tiny gray-haired woman, crouching there with a dirty thermal blanket wrapped around her. She shivered repeatedly. Sick and hiding from the foreman. I squatted beside her.

The woman started and her eyes got big with terror. She scrambled backwards toward the steps, almost falling over. I grabbed her arm and steadied her; her flesh felt as if it was burning up. "Don't be scared," I said.

Her eyes moved from me to Shar. Little cornered bunny-rabbit eyes, red and full of the awful knowledge that there's no place left to hide. She babbled something in a tongue that I couldn't understand. I put my arms around her and patted her back—universal language. After a bit she stopped trying to pull away.

I whispered, "Do you know Mae Jones?"

She drew back and blinked.

"Mae Jones?" I repeated.

Slowly she nodded and pointed to the door off the next landing.

So Tommy's mother *was* here. If we could get her out, we'd have an English-speaking witness who, because she had her permanent green card, wouldn't be afraid to go to the authorities and file charges against the owners of this place. But there was no telling who or what was beyond that door. I glanced at Shar. She shook her head.

The sick woman was watching me. I thought back to yesterday morning and the way Darrin Boydston had communicated with the boy he called Daniel. It was worth a try.

I pointed to the woman. Pointed to the door. "Mae Jones." I pointed to the door again, then pointed to the floor.

The woman was straining to understand. I went through the routine twice more. She nodded and struggled to her feet. Trailing the ratty blanket behind her, she climbed the stairs and went through the door.

Shar and I released sighs at the same time. Then we sat down on the steps and waited.

❖ ❖ ❖

It wasn't five minutes before the door opened. We both ducked down, just in case. An overly thin woman of about thirty-five rushed through so quickly that she stumbled on the top step and caught herself on the railing. She would have been beautiful, but lines of worry and pain cut deep into her face; her hair had been lopped off short and stood up in dirty spikes. Her eyes were jumpy, alternately glancing at us and behind her. She hurried down the stairs.

"You want me?"

"If you're Mae Jones." Already I was guiding her down the steps.

"I am. Who are—"

"We're going to get you out of here, take you to Tommy."

"Tommy! Is he—"

"He's all right, yes."

Her face brightened, but then was taken over by fear. "We must hurry. Lan faked a faint, but they will notice I'm gone very soon."

We rushed down the stairs, along the hall toward the storage room. We were at its door when a man called out behind us. He was coming from the sewing room at the far end.

Mae froze. I shoved her, and then we were weaving through the stacked cartons. Shar got down on her knees, helped Mae into the duct, and dove in behind her. The door banged open.

The man was yelling in a strange language. I slid into the duct, pulling myself along on its riveted sides. Hands grabbed for my ankles and got the left one. I kicked out with my right foot. He grabbed for it and missed. I kicked upward, hard, and heard a satisfying yelp of pain. His hand let go of my ankle and I wriggled forward and fell to the ground outside. Shar and Mae were already running for the fence.

But where the hell was Willie?

Then I saw him: a shadowy figure, motioning with both arms as if he were guiding an airplane up to the jetway. There was an enormous hole in the chain-link fence. Shar and Mae ducked through it.

I started running. Lights went on at the corners of the building. Men came outside, shouting. I heard a whine, then a crack.

Rifle, firing at us!

Willie and I hurled ourselves to the ground. We moved on elbows and knees through the hole in the fence and across the sidewalk to the shelter of a van parked there. Shar and Mae huddled behind it. Willie and I collapsed beside them just as sirens began to go off.

"Like 'Nam all over again," he said.

I stared at him in astonishment. Willie had spent most of the war hanging out in a bar in Cam Ranh Bay.

Shar said, "Thank God you cut the hole in the fence!"

Modestly he replied, "Yeah, well, you gotta do something when you're bored out of your skull."

❧ ❧ ❧

Because a shot had been fired, the SFPD had probable cause to search the building. Inside they found some sixty Asian women —most of them illegals—who had been imprisoned there, some as long as five years, as well as evidence of other sweatshops the owners were running, both here and in southern California. The INS was called in, statements were taken, and finally at around five that morning Mae Jones was permitted to go with us to be reunited with her son.

Darrin Boydston greeted us at the Cash Cow, wearing electric-blue pants and a western-style shirt with the bucking-bull emblem embroidered over its pockets. A polyester cowboy. He stood watching as Tommy and Mae hugged and kissed, wiped a sentimental tear from his eye, and offered Mae a job. She accepted, and then he drove them to the house of a friend who would put them up until they found a place of their own. I waited around the pawnshop till he returned.

When Boydston came through the door he looked down in the mouth. He pulled up a stool next to the one I sat on and said, "Sure am gonna miss that boy."

"Well, you'll probably be seeing a lot of him, with Mae working here."

"Yeah." He brightened some. "And I'm gonna help her get him into classes. Stuff like that. After she lost her Navy benefits when that skunk of a husband walked out on her, she didn't know about all the other stuff that's available." He paused, then added, "So what's the damage?"

"You mean, what do you owe us? We'll bill you."

"Better be an honest accounting, little lady," he said. "Ma'am, I mean," he added in his twangiest Texas accent. And smiled.

I smiled, too.

# ONE FINAL ARRANGEMENT
## (Mick Savage)

Devil's Slide, south of San Francisco, is a stretch of highway where you don't want to push your luck, but I was pushing mine on the Yamaha, even though I had Lottie—my lady, Charlotte Keim—snuggled up behind me. It was a killer day, clear and crisp, and there wasn't a shred of cloud in the sky. We hugged the curves above the sea, really leaned into them, and left the city and work far behind us.

At least Lottie—who's one of my fellow operatives at McCone Investigations—had left work behind. I was still steamed after having spent last night hunkered down in the rhododendrons at some guy's Hillsborough estate, watching him go through the same damn motions that he had been going through for over a week. Watching him on a damp October night whose every chill breeze whispered the word *pneumonia*. And I was even more steamed about the conversation I'd had this morning with my aunt and boss, Sharon McCone.

Just thinking about it made me come up too fast at the start of a hairpin curve. I corrected in time, but Lottie's arms tightened around me, and she said, "For God's sake, Mick!" After that I took it slower until we got the state beach at San Gregorio. While I was securing the bike in the parking area, Lottie ran off toward the sand.

By the time I followed her, Lottie was dancing along the water's edge, her long dark-brown curls flaring and bouncing. She saw me and called, "Last one in's a lovesick armadillo!" Lottie's got seven years on me, but sometimes she's as much a kid as my littlest sister, and when she gets excited, the Texas accent she tried to leave behind in Archer City comes out—along with what Shar calls Lottie's "Texasisms." Today Lottie was as Texas as Lone Star beer.

We didn't really plan to go in the water; it's cold along the northern California coast, even in summer. So I caught up with her and grabbed her hand, and we strolled south to where the beach backed up against the cliffs. There were only three people around —a daddy and two little kids, maybe around seven and eight. The kids were building sand castles, and the daddy was lying on his back, his head propped on a driftwood log. Lottie and I parked it on another log and watched the construction project.

"You want to tell me about it?" she asked.

"About what?"

"Whatever's got you tryin' to see if that bike can fly."

"Just a problem at work, is all. No big deal. Shar's got me on this case that's going no place, no way, no how. You'd think she'd give up. The woman's fixated."

Lottie waited.

"Okay," I said after a minute, "this is the situation. There's this dude, seriously weird. Name of Harry Homestead. Lives all alone in this mansion down the Peninsula that makes my dad's place looks like a homeless shelter."

"Hard to believe that." Lottie's a little in awe of my father, who makes an obscene heap of money as a country singer.

"Well, believe it. Seven and a half years ago this dude married big bucks. Older lady, Susan Cross, of the oil and banking family. Way back when, her forebears robbed practically everybody dumber than them who ever trekked through Emigrant Gap. Harry, though, he was kind of questionable, being from someplace nobody ever heard of in Nebraska and having—among other things —run a carnival concession and done a stint as a dealer in Vegas. That's where Susan met him, Vegas. And she married him a few weeks later, without a prenup. Maybe she thought he was exotic, after years of boring high-society life with her late husband. Who knows what makes people get together?"

Lottie grinned and squeezed my hand. A lot of people thought we were an unlikely couple.

"Anyway," I went on, "one thing the two of them had in common was gardening. Harry and Susan loved flowers and spent a lot of time in the greenhouse at her Hillsborough estate. A couple of months after the wedding, one of her arrangements won what I guess you'd call the Grammy of gardening, and the picture in our file shows them with it, smiling like it was their firstborn and looking in love."

"I take it the wedded bliss didn't last?"

"You got it. Four months later, to the day, Susan disappeared. Vanished totally, without a trace. Leaving Harry in the Hillsborough mansion with the joint checkbooks. Everybody knew he'd murdered her, and that it was only a matter of time till he looted the accounts and split."

"But he didn't."

"Nope. Harry stayed put. He didn't even spend much money, just stayed on in the mansion and let the trust department of the bank pay the bills like they always did. He puttered around in the greenhouse, didn't date, didn't travel. Nobody knew if he was grieving, because he didn't have any friends. He just lay low and cooperated with the cops who were investigating his wife's disappearance."

"So maybe he didn't kill her after all."

"Wrong again. At least, according to Shar. She and her client, Susan Cross's attorney, claim Harry's a very patient man. He's been waiting, they say, for the seven years to pass so he can get Susan declared legally dead. And if he has, all that waiting'll pay off next week when he goes to court. Then all the loot'll belong to him."

"So that's what's kept you so busy lately. Trying to get the goods on Harry."

"Yep. Shar says that all people leave traces of their crimes, and it's just a matter of pinpointing and interpreting them. She's sure that Harry's feeling secure as his court date approaches and that he's bound to do something stupid."

"After seven years of being careful? I don't think so."

"That's what I told Shar. You'd think she'd give up, wouldn't you?"

Lottie shrugged. "Maybe, maybe not. I have a hard time giving up on anything. Even you."

Now what the hell did that mean? I didn't want to ask. Instead I watched the kids build their castles, and brooded about my morning conference with my aunt Sharon.

✣ ✣ ✣

"So what've got here, Mick?" Shar had asked me.

She looked bright-eyed and pretty and sexy—for an old broad of forty. Her boyfriend, Hy Ripinsky, must've been in town. "What we've got is zilch," I said.

She gave me a look that said, *Impossible.*

"Zilch," I said again, but not as firmly. "Here's how it went: Harry came out of the mansion at seven-thirty and went to the greenhouse. Stayed there till close to nine. Went inside and spent a couple hours in the room the house plans call the library." I'd got hold of the plans in a perfectly legal way, since the mansion was registered as a state historical building. "Then he went to the master-bedroom wing, and the lights there went out around midnight."

Shar seemed to be waiting.

"That's all there is." I couldn't hold back any longer. "This surveillance is idiotic, and on top of that, I think I've caught a cold."

Now she looked sad. Oh, hell, was she thinking I didn't have what it takes for the business? Normally, I don't get to do much field work, just sit at the computer, and she told me this case was a chance to prove my abilities. "Mick," she said after a minute, "maybe it'll help to review the case from day one."

"Whatever." I slumped down in my chair, resigned to the rehash of details I already knew by heart.

Shar opened the file in front of her, paged through it. "Susan Cross disappeared on October nineteen, six months and five days after she married Harry Homestead. That morning she drove to the city, left her car for an oil change at the Sutter-Stockton garage, and kept a nine-thirty appointment at Yosh for Hair on Maiden Lane. According to Homestead, he was to meet her in the lobby of the Saint Francis at twelve-thirty and take her to a nearby restaurant for lunch. Cross never showed.

"Homestead waited at the hotel till one-thirty. Staff members saw him arrive and later go to the phones. He called the beauty salon, and they told him Cross left around eleven. He checked with the garage and learned the car was still being serviced. Next he called home to see if she'd left a message there for him; phoned the restaurant, thinking they'd got their signals crossed about where to meet; called several of her friends, her attorney, and her banker, on the chance she'd stopped to see one of them and got held up. Nobody had seen her. Finally, he called the police."

To speed things up, I said, "The cops treated it as routine, told him to wait seventy-two hours and then report her missing. Next day her lawyer stepped in, and they took it more seriously. Cops talked to the people at Yosh's, and that's when the one weird thing came out."

Shar nodded. "Cross told her stylist that she was going to meet Homestead's mother later that day, and added that the woman was living in horrible circumstances. She said she hoped Mrs. Homestead would allow Harry and her to do something to help out. But when the stylist pressed for details, Cross changed the subject."

"And later it came out that Homestead's mother had died ten years earlier. He claimed he didn't know why his wife would tell the stylist something like that."

Shar flipped through the rest of the pages and closed the file. "The police started focusing their investigation on Homestead within the week. They searched the house and grounds of the estate; no body turned up. They did a complete background check on him. He came up clean except for a couple of old DUI's. He agreed to take a polygraph test and passed. But as we know, some people can fool the lie detector."

"Shar—"

"Cross's family hired private detectives to try to get something on Homestead," she went on. "Nothing. A reward was offered, and the usual nut cases come out of the woodwork. No leads. Homestead had no assets of his own, but he didn't seem inclined to tap into his wife's money. He's kept a low profile for seven years, and if we don't get something on him, next week he's going to be handsomely rewarded for murder."

"Did you ever consider that he didn't do it?"

"He did."

"Or that you might be just a tiny bit obsessed with—"

"I'm not. Harry Homestead killed his wife."

I threw up my hands. The woman can be so exasperating! "Okay! Whatever you say! He killed her. But we can't prove it. This case is impossible."

"I thought I taught you better than that. No case is impossible." She fixed me with that steely look of hers, the one that makes me feel like I'm still a five-year-old who won't pick up his toys. "I think you're burned out on this, Mick. Why don't you take the rest of the day off?"

"I'm not burned out, Shar! I'm just . . . realistic."

Her mouth twitched. It does that only when she's mad or worried. And I knew for sure she wasn't worried. "All right, I'll take the rest of the day off!" I got up and stomped out of there—fast.

❖   ❖   ❖

Lottie said, "Give it a rest, Mick. Stop fretting about the case and enjoy the afternoon." She motioned at the kids. "You ever do that?"

"Play in the sand? Who doesn't? We used to have contests to see who could build the best castle."

"Who won?"

"Me, of course."

"Of course." She poked me in the ribs. I put my arm around her for self-protection, and we kept on watching the kids. They sure were enterprising. The boy finished his castle, marked out a subdivision, and started building another. The girl saw what he was up to, left her castle, and laid a sandy cornerstone.

"Hey," the boy said to her, "you can't have two castles!"

"You've got two."

"That's different. I'm a boy and you're a girl. And girls don't got any money."

Lottie muttered, "A sexist, already!"

The little girl gave her brother a snotty look—the kind I've seen plenty of times, from all four of my sisters. "You think I don't have money," she told him. "I've got lots of stuff you don't know about." That was when he grabbed her bucket and dumped sand over her head, and she screamed, and the daddy jumped up and clobbered both of them.

And that was when something I hadn't thought of before occurred to me, and I jumped up from the log, then pulled Lottie to her feet. "Hey, let's go home."

"Now? Why?"

"I want to play with my laptop."

It was getting dark by the time we got to my condo on the Embarcadero, not far from McCone Investigations' offices. I went straight to my computer, not even bothering to take off my jacket, and Lottie joined me. By then, she'd figured out a few things too. "You doing a real estate data search?" she asked.

I nodded without looking up from the computer keyboard.

"Search by owner's name? San Francisco County?"

"Uh-huh."

She sat down on the couch and waited while data scrolled in front of me on the monitor. Within a few minutes I had the information: Parcel 019 140-50. Owner: Harry Homestead. I turned and smiled at Lottie.

"Mick," she drawled, "you're grinnin' like a jackass eatin' sweetbrier!"

"Well come and look where this property's located."

She scanned the screen. "Ingleside district. Isn't that the area of nice houses that drug dealers've taken over? Where the property values aren't worth squat anymore because of the crime factor?"

"Yep."

"So why would Homestead buy property there when he's got a perfectly good mansion down the Peninsula?"

"I can think of one reason."

Her eyes met mine, and then she shook her head. "You didn't read carefully, Mick. Homestead bought that property three years after his wife disappeared."

I looked where she was pointing. Damn!

"Wonder who owned the place before he bought it?" she said.

"This database doesn't show."

"County registrar of deeds is online."

My Lottie thinks faster on her feet than I do.

"Wolfgang Trujillo. What kind of a name is that?"

Lottie smiled. "One that's easy to trace. How many Wolfgang Trujillos can there be in San Francisco?"

"If he still lives here."

"Try Information." She handed me the phone. I got a number and called. No answer.

"Okay, Trujillo's not home, but I left a message on his machine. I'll try him again after I take a look at that Ingleside district address."

Lottie was already putting on her jacket. I went over and hugged her. "Sorry for ruining the afternoon and evening."

"I don't consider them ruined, not when we're nipping at the heels of a wife-killer."

"We?" I stepped back.

"Yeah, we. You're not keeping me out of this one. Besides, you might need me." She patted her oversized purse.

Yeah, I might. Lottie's firearms-qualified and has a carry permit for her .357 Magnum. I can't shoot straight to save my life. Plus she's better at interviewing witnesses that I am. Come to think of it, she's my equal or better at almost anything we do. Which is what makes the relationship interesting.

It was already the dangerous hour by the time we got to Harry Homestead's street on the other side of the city.

Three of those big old boats of cars that drug dealers seem to favor were parked in front of a house with a weedy front yard in the middle of the block. Guys who looked straight out of the Thugs "R" Us catalog lounged around on them, smoking and swapping lies while they waited for their clientele. Most of the houses there were big two-story stucco places, set back from the sidewalk on a little grassy rise. They must've been nice once, but now they had bars on their windows and FOR SALE signs on their lawns.

A couple of the dealers glanced at Lottie and me as we drove in, but the Yamaha and our leathers were what Shar called "protective coloration." Meaning that we looked like we belonged, so they didn't try to mess with us. A good thing, too, because the odds would've been with Lottie and her Magnum.

Harry's house was sunk way back behind a clump of yew trees. I pulled the bike up the drive and under them, and shut it down. Then we sat astride it, looking at the house. It was tall and narrow, cream stucco with dark timbers and leaded glass windows covered with heavy iron mesh. The light from the moon glinted off the glass, but otherwise it was dark.

"Nobody home," I whispered, "except maybe a ghost."

Lottie didn't answer. She was fumbling around in her purse. "Wait here," she whispered, and got off the bike.

"Where're you—" But she'd already disappeared into the yews. Dammit, what was she doing? This was my case. I should be calling the shots.

A few seconds later I spotted her slipping up the steps to the entry, flashlight in hand. She disappeared through an archway, and I saw the beam swing around, stop, swing some more. Then she came off the steps at a trot and hurried back to me. "House is protected by Bay Alarm. We don't want to mess with it," she said.

"I wasn't planning to break and enter." I probably sounded as pissed off as I felt.

"The hell you weren't!" She slid onto the seat behind me.

"Well, maybe I would, if it was an easy in-and-out. If we're right about this place, Harry hasn't been near it for years."

"There's still the problem of the timing. He bought it long after the missus disappeared."

"Maybe Wolfgang Trujillo can shed some light on that." I took out my cell phone and punched out his number.

❖  ❖  ❖

Wolfgang Trujillo lived in a residential hotel on Nob Hill, close to downtown and the theater district. His living room was so full of books and magazines and playbills and newspaper clippings that there was only one place to sit—an old armchair with busted springs. He offered the chair to Lottie, and she perched on its edge.

I leaned against the sill of a painted-shut window that stared smack at the wall of the next building, and watched Mr. Trujillo pace around the room. He must've been in his seventies, tall and skinny, with a sunken chest and a wild mop of white hair, and he liked to wave his arms around while he talked.

"Mr. Homestead bought the Ingleside house on the advice of my former tenant, James Chaffee," he said in response to Lottie's first question. "I never met Homestead. The transaction was handled through Coldwell Banker."

"The house was rented to Mr. Chaffee for how long?"

"Three, three and a half years before Mr. Homestead bought it. My wife had died, and I wanted to be closer to downtown, but I'd had difficulty selling, so I let it out instead."

"What can you tell me about Mr. Chaffee?"

"He was a good tenant, kept the house and yard up. He installed an alarm system and didn't ask for reimbursement. He paid his rent on a six-month basis, with a cashier's check drawn on Wells Fargo Bank."

"I suppose you ran a credit check on him before he took possession?"

Mr. Trujillo stopped pacing and gave Lottie a stern, somewhat astonished look. "Young woman, are you familiar with that neighborhood?"

"Uh, sort of."

"Then you must be aware of the problems involved in owning property there. A house is very difficult to rent when drug dealers are camping on its front lawn, intimidating everyone who comes and goes. Mr. Chaffee gave me a cash deposit as soon as he looked at the place. He returned within the hour with a bank check for the balance. Frankly, I wouldn't have cared if he had the credit rating of Saint Anthony."

"Huh?"

"Patron saint of paupers," I explained. I was raised Catholic, although most of it didn't take.

"Oh."

Lottie seemed thrown off her stride, so I questioned Mr. Trujillo. "Can you describe James Chaffee?"

"Certainly. He was around forty. Five-foot ten or thereabouts, slender build. He had blond hair that looked like a toupee, or maybe a wig. Very regular features."

"Anything else? Facial hair? Distinguishing marks?" So far, the description could've fit a lot of people.

Mr. Trujillo thought, staring up at the ceiling. "There was . . . Yes! He had a mole on his right earlobe. Quite a large one. I couldn't help but stare at it, and that seemed to make him uncomfortable."

As Lottie and I exchanged looks, the phone rang. Mr. Trujillo went to dig it out from behind a mound of clippings on the desk. He spoke with his back to us, then held out the receiver to me. "It's your employer, Ms. McCone."

How the hell had Shar known to call here? "So you're one step ahead of me," she said when I picked up.

"You found out about the house in Ingleside, and Mr. Trujillo?"

"Uh-huh. After you left I decided to run another background check on Homestead, in case the police missed something."

"Were you messing around with my computer?" Shar's only now becoming computer literate, and she doesn't really know what she's doing. Besides, nobody but me touches my office computer or laptop.

"It's the agency's machine, Mick."

And that was that. She wasn't going to tell me how she came up with the information. Sometimes I think the only reason she resists technology is to bother me.

I decided to one-up her. "Well, Lottie and I have found out that at the time his wife disappeared, Homestead was renting the Ingleside house under an assumed name. Here's what I think happened: Old Harry had arranged to meet Susan someplace other than the Saint Francis that day. After all, we've only got his word about their lunch date. She thought he was gonna take her to meet his mother, who was living in what she called horrible circumstances."

"In a house held siege by drug dealers."

"Right. He took Susan there, whacked her, hid the body— maybe in a freezer. Then he activated the alarm system he'd had installed and went to the Saint Francis, where he made sure the staff saw him. And then he put on his act for the people he called and the cops."

"So the body's been in the house for all seven years?"

"Protected by the alarm system. For added insurance, Harry bought the place after enough time had gone by that the cops had back-burnered Susan's disappearance. If he's visited since, he's been real careful."

Shar didn't say anything. Sometimes those silences of hers unnerve me. "So do we go to the cops with this?" I asked.

"I think you're right about what happened," she said, "but it'll appear an iffy scenario at best to the police. And there'd be nothing they could do. No judge would issue a search warrant without probable cause. We'll have to see if we can get Homestead to visit the house again—in front of the right witnesses."

Shar spent the next morning in conference with Susan Cross's attorney, an inspector from the SFPD homicide detail, and a representative of Bay Alarm. I spent the afternoon at the florist's.

Not just any florist, mind you, but Sylvester Piazza, arranger to the glitterati. His fancy shop on Post Street was chock-full of flowers and plants that I'd never seen before, and every customer who came in dropped more bucks than I spend on rent each month. Sylvester himself was a hoot, as Lottie would say: a tubby little guy with thinning blow-dried hair. He scurried around his workroom in his black velvet jumpsuit, plucking a blossom from here, a piece of greenery from there, and mumbling about what an honor it was to be asked to replicate Susan Cross's masterpiece. La Cross—he actually called her that—had been a divine floral "artiste."

I sat on a stool and watched as he consulted the color photo of Susan's prize-winning arrangement that her lawyer had given us, and wondered why I'm always the one who gets the weird assignments at McCone Investigations. Sylvester arranged happily, humming opera and occasionally bursting into song. Finally he stepped back and eyeballed his work, nodded, and announced, "Now for the piece de resistance!" He went to one of his glass cases and rustled through the flowers stored there. Suddenly he stopped, clutched his heart, and let out a strangled howl.

I was off the stool right away, thinking he was having some sort of attack. As he doubled over, I rushed to steady him. "What's wrong?"

"The *Strelitzia!*" he sobbed.

A fatal disease? Some body part gone out of whack? "Say what?"

"Bird of paradise! It's the focal point of the arrangement, what gives it its meaning! And I have none! One of my dunderheaded assistants must have used it!"

"If that's the problem, my dad has one of those plants that he brought back from Hawaii—"

"No, you imbecile, I'm talking about the giant bird of paradise! *Strelitzia nicolai.* The bananalike leaves, the purple floral envelope! Without it, this arrangement is nothing! Even if I could locate a proper plant, getting the cuttings here on time would be impossible."

"Can't you substitute—"

Sylvester's face scrunched up and got red, and he shrieked, "Substitute?"

Right then Lottie breezed in. "Shar sent me to—what's his problem?"

"No *Strelitzia.* I'll let him explain." I went outside and took a walk over to Union Square. The most zoned-out homeless guy there looked normal after old Sylvester.

When I got back to the florist's shop, Lottie was on the phone, and Sylvester lay on the floor doing deep-breathing exercises. "Bird of paradise," Lottie was saying. "No, the giant variety . . . You don't? Well, thanks anyway." She hung up and gave me the evil eye. "While you've been out I've called thirty-three florists. Seems giant bird of paradise is in short supply."

"So use something else."

Sylvester moaned dramatically. Lottie rolled her eyes. "He says the arrangement won't look right, and that'll ruin its effect." She consulted a list, picked up the receiver again and punched in a number.

Till then I'd never realized how much like Shar she is. Single-minded and stubborn in the extreme. I watched as she went through the whole list without turning up any giant *Strelitzia*. Then she grabbed one of Sylvester's reference books and stuck her nose into it. "There's got to be something," she muttered.

You'd think she'd give up. Wouldn't you?

❖ ❖ ❖

At around ten that night I was once again hunkered down in shrubbery—this time in the yew trees at the Ingleside house, with Shar on one side of me and Lottie on the other. The guy from Bay Alarm had already called Harry Homestead to tell him about a malfunction in the security system and the huge floral arrangement sitting on the front porch. Now he was waiting on the walk for Harry to arrive. And not far away, in deepest shadow, lurked a couple of San Francisco's finest.

"You really think this'll work?" I whispered.

"Yes," Shar and Lottie said in unison.

I looked from one to the other. Their expressions were so fierce that I was reminded of a horror movie where these harpies ripped a poor helpless male to shreds.

A few minutes more and a car turned into the driveway. Its headlights moved over the yew trees, and even though we were well hidden, I ducked my head. The car door slammed, footsteps tapped on the concrete, and a figure in a trench coat hurried up the walk to the security guy. From my past surveillances, I recognized old Harry.

"What's going on here?" he demanded.

The security man said something I couldn't hear, turned on his flashlight, and shone it up the steps at the porch where the flowers were.

Homestead went stiff. He took a step toward the house, stopped and said, "How long has that been here?"

"It was here when I checked the place around nine. The malfunction came up on our command center screens at eight-fifteen."

Homestead was still staring at the floral arrangement. "You sure it wasn't a break-in?"

"Well, we can't be a hundred percent certain, but there's no evidence of tampering. All the same, if you'll give me your keys, I'll check around inside—"

"No! I mean, don't go to the trouble. I'll take it from here."

"It's no trouble—"

"Just go. Please." The security guy shrugged and went down the driveway to his car.

Harry stayed where he was, staring at the dark porch. Finally he squared his shoulders and started up there. At the top of the steps he took out what I guessed was a Bic and flicked it. The flame flared, wavered and went out as he dropped the lighter. And Harry let out a sound that made the hair on the back of my neck stand up. "Got him!" Lottie whispered.

Next I heard Harry fumbling with the lock. The door opened and banged back against the inside wall. Light came on overhead, and Harry pushed the flower arrangement aside and stumbled down the hallway. Other lights flashed on, progressing from the front to the back of the house. Lottie murmured, "I'd say he's as nervous as a long-tailed cat in a room full of rockers."

A few seconds later the cops who had been watching nearby stepped out of the shadows and flashed us a thumbs-up sign. Hands on their holstered guns, they climbed the steps to investigate whoever it was who'd entered a long-unoccupied house in one of the city's most crime-ridden areas.

Shar stood up and brushed a piece of yew tree out of her hair. "The flowers really spooked him! Sylvester Piazza must've done

one hell of a job."

"Actually, the arrangement doesn't exactly match Susan Cross's original," Lottie said.

"Oh?" Shar's eyes were on the house.

"Yeah. Sylvester couldn't get any giant bird of paradise, so I came up with the idea of substituting something even more effective. *Sansevieria.*"

"What's that?"

Lottie grinned wickedly. "Something that's highly appropriate, given that Harry lured his wife here on the pretext that she was to meet his mother. The common name for *Sansevieria* is mother-in-law's tongue."

Shar started to laugh, and she was still laughing when the cops dragged a handcuffed Harry from the garage. They'd found him checking the freezer to make sure Susan Cross hadn't risen from the dead to create one last flower arrangement.

# UP AT THE RIVERSIDE
## (Ted Smalley)

"**D**uck if you see a cop, Ted."
And so we were off on our mission: my boss, Sharon McCone; my partner, Neal Osborn; and me, Ted Smalley. She, the issuer of my orders, drove her venerable MG convertible. He sat slouched and rumpled beside her. I was perched on the backseat, if you could call it that, which you really can't because it's nothing more than a shelf for carrying one's groceries and such. And illegal for passengers, which is why I had to keep a keen eye out for the law.

❖ ❖ ❖

I think our minor vehicular transgression made Shar feel free—far away from her everyday concerns about clients and caseloads at the investigative agency she owns. I knew our excursion was taking Neal's mind off the rising rent and declining profits of his used bookstore. And even though I entertained an image of myself as a sack from Safeway, my thinning hair ruffling like the leaves of a protruding bunch of celery, I still felt like a kid cutting school. A kid who had freed himself from billing and correspondence, to say nothing of keeping five private investigators and the next-door law firm in number-two pencils and scratch pads.

Soon we were across the Golden Gate Bridge and speeding north on Highway 101. It was a summer Friday and traffic was heavy, but Shar made the MG zip from lane to lane and we outdistanced them all. Our mission was a pleasurable one: a stop along the Russian River to look at and perhaps purchase the jukebox of Neal's and my dreams, then a picnic on the beach at Jenner.

Our plans had been formulated that morning when Shar called us at the ungodly hour of six, all excited. "One of those jukeboxes you guys want is advertised in today's classified," she said.

"Seeburg Trashcan, and you won't believe this: It's almost within your price range."

While I primed my brain into running order, Neal went to fetch our copy of the paper. "Phone number's in the 707 area code," he said into the downstairs extension. "Sonoma County."

"Nice up there," Shar said wistfully.

"Maybe Ted and I can take a drive on Sunday, check it out."

I issued a Neanderthal grunt of agreement. Till I have at least two cups of coffee, I'm not verbal. "I've a feeling somebody'll snap it up before then," she said.

"Well, if you'll give Ted part of the day off, I can ask my assistant to mind the store."

"I . . . oh, hell, why don't the three of us take the whole day off? I'll pack a picnic. You know that sourdough loaf I make, with all the melted cheese and stuff?"

"Say no more."

Shar exited the freeway at River Road and we sped through vineyards toward the redwood forest. When we rolled into the town of Guerneville, its main street mirrored our holiday spirits. People roamed the sidewalks in shorts and t-shirts, many eating ice cream cones or by-the-slice pizza; a flea market in the parking lot of a supermarket was doing a brisk business; rainbow flags flapped in the breeze outside gay-owned businesses.

The town has been the hub of the resort area for generations; rustic cabins and summer homes line the riverbank and back up onto the hillsides. In the seventies it became a vacation-time mecca for gays, and the same wide-open atmosphere as in San Francisco's Castro district prevailed, but by the late eighties the AIDS epidemic, a sagging economy, and a succession of disastrous floods had taken away the magic. Now it appeared that Guerneville was bouncing back as an eclectic and bohemian community of hardy folk who are willing to yearly risk cresting flood waters and mud slides. I, the grocery sack, smiled benevolently as we cruised along.

❖ ❖ ❖

Outside of town the road wound high above the slow-moving river.

At the hamlet of Monte Rio, we crossed the bridge and turned down a narrow lane made narrower by encroaching redwoods and vehicles pulled close to the walls of the mainly shabby houses. Neal began squinting at the numbers. "Dammit, why don't they make them bigger?" he muttered.

I refrained from reminding him that he was overdue for his annual checkup at the optometrist's.

Shar was the one who spotted the place: a large sagging three-story dirty-white clapboard structure with a parking area out front. The roof was missing a fair number of its shingles, the windows were hopelessly crusted with grime, and one column of the wide front porch leaned alarmingly. On the porch, to either side of the double front door, sat identical green wicker rockers, and in each sat a scowly-looking man. Between them, extending from the door and down the steps, was a series of orange cones such as highway department crews use. A yellow plastic tape strung from cone to cone bore the words DANGER DO NOT CROSS DANGER DO NOT CROSS DANGER DO NOT CROSS . . .

In as reverent a tone as I'd ever heard him use, Neal said, "Good God, it's the old Riverside Hotel!"

While staring at it Shar had overshot the parking area. As she drove along looking for a place to turn around she asked, "You know this place?"

"From years ago. Was built as a fancy resort in the twenties. People would come up from the city and spend their entire vacations here. Then in the seventies the original owner's family sold it to a guy named Tom Atwater, who turned it into a gay hotel. Great restaurant and bar, cottages with individual hot tubs scattered on the grounds leading down to the beach, anything-goes atmosphere."

"You stayed there?" I asked.

Neal heard the edge in my voice. He turned his head and smiled at me, laugh lines around his eyes crinkling. It amuses and flatters him that I'm jealous of his past. "I had dinner there. Twice."

Shar turned the MG in a driveway and we coasted back toward

the hotel. The men were watching us. Both were probably in their mid fifties, dressed in shorts and t-shirts, but otherwise—except for the scowls—they were total opposites. The one on our left was a scarecrow with a shock of long gray-blond hair; the one on the right reminded me of Elmer Fudd, and had just as bald a pate.

When we climbed out of the car—the grocery sack needing a firm tug—Neal called, "I phoned earlier about the jukebox."

The scarecrow jerked his thumb at Fudd and kept scowling. Fudd arranged his face into more pleasant lines and got up from the rocker.

"I'm Chris Fowler," he said. "You Neal and Ted?"

"I'm Neal, this is Ted, and that's Sharon."

"Come on in, I'll show you the box."

" 'Come on in, I'll show you the box,' " the scarecrow mimicked in a high nasal whine.

"Jesus!" Chris Fowler exclaimed. He led us through his side of the double front door.

Inside was a reception area that must've been magnificent before the oriental carpets faded and the flocked wallpaper became water stained and peeling. In its center stood a mahogany desk backed by an old fashioned pigeonhole arrangement, and wide stairs on either side led up to the second story. The yellow tape continued, from the door to the pigeonholes, neatly bisecting the room.

Shar stopped and stared at it, frowning. I tugged her arm and shook my head. Sometimes the woman can be so rude. Chris Fowler didn't notice though, just turned right into a dimly lighted barroom. "There's your jukebox," he said.

A thing of beauty, it was. Granted, a particular acquired-taste kind of beauty: shaped like an enormous trash can of fake blond wood, with two flaring red plastic side panels and a gaudy gilt grille studded with plastic gems. Tiny mirrored squares surrounded the grille, and the while thing was decked out with enough chrome as a 1950s Cadillac. I went up to it and touched the coin slot. Five plays for a quarter, two for a dime, one for a nickel. Those were the days.

Instantly I fell in love.

When I looked at Neal, his eyes were sparkling. "Can we play it?" he asked Chris.

"Sure." He took a nickel from his pocket and dropped it into the slot. Whirrs, clicks, and then mellow tones crooned, "See the pyramids across the Nile . . ."

Shar shook her head, rolled her eyes, and wandered off to inspect a pinball machine. She despairs of Neal's and my campy tendencies.

"So what d'you think?" Chris asked.

I said, "Good sound tone."

Neal said, "The price is kind of steep for us, though."

Chris said, "I'll throw in a box of extra 78s."

Neal said, "I don't know . . ."

And then Shar wandered back over. "What's with the tape?" she asked Chris. "And what's with the guy on the other side of it?"

Neal looked as if he wanted to strangle her. I stifled a moan. A model of subtlety, Shar, and right when we were trying to strike a deal.

Chris grimaced. "That's my partner of many years, Ira Sloan. We've agreed to disagree. The tape's my way of indicating my displeasure with him."

"Disagree over what?"

"This hotel. We jointly inherited it six months ago from Tom Atwater. Did either of you guys know him?"

I shook my head, but Neal nodded. He said, "I met him." Grinned at me and added, "Twice."

"Well," Chris said, "Tom was an old friend. In fact, he introduced Ira and me, nearly twenty years ago. When he left the place to us we said, 'What a great way to get out of the city, have our own business in an area that's experiencing a renaissance.' So we sold our city house, moved up here, called in the contractors, and got estimates of what it would take to go upscale and reopen. The building's run down, but the construction's solid. All it needs outside is a new roof and paint job. The cottages were swept away in the floods, but eventually they can be rebuilt. Inside here, all it would take is redecorating, a new chimney and fireplace in the common room on the other side, and updated kitchen equipment. So then what does my partner decide to do?"

All three of us shook our heads, caught up in his breathless monologue.

"My loving partner decides we're to do nothing. Even though we've got more than enough money to fix the place up, he wants to leave it as is and live out our golden years here in Faulkneresque splendor while it falls down around us!"

Neal and I looked properly horrified, but Shar asked, "So why'd you put up the tape?" Maybe a singleminded focus is an asset in a private investigator, but it seems to me it plays hell with interpersonal relations.

Chris wanted to talk about the tape, however. "Ira and I divided the place, straight down the middle. He took the common room, utility room, and the area on the floors above it. I took the restaurant, kitchen, bar, and above. I prepare the meals and slip his under the tape on the reception desk. He washes our clothes and pushes mine over here to me. I'll tell you, it's quite a life!"

"And in the meantime, you're selling off the fixtures in your half?"

"Only the ones that won't fit the image I want to create here."

"How can you create it in half a hotel?"

"I can't, but I'm hoping Ira'll come around eventually. I wish I knew why he has this tic about keeping the place the way it is. If I did, I know I could talk him out of the notion."

Shar was looking thoughtful now. She walked around the jukebox, examining its lovely lines and gnawing at her lower lip. She peered through the glass at the turntable where the 78 of "You Belong to Me" now rested silently. She glanced through the archway at the yellow plastic tape.

"Chris," she said, "what would it be worth to you to find out what Ira's problem is?"

"A lot."

"A reduction of price on this jukebox to one my friends can afford?"

I couldn't believe it! Yes, she was offering out of the goodness of her heart, because she'd seen how badly Neal and I wanted the jukebox, and she knew the limits of our budget. But she was also doing it because she never can resist a chance to play detective.

Chris looked surprised, then grinned. "A big reduction, but I don't see how—"

She took one of her business cards from her purse and handed it to him. Said to me, "Come on, Watson. The game's afoot."

♣ ♣ ♣

"Mr. Sloan?" Shar was standing at the tape on the porch. I was trying to hide behind her.

Ira Sloan's eyes flicked toward us, then straight ahead.

"Oh, Mr. Sloan!" Now she was waving, for heaven's sake, as if he wasn't sitting a mere five feet away!

His scowl deepened.

Shar stepped over the tape. "Mr. Sloan, d'you suppose you could give Ted and me a tour of your side of the hotel? We love old places like this, and we both think it's a shame your partner wants to spoil it."

He turned his head, looking skeptical but not as ferocious.

Shar reached back and yanked on my arm so hard that I almost tripped over the tape. "Ted's partner, Neal, is in there with Chris, talking upscale. I had to remove Ted before they end up with a tape down the middle of their apartment."

Ira Sloan ran his hand through his longish hair and stood up. He was very tall—at least six-four—and so skinny he seemed to have no ass at all. Had he always been so thin, or was it the result of too many cooling meals shoved across the reception desk?

He said, "The tape was his idea."

"So he told us."

"Thinks it's funny."

"It's not."

"I like people who appreciate old things. It'll be a pleasure to show you around."

♣ ♣ ♣

The common room was full of big maple furniture with wide wooden arms and thick floral chintz-covered cushions, faded now.

The chairs and sofas would've been fashionable in the thirties and forties, campy in the seventies. Now they just looked tired. Casement windows overlooked the lawn and the river, and on the far side of the room was a deep stone fireplace whose chimney showed chinks where the mortar had crumbled. Against the stones hung an oval stained-glass panel in muddy looking colors. It reminded me of the stone in one of those mood rings that were popular in the seventies.

By the time we'd inspected the room, Shar and Ira Sloan were chattering up a storm. By the time we got upstairs to the guestrooms, they were old friends.

The guestrooms were furnished with waterbeds, another cultural icon of the sybaritic decade. Now their mattresses were shriveled like used condoms. The suites had Jacuzzi tubs set before the windows, once brightly colored porcelain, but now rust-stained and grimy. The balconies off the third-story rooms were narrow and cobwebby, and the webbing on their lounge chairs had been stripped away, probably by nesting birds.

Shar asked, "How long was the hotel in operation?"

"Tom closed it in 'eighty-three."

"Why?"

"Declining business. By then . . . well, a lot of things were over."

It made me so sad. The Riverside Hotel's brief time in the sun had been a wild, tumultuous, drug-hazed era—but also curiously innocent. A time of experimentation and new found freedom. A time to adopt new lifestyles without fear of reprisal. But now the age of innocence was over, harsh reality had set in. Many of the men who had stayed here were dead, many others decaying like this structure.

Why would Ira Sloan want to keep intact this monument to the death of happiness?

❖ ❖ ❖

Back downstairs Shar whispered to me, "Stay here. Talk with him." Then she was gone into the reception room and over the tape.

I turned, trying to think of something to say to Ira Sloan, but he'd vanished into some dark corner of the haunted place, possibly to commune with his favorite ghost. I sat down on one of the chairs amid a cloud of rising dust to see if he'd return. Against the chimney the stained-glass mood-ring stone seemed to have darkened. My mood darkened with it. I wanted out of this place and into the sun.

In about ten minutes Ira Sloan still hadn't reappeared. I heard a rustling behind the reception desk. Shar—who else? She was removing a ledger from a drawer under the warning tape and spreading it open.

"Well, that's interesting," she muttered after a couple of minutes. "Very interesting."

A little while more and she shut the ledger and stuffed it into her tote bag. Smiled at me and said, "Let's go now. You look as though you can use some of my famous sourdough loaf and a walk by the sea."

❖ ❖ ❖

When we were ensconced on the sand with our repast spread before us, I asked Shar, "What'd you take from the desk?"

"The guest register." She pulled it from her tote and handed it to me.

"You stole it?"

Her mouth twitched—a warning sign. "Borrowed it, with Chris's permission."

"Why?"

"Well, when I went back to talk with him some more, I asked how the two of them decided who got what. He said Ira insisted on his side of the hotel, and Chris was glad to divide it that way because he likes to cook."

Neal poured wine into plastic glasses and handed them around. "Bizarre arrangement, if you ask me."

Shar was cutting the sourdough loaf, in imminent danger of sawing off a finger as well. I took the knife from her and performed culinary surgery.

"Anyway," she went on, "then I asked Chris if Ira had insisted on getting anything else. He said only the guest register. But by then Chris'd gotten his back up, and he pointed out that the ledger was kept in a drawer of the desk that's bisected by the tape. So they agreed to leave it there and hold it in common. Ira wasn't happy with the arrangement."

I filled paper plates with slices of the loaf. Its delicious aroma was quickly dispelling my hotel-induced funk.

"And did the register tell you anything?" Neal asked.

"Only that somebody—I assume Ira—tore the pages out for the week of August 13, 1978. Recently."

"How d'you know it was recent?"

"Fresh tears look different than old ones. The edges of these aren't browning." She flipped the book open to where the pages were missing.

"So now what?"

"I try to find out who was there and what happened that week. Maybe some well known who was still in the closet stayed there. Or somebody who was with a person he wasn't supposed to be."

I asked, "How're you going to find out, if the pages're missing?"

She stabbed her finger at the first column on the ledger page, then at the last. "Date checked in, date checked out. Five individuals who checked in before the thirteenth checked out on the eighteenth. My job for this weekend is to try to locate and talk with them."

"Hey, Ted, come along with me!"

Shar was in the driver's seat of the agency van parked on the floor of Pier 24½, where we have our offices. I was dragging tail down the iron stairway from the second level, intent on heading home after a perfectly outlandish Monday. I went over to the van and leaned in the open window. "What's happening?"

"With any luck, you and I are going to collect your jukebox this evening and have it back at your place by the time Neal closes the store." Anachronism, Neal's used bookstore, is open till nine on Mondays.

I jumped into the van, the day's horrors forgotten. "You find out what Ira Sloan's problem is?"

"Some of it. The rest is about to unfold."

I got my seatbelt on just as she swerved into traffic on the waterfront boulevard outside the pier. Thanked God I was firmly strapped in, a grocery sack no longer.

❖ ❖ ❖

The house was on a quiet street on the west side of Petaluma, a small city some forty minutes north of the Golden Gate. It used to be called the Egg Basket of the World, before the chicken boom went bust. From what I hear lately, it's turning into Yuppie Heaven.

As we got out of the van I looked up at the gray Victorian. It had a wide porch, high windows, and a fan-like pediment over the door that was painted in the colors of the rainbow. This, Shar had told me, was the home of Mark Curry, one of the men who had stayed at the Riverside during the second week of August, 1978. Surprisingly, given the passage of time, she'd managed to locate three of the five who'd signed the register before the missing week, and to interview two so far.

"Ted," she said, "how long have gays been doing that rainbow thing?"

"You mean the flags and all? Funny—since 1978. The first rainbow flag was designed by a San Francisco artist, Gilbert Baker, as a sign of the gay community's solidarity. A version of it was flown in the next year's Pride Parade."

"I didn't realize it went back that far." She started up the walk, and I followed.

The man who answered the door was slender and handsome, with a fine-boned face and a diamond stud in one nostril, and a full head of wavy gray hair that threatened to turn me green with envy. His wood-paneled parlor made me envious too: full of Chippendale furniture, with a gilt harp in the front window. Mark Curry seated us there, offered coffee, and went to fetch it.

Shar saw the way I was looking at the room. "It's not you," she said. "In a room like this that jukebox would look—"

"Like a wart on the face of an angel. But in our place—"

"It'll still look like a trashcan."

Mark Curry came back with a silver coffee service, and got down to business while he poured. "After you phoned, Ms. McCone, I got in touch with Chris Fowler. He's an old friend, from the time we worked as volunteers at an AIDS hospice. He vouched for you, so I dug out my journal for 1978 and refreshed my memory about August's stay at the Riverside."

"You arrived there August eleventh?"

"Yes."

"Alone?"

"No, with my then partner, Dave Howell. He's been dead . . . do you believe nearly sixteen years now?"

"I'm sorry."

"Thanks. Sometimes it seems like yesterday."

"Were you and Mr. Howell staying in a cottage or the main building?"

"Main building, third floor, river side. Over the bar."

"D'you recall who else was there?"

"Well, the place was always full in the summertime, and a lot of the men I didn't know. And even more people came in over the weekend. There was to be a canoeing regatta on Wednesday the sixteenth, with a big barbecue on the beach that evening, and they were gearing up for it.

I said, "*Canoeing* regatta?"

Mark Curry winked at me. "A bunch of guys, stoned and silly, banging into each other and capsizing and having a great time of it."

"Sounds like fun."

Shar said, "So who do you remember?"

"Well, Tom Atwater, of course. His lover, Bobby Gardena, showed up on Tuesday. Bobby had a house in the city, divided his time between there and the river. Ira Sloan, one of Tom's best friends, and the guy who inherited that white elephant along with Chris. He was alone, had just broken off a relationship, and seemed pretty unhappy, but a few months later Tom introduced him to Chris, and they've been together ever since. Then there was Sandy Janssen. Darryl Williams. And of course there was . . ."

Shar dutifully noted the names, but I sensed she'd lost interest in them. No well known who customarily hid in the closet, no scandalous mispairing. When Mark Curry ran out of people, she said, "Tell me about the week of the thirteenth. Did anything out of the ordinary happen?"

Mark Curry laughed. "Out of the ordinary was de rigeur at the Riverside."

"More out of the ordinary than usual."

Her serious—and curiously intense—tone sobered him. He stared into his coffee cup, recapturing his memories. When he spoke, his voice was subdued.

"The night of the regatta, you know? Everybody was on the beach, carrying on till all hours. A little before two Dave and I decided we wanted to have a couple of quiet drinks alone, so we slipped away from the party. I remember walking up the slope from the beach and across the lawn to the hotel. Everything was so quiet. I suppose it was just the contrast to the commotion on the beach, but it gave me the shivers. Dave, too. And when we went inside, it was still quiet, but . . ."

"But what, Mr. Curry?"

"There was a . . . an undercurrent. A sense of whispers and footfalls, but you couldn't really identify whose or where they were. Like something was going on, but not really. You know how that can be?"

Shar's face was thoughtful. She's had a lot of unusual experiences in her life, and I was sure she did know how that could be.

Mark Curry added, "Dave and I went into the bar and sat down. Nobody came. We were about to make our own drinks— you could do that, so long as you signed a chit—when Ira Sloan stepped out of the kitchen and told us the bar was closed."

"But this was after legal closing time."

He shook his head. "The bar at the Riverside never closed. It was immune to the dictates of the state lawmakers—some of whom were its frequent patrons."

"I see. Did Ira give you any explanation?"

"No. He asked if we wanted to buy a bottle, so we did, and

took it up to our room and consumed it on our balcony. And all night the noisy party on the beach went on. But the quiet in the hotel was louder than any cacophony I've ever experienced."

❖ ❖ ❖

When we got back to the van, Shar took out her phone and made a call. "Hi, Mick," she said. "Anything?"

Mick Savage, her nephew, computer specialist, and fastest skiptracer in the west.

"I see . . . Uh-huh . . . Right . . . No evidence about a gas leak on Friday the eighteenth? . . . Yes, I thought as much . . . No, nothing else. And thanks."

She broke the connection, stuffed the phone back into her bag, and looked at me. Her expression was profoundly sad.

"You've got yourself a jukebox," she said.

❖ ❖ ❖

"Before I go into this," Shar said to Chris Fowler, "there's something I ought to say."

The three of us were seated at a table in the bar at the Riverside. The dim lighting made Chris look curiously young and hopeful.

"Secrets," Shar went on, "are not necessarily harmful, so long as they remain secrets. But once you put them into words, they can't be taken back. Ever."

Chris nodded. "I understand what you're trying to tell me, but I need to know."

"All right, then. I spoke with three men who were present at the hotel on Wednesday, August 16, 1978. Each gave me bits and pieces of a story, that led me to suspect what happened. A check I had run on a fourth man pretty much confirmed my suspicions.

"On August sixteenth of that year, a canoeing regatta was held at this hotel—a big yearly event. The cottages and rooms were all full, but we're only concerned with a few people: Tom Atwater and his lover, Bobby Gardena. Ira. And my witnesses: Mark Curry, Darryl Williams, and Sandy Janssen.

"All three witnesses came up here the Friday before the regatta. Ira arrived on Sunday, Bobby Gardena on Tuesday. It soon became apparent to everybody that Tom and Bobby weren't getting on.

Bobby was baiting Tom. They quarreled frequently and publicly. Bobby confided to Sandy Janssen that he'd told Tom he'd quit his job and put his San Francisco house up for sale, with the intention of moving to New Orleans. Tom accused him of being involved with somebody else, and Bobby wouldn't confirm or deny it. He taunted Tom with the possibility.

"After the regatta there was a barbecue on the beach. Everybody was there except for Tom, Bobby, and Ira. Bobby had told Darryl Williams he planned to pack and head back to the city that night. Ira was described by Mark Curry as alone and unhappy."

I heard a noise in the reception area and looked that way. A thin scarecrow's shape stood deep in shadow on the other side of the desk. Ira Sloan. I started to say something, then thought, No. Shar and Chris are discussing him. He has a right to hear, doesn't he?

"Something unusual happened that night," Shar continued. "Mark Curry noticed it when he returned to the hotel around two. Sandy Janssen described a strange atmosphere that kept him from sleeping well. Darryl Williams talked about hearing whispers in the corridors. The next morning Tom told everybody that Bobby had left early for the city, but Darryl claims he saw Bobby's car in the lot when he looked out his window around nine. An hour later it was gone. None of my three witnesses ever heard from or saw Bobby again. The skip trace I had run on him turned up nothing. The final closing on the sale of his city house was handled by Tom, who had his power-of-attorney."

Chris Fowler started to say something, but Shar held up her hand. "And here's the most telling point: On Thursday night, all the guests received notice that they had to vacate the premises on Friday morning, due to a potentially dangerous gas leak that needed to be worked on. A leak that PG&E has no record of. The only men who remained behind were Tom and Ira."

Chris sat very still, breathing shallowly. I looked at the reception area. The scarecrow figure in the shadows hadn't moved.

"I think you can draw your own conclusions," Shar added. She spoke gently and sadly—not the usual trumpeting and crowing that I hear from her when she solves a case.

Slowly Chris said, "God, I can't believe Tom killed Bobby! He was a gentle man. I never saw him raise his hand to anybody."

"It may have been self defense," Shar said. "Darryl Williams told me one of his friends had an earlier relationship with Bobby, an abusive one. Bobby always threw the first punches."

"So an argument, a moment of violence . . ."

"Is all it takes."

"Naturally he would've turned to Ira to help him cover up. They were best friends, had been since grade school. But that doesn't make Ira a murderer."

"No, it doesn't."

"Anyway, you can't prove it."

"Not without Bobby's remains—which are probably somewhere in this hotel."

Chris glanced around, shivering slightly. "And as long as they're here, Ira and I will be at a stalemate, estranged for the rest of our lives. That's how long he'll guard them."

I was still staring at Ira Sloan's dark figure, but now I looked beyond it, into the common room. The stained-glass oval hanging on the fireplace chimney, that I'd fancifully thought of as the stone in a mood ring, gleamed in the rays from a nearby floor lamp: pink, red, orange, yellow, green, blue, indigo. The seven colors of the rainbow.

I said, "I know where Bobby's buried."

"When I saw this stained glass yesterday," I said, "I couldn't tell the colors, on account of it being hung where no light could pass through. A strange place, and that should've told Shar or me something right then. Tonight, with the lamp on, I see that it's actually the seven colors of the rainbow."

We—Shar, Chris, and I—were standing in front of the fireplace. I could feel Ira Sloan's presence in the shadows behind us.

"It's the only rainbow symbol in the hotel," I went on, "and it was probably commissioned by Tom Atwater sometime in 1978."

"Why then?" Shar asked.

"Remember I told you that the first rainbow flag was designed in '78? And that a version of it was flown in the '79 Pride Parade?"

She nodded.

"The '78 flag was seven colors, like this panel. Respectively, they symbolized sexuality, life, healing, sun, nature, art, harmony, and spirit. But the flag that was flown at the parade only had six colors. They dropped indigo so there would be exactly three stripes on either side of the street. That's the one that's become popular and is recognized by the International Congress of Flag Makers."

Chris said, "So Tom and Ira put Bobby's body someplace temporary the night of the murder—maybe the walk-in freezer—and after Tom closed the hotel, they walled him in behind the fireplace. But Tom was a sentimental guy, and he loved Bobby. He'd've wanted some monument."

Behind us there was a whisper of noise, such as I imagined had filled this hotel the night of August 16, 1978. Shar heard it—I could tell from the way she cocked her head—but Chris didn't.

Bitterly he said, "It couldn't've been self defense. If it was, Tom or Ira would've called the county sheriff."

"It wasn't self defense," Ira's voice said. "It was an accident. I was there. I saw it."

Slowly we turned toward the reception area. Ira Sloan had come out of the shadows and was backed up against the warning tape, his face twisted with the despair of one who expects not to be believed.

"Bobby was leaving to go back to the city," he added. "He was taunting Tom about how he'd be seeing his new lover. They were at the top of the stairs. Tom called Bobby an ugly name, and Bobby went to hit him. Tom ducked, Bobby lost his balance. He fell, rolled over and over, and hit his head on the base of the reception desk." He motioned at the sharp corner near the stairway.

Shar asked, "Why didn't you call the sheriff?"

"Tom had been outspoken about gay rights. Outspoken and

abrasive. He had enemies on the county board of supervisors and in the sheriff's department. They'd have seen to it that he was charged with murder. Tom was afraid, so I did what any friend would do."

Chris said, "For God's sake, Ira, why didn't you tell me this when we inherited the hotel?"

"I wanted to preserve Tom's memory. And I was afraid what you might think of me. What you might do about it."

His partner was silent for a moment. Then he said, "I should've let you keep your secret."

"Maybe not," Shar told him. "Secrets that tear two people apart are destructive and potentially dangerous."

"But—"

"The fact is, Chris, that secrets come in all varieties. What you do about them, too. You can expose them, and then everybody gets hurt. You can make a tacit agreement to keep them, and by the time they come out, nobody cares, but keeping them's still exacted its toll on you. Or you can share them with a select group of trusted people and agree to do something about them."

"What're you trying to tell me?"

"The group of people in this room is a small and closed-mouthed one. We all know Ira can keep his own counsel. Bobby Gardena's been in his tomb a long time, but I doubt he's rested easily. Perhaps it would release him if you moved his remains to a more suitable place on the property, and created a better monument to him."

I said, "A better monument, like a garden in the colors of the rainbow."

Chris nodded. A faint ray of hope touched Ira's tortured features.

I added, "Of course, a fitting monument to both Bobby and Tom would be if you renovated this hotel like you planned and reopened it to the living."

Chris nodded again. Then he went to Ira, grasped the warning tape, and tore it free from where it was anchored to the pigeonholes.

❖ ❖ ❖

I rode in the back of the van on our way home to the city, making sure the Seeburg Trashcan didn't slip its moorings. Both Shar and I were quiet as we maneuvered it up my building's elevator and into the apartment.

Later, after Neal promised to become the fifth party to a closely held secret, I told him the story of August 16, 1978. He was quiet too.

But still later, when we'd jockeyed the Trashcan into position in our living room and plugged it in, the nostalgic tunes of happier times played long into the night, heralding happy times to come.

# KNIVES AT MIDNIGHT
## (Sharon McCone)

My eyes were burning, and I felt not unlike a creature that spends a great deal of its life underground. I marked the beat-up copy of last year's *Standard California Codes* that I'd scrounged up at a used bookstore on Adams Avenue, then shut it. When I stood up, my limbs felt as if I were emerging from the creature's burrow. I stretched, smiling. *Well, McCone,* I told myself, *at last one of your peculiarities is going to pay off.*

For years, I'd taken what many considered a strange pleasure in browsing through the tissue-thin pages of both the civil and penal codes. I had learned many obscure facts. For instance: it is illegal to trap birds in a public cemetery; anyone advertising merchandise that is made in whole or in part by prisoners must insert the words "convict-made" in the ad copy; stealing a dog worth $400 or less is petty theft, while stealing a dog worth more than $400 is grand theft. Now I could add another esoteric statute to my store of knowledge, only this one promised a big payoff.

Somebody who thought himself above the law was about to go down—and I was the one who would topple him.

Two nights earlier, I'd flown into San Diego's Lindbergh Field from my home base in San Francisco. Flown in on a perilous approach that always makes me, holder of a both single-and a multi-engine rating, wish I didn't know quite so much about pilot error. On top of a perfectly natural edginess, I was aggravated with myself for giving in to my older brother John's plea. The case he wanted me to take on for some friends sounded like one where every lead comes to a dead end; besides, I was afraid that in my former hometown I'd become embroiled in some family crisis. The McCone clan attracts catastrophe the way normal people attract stray kittens.

John was waiting for me at the curb in his old red International Scout. When he saw me, he jumped out and enveloped me in a bear hug that made me drop both my purse and my briefcase. My travel bag swung around and whacked him on his back; he released me, grunting.

"You're looking good," he said, stepping back.

"So're you." John's a big guy—six-foot-four—and sometimes he bulks up from the beer he's so fond of. But now he was slimmed down to muscle and sported a new closely trimmed beard. Only his blond hair resisted taming.

He grabbed my bag, tossed it into the Scout, and motioned for me to climb aboard. I held my ground. "Before we go anyplace— you didn't tell Pa I was coming down, did you?"

"No."

"Ma and Melvin? Charlene and Ricky?"

"None of them."

"Good. Did you make me a motel reservation and reserve a rental car?"

"No."

"I asked you—"

"You're staying at my place."

"John! Don't you remember—"

"Yeah, yeah. Don't involve the people you care about in something that could get dangerous. I heard all that before."

"And it *did* get dangerous."

"Not very. Anyway, you're staying with me. Get in."

John can be as stubborn as I when he makes up his mind. I opted for the path of least resistance. "Okay, I'll stay tonight— only. But what am I supposed to drive while I'm here?"

"I'll loan you the Scout."

I frowned. It hadn't aged well since I last borrowed it.

He added, "I could go along, help you out."

"John!"

He started the engine and edged into the flow of traffic.

"You know, I've missed you." Reaching over and ruffling my hair, he grinned broadly. "McCone and McCone—the detecting duo. Together again."

I heaved a martyred sigh and buckled my seat belt.

❖ ❖ ❖

The happy tone of our reunion dissipated when we walked into the living room of John's little stucco house in nearby Lemon Grove. His old friends, Bryce and Mari Winslip, sat on the sofa in front of the corner fireplace; their hollow eyes reflected weariness and pain and—when they saw me—a kind of hope that I immediately feared was misplaced. While John made the introductions and fetched wine for me and freshened the Winslips' drinks, I studied them.

Both were a fair number of years older than my brother, perhaps in their early sixties. John had told me on the phone that Bryce Winslip was the painting contractor who had employed him during his apprenticeship; several years ago, he'd retired and they'd moved north to Oregon. Bryce and Mari were white-haired and had the bronzed, tough-skinned look of people who spent a lot of time outdoors. I could tell that customarily they were clear-eyed, mentally acute, and vigorous. But not tonight.

Tonight the Winslips were gaunt-faced and red-eyed; they moved in faltering sequences that betrayed their age. Tonight they were drinking straight whiskey, and every word seemed an effort. Small wonder: they were hurting badly because their only child, Troy, was violently dead.

Yesterday morning, twenty-five-year-old Troy Winslip's body had been found by the Tijuana, Mexico, authorities in a parking lot near the bullring at the edge of the border town. He had been stabbed seventeen times. Cause of death: exsanguination. Estimated time of death: midnight. There were no witnesses, no suspects, no known reason for the victim to have been in that place. Although Troy was a San Diego resident and a student at San Diego State, the SDPD could do no more than urge the Tijuana authorities to pursue an investigation and report their findings. The TPD, which would have been overworked even if it wasn't notoriously corrupt, wasn't about to devote time to the murder of a *gringo* who shouldn't have been down there in the middle of the night anyway. For all practical purposes, case closed.

So John had called me, and I'd opened my own case file.

When we were seated, I said to the Winslips, "Tell me about Troy. What sort of person was he?"

They exchanged glances. Mari cleared her throat. "He was a good boy . . . man. He'd settled down and was attending college."

"Studying what?"

"Communications. Radio and TV."

"You say he'd 'settled down.' What does that mean?"

Again the exchanged glances. Bryce said, "After high school, he had some problems that needed to be worked through—one of the reasons we moved north. But he's been fine for at least five years now."

"Could you be more specific about these problems?"

"Well, Troy was using drugs."

"Marijuana? Cocaine?"

"Both. When we moved to Oregon, we put him into a good treatment facility. He made excellent progress. After he was released, he went to school at Eugene, but three years ago he decided to come back to San Diego."

"A mistake," Mari said.

"He was a grown man; we couldn't stop him," her husband responded defensively. "Besides, he was doing well, making good grades. There was no way we could have predicted that . . . this would happen."

Mari shrugged.

I asked, "Where was Troy living?"

"He shared a house on Point Loma with another student."

"I'll need the address and the roommate's name. What else can you tell me about Troy?"

Bryce said, "Well, he is . . . was athletic. He liked to sail and play tennis." He looked at his wife.

"He was very articulate," she added. "He had a beautiful voice and would have done well in radio or television."

"Do you know any of his friends here?"

" . . . No. I'm not even sure of the roommate's name."

"What about women? Was he going with anyone? Engaged?"

Head shakes.

"Anything else?"

Silence.

"Well," Bryce said after a moment, "he was a very private person. He didn't share many of the details of his life with us, and we respected that."

I was willing to bet that the parents hadn't shared many details of their life with Troy, either. The Winslips struck me as one of those couples who have formed a closed circle that admits no one, not even their own offspring. The shared glances, their body language, the way they consulted nonverbally before answering my questions—all that pointed to a self-sufficient system. I doubted they'd known their son very well at all, and probably hadn't even realized they were shutting him out.

Bryce Winslip leaned forward, obviously awaiting some response on my part to what he and Mari had told me.

I said, "I have to be frank with you. Finding out what happened to Troy doesn't look promising. But I'll give it a try. John explained about my fee?"

They nodded.

"You'll need to sign one of my standard contracts, as well as a release giving me permission to enter Troy's home and go through his personal effects." I took the forms from my briefcase and began filling them in.

After they'd put their signatures on the forms and Bryce had written me a check as a retainer, the Winslips left for their hotel. John had fetched me another glass of wine and a beer for himself and sat in the place Mari had vacated, propping his feet on the raised hearth.

"So," he said, "how're we going to go about this?"

"You mean how am _I_ going to go about this. First _I_ will check with the SDPD for details on the case. Do you remember Gary Viner?"

"That dumb-looking friend of Joey's from high school?"

All of our brother Joey's friends had been dumb-looking. "Sandy-haired guy, one of the auto shop crowd."

"Oh, yeah. He used to work on Joey's car in front of the house and ogle you when he thought you weren't looking."

I grinned." That's the one. He used to ogle me during cheer-leading, too. When I was down here on that kidnaping case a couple of years ago, he told me I had the prettiest bikini pants of anybody on the squad."

John scowled indignantly, like a proper big brother. "So what's this underwear freak got to do with the Winslip case?"

"Gary's on Homicide with the SDPD now. It's always best to check in with the local authorities when you're working a case on their turf, so I'll stop by his office in the morning, see what he's got from the TJ police."

"Well, just don't wear a short skirt. What should I do while you're seeing him?"

"Nothing. Afterward, *I* will visit Troy's house, talk with the roommate, try to get a list of his friends and find out more about him. Plus go State and see what I can dig up there."

"What about me?"

"You will tend to Mr. Paint." Mr. Paint was the contracting business he operated out of his home shop and office.

John's lower lip pushed out sulkily.

I said, "How about dinner? I'm starving."

He brightened some. "Mexican?"

"Sure."

"I'll drive."

"Okay."

"You'll pay."

"John!"

"Consider it a finder's fee."

❖ ❖ ❖

Gary Viner hadn't changed since I'd seen him a couple of years earlier, but he was very different from the high school kid I remembered. Gaining weight and filling out had made him more attractive; he'd stopped hiding his keen intelligence and learned to tone down his ogling to subtly speculative looks that actually flattered me. Unfortunately, he had no more information on the

Winslip murder than what John had already told me.

"Is it okay if I look into this for the parents?" I asked him.

"Feel free. It's not our case, anyway. You go down there"—he motioned in the general direction of Baja California—"you might want to check in with the TJ authorities."

"I won't be going down unless I come up with something damned good up here."

"Well, good luck, and keep me posted." As I started out of his cubicle, Gary added, "Hey, McCone—the last time I saw you, you never did answer my question."

"Which is?"

"Can you still turn a cartwheel?"

I grinned at him. "You bet I can. And my bikini pants are still the prettiest ever."

It made me feel good to see a tough homicide cop blush.

❖ ❖ ❖

My first surprise of the day was Troy Winslip's house. It was enormous, sprawling over a double lot that commanded an impressive view of San Diego Bay and Coronado Island. Stucco and brick and half-timbers, with a terraced yard landscaped in brilliantly flowering iceplant, it must have been at least six thousand square feet, give or take a few.

A rich roommate? Many rich roommates? Whatever, it sure didn't resemble the ramshackle brown-shingled house that I'd shared with what had seemed a cast of thousands when I was at UC Berkeley.

I rang the bell several times and got no response, so I decided to canvass the neighbors. No one was home at the houses to either side, but across the street I got lucky. The stoop-shouldered man who came to the door was around seventy and proved to like the sound of his own voice.

"Winslip? Sure, I know him. Nice young fellow. He's owned the place for about a year now."

"You're sure he owns it?"

"Yes. I knew the former owners. Gene and Alice Farr—nice people, too, but that big house was too much for them, so they sold it and bought one of those condos. They told me Winslip paid cash."

Cash? Such a place would go for many hundreds of thousands. "What about his roommate? Do you also know him?"

The old man leered at me. "Roommate? Is that what you call them these days? Well, he's a she. The ladies come and go over there, but none're very permanent. This last one, I'd say she's been there eight, nine weeks."

"Do you know her name?"

He shook his head. "She's a good-looking one, though—long red hair, kind of willowy."

"And do you know what either she or Mr. Winslip do for a living?"

"Not her, no. And if he does anything, he's never talked about it. I suspect he inherited his money. He's home a lot, when he's not sailing his boat."

"Where does he keep his boat?"

"Glorietta Bay Marina, over on Coronado." The man frowned now, wrinkles around his eyes deepening. "What's this about, anyway?"

"Troy Winslip's been murdered, and I'm investigating it."

"What?"

"You didn't read about it in the paper?"

"I don't bother with the paper. Don't watch TV, either. With my arthritis, I'm miserable enough; I don't need other humans' misery heaped on top of that."

"You're a wise man," I told him, and hurried back to where I'd left the Scout.

Glorietta Bay Marina sits at the top of the Silver Strand, catty-corner from the Victorian towers of the Hotel Del Coronado. It took me more than half an hour to get there from Point Loma, and when I drove into the parking lot, I spotted John leaning against his motorcycle. He waved and started toward me.

I pulled into a space and jumped out of the Scout. "What the hell are *you* doing here?"

"Nice way to greet somebody who's helping you out. While you were futzing around at the police department and Troy's place, I went over to State. Talked with his adviser. She says he dropped out after one semester."

"So how did that lead you here?"

"The adviser sails, and she sees him here off and on. He owns a boat, the *Windsong*."

"And I suppose you've already checked it out."

"No, but I did talk with the marina manager. He says he'll let us go aboard if you show him your credentials and the release from Bryce and Mari."

"Good work," I said grudgingly. "You know," I added as we started walking toward the manager's office, "it's odd that Troy would berth the boat here."

"Why?"

"He lived on Point Loma, not far from the Shelter Island yacht basin. Why would he want to drive all the way around the bay and across the Coronado Bridge when he could have berthed her within walking distance of his house?"

"No slips available over there? No, that can't be; I've heard the marinas're going hungry in this economy."

"Interesting, huh? And wait till you hear what else—" I stopped in my tracks and glared at him. "Dammit, you've done it again!"

"Done what? I didn't do anything! What did I do?"

"You know *exactly* what you've done."

John's smile was smug.

I sighed. "All right, other half of the 'detecting duo'—lead me to the manager."

❖ ❖ ❖

My unwanted assistant and I walked along the outer pier toward the *Windsong's* slip. The only sounds were the cries of seabirds and the rush of traffic on the Strand. Our footsteps echoed on the aluminum walkways and set them to bucking on a slight swell. No one was around this Wednesday morning except for a pair of artists sketching near the office; the boats were buttoned up tightly, their sails furled in sea-blue covers. Troy Winslip's yawl was a big one, some thirty feet. I crossed the plank and stepped aboard; John followed.

"Wonder where he got his money," he said. "Bryce and Mari're well off, but not wealthy."

"I imagine he had his ways." I tried the companionway door and found it locked.

"What now?" my brother asked. "Standing around on deck isn't going to tell us anything."

"No." I felt through my bag and came up with my set of lock picks.

John's eyes widened. "Aren't those illegal?"

"Not strictly." I selected one with a serpentine tip and began probing the lock. "It's a misdemeanor to possess lock picks with intent to feloniously break and enter. However, since I intend to break and enter with permission from the deceased owner's next of kin, we're in kind of a gray area here."

John looked nervously over his shoulder. "I don't think cops recognize gray areas."

"For God's sake, do you see any cops?" I selected a more straight-tipped pick and resumed probing.

"Where'd you get those?" John asked.

"An informant of mine made them for me; he even etched my initials on the finger holds. Wiley 'the Pick' Pulaski. He's currently doing four-to-six for burglary."

"My little sister, consorting with known criminals."

"Well, Wiley wasn't exactly known when I was consorting with him. Good informants can't keep a high profile, you know." I turned the lock with a quick flick of my wrist. It yielded, and I removed the pick and opened the door. "After you, big brother."

The companionway opened into the main cabin—a compactly arranged space with a galley along the right bulkhead and a seating area along the left. I began a systematic search of the lockers but came up with nothing interesting. When I turned, I found John sitting at the navigator's station, studying the instruments.

"Big help you are," I told him. "Get up; you're blocking the door to the rear cabin."

He stood, and I squeezed around him and went inside.

The rear cabin had none of the teak-and-brass accoutrements of the main; in fact, it was mostly unfinished. The portholes were masked with heavy fabric, and the distinctive trapped odor of marijuana was enough to give me a contact high. I hadn't experienced its like since the dope-saturated seventies in Berkeley.

John, who cultivated a small crop in his backyard, smelled it, too. "So that's what pays the mortgage!"

"Uh-huh." My eyes were becoming accustomed to the gloom, but not fast enough. "You see a flashlight anyplace?"

He went away and came back with one. I flicked it on and shined it around. The cabin was tidy, the smell merely a residue of the marijuana that had been stored there, but crumbled bits of grass littered the floor. I handed John the flashlight, pulled an envelope from my bag, and scraped some of the waste matter into it. Then I moved forward, scrutinizing every surface. Toward the rear under the sharp cant of the bulkhead, I found a dusting of white powder. After I tasted it, I scraped it into a second envelope.

"Coke, too?" John asked.

"You got it."

"Mari and Bryce aren't going to like this. They thought he'd kicked his habit."

"He wasn't just feeding a habit here, John. Or dealing on a small scale. He was distributing, bringing it in on this boat in a major way."

"Yeah." He fell silent, staring grimly at the littered floor. "So what're you going to do—call the cops?"

"They'll have to know eventually, but not yet. The dealing in itself isn't important anymore; its bearing on Troy's murder is."

❖ ❖ ❖

Back on Point Loma, I waited just out of sight of Troy Winslip's house in the Scout. John had wanted to come along and help me stake the place out, so in order to otherwise occupy him, I'd sent him off on what I considered a time-consuming errand. The afternoon waned. Behind me, the sky's blue deepened and the lowering sun grew bright gold in contrast. Tall palms bordering the Winslip property cast long easterly shadows. At around six, a white Dodge van rounded the corner and pulled into Troy's driveway. A young woman—red-haired, willowy, clad in jeans and a black-and-white African print cape—jumped out and hurried into the house. By the time I got to the front door, she was already returning, arms full of clothing on hangers. She started when she saw me.

I had my identification and the release from Troy's parents ready. As I explained what I was after, the woman barely glanced at them. "All I want is my things," she said. "After I get them out of here, I don't care what the hell you do."

I followed her, picking up a purple silk tunic that had slipped from its hanger. "Please come inside. We'll talk. You lived with Troy; don't you care why he was killed?"

She laughed bitterly, tossed the armload of clothing into the back of the van, and took the tunic from my outstretched hand. "I care. But I also care about myself. I don't want to be around here any longer than necessary."

"You feel you're in danger?"

"I'd be a fool if I didn't." She pushed around me and hurried up the walk. "Those people don't mess around, you know."

I followed her. "What people?"

She rushed through the door, skidding on the polished marble of the foyer. A few suitcases and cartons were lined up at the foot of a curving staircase. "You want to talk?" the woman said. "We'll talk, but you'll have to help me with this stuff."

I nodded, picked up the nearest box, and followed her back to the van. "I know that Troy was dealing."

"Dealing?" She snorted. "He was supplying half the county. He and Daniel were taking the boat down to Baja three, four nights a week."

"Who's Daniel?"

"Daniel Pope, Troy's partner." She took the box from my hands, shoved it into the back of the van, and started up the walk.

"Where can I find him?"

"His legit business is a surf shop on Coronado—Danny P's."

"And the people who don't mess around—who are they?"

We were back in the foyer now. She thrust two suitcases at me. "Oh, no, you're not getting me involved in *that*."

"Look—what's your name?"

"I don't have to tell you." She hefted the last carton, took a final look around, and tossed her hair defiantly. "I'm out of here."

Once again, we were off at a trot toward the van. "You may be out of here," I said, "but you're still afraid. Let me help you."

She stowed the carton, took the suitcases from me, and shook her head. "Nobody can help me. It's only a matter of time. I know too much."

"Then share it—"

"No!" She slammed the van's side door, slipped quickly into the driver's seat, and locked the door behind her. For a moment, she sat with her head bowed, her hands on the wheel; then she relented and rolled down the window a few turns. "Why don't you go talk to Daniel? If he's not at the surf shop, he'll be at home; he's the only Pope on C Street in Coronado. Ask him . . ." She hesitated, looking around as if someone could hear her. "Ask him about Renny D."

"Ronny D?"

"No, Renny, with an e. It's short for Reynaldo." Quickly, she cranked up the window and started the van. I stepped back in time to keep from getting my toes squashed.

The woman had left the front door of the house open and the keys in the lock. For a moment, I considered searching the place, then concluded it was more important to talk to Daniel Pope. I went back up the walk, closed the door, turned the deadbolt, and pocketed the keys for future use.

❖ ❖ ❖

Daniel Pope wasn't at his surf shop, and he wasn't at his home on C Street. But John was waiting two houses down, perched on his cycle in the shade of a jacaranda tree.

I raised my eyes to the heavens and whispered to the Lord, "Please, not again!"

The Lord, who in recent years had been refusing to listen to my pleas, failed to eradicate my brother's presence.

I parked the Scout behind the cycle. John sauntered back and leaned on the open window beside me. "Daniel Pope owns a half interest in the *Windsong*," he said out of the corner of his mouth, eyes casing the house like an experienced thief.

I'd assigned him to check into the yawl's registry, but I hadn't expected him to come up with anything this quickly.

John went on, "He and Troy bought the boat two years ago for 90,000 dollars cash from the yacht broker at Glorietta Bay. They took her out three or four times a week for about eight hours a stretch. In between, they partied. Men would come and go, carrying luggage. Some of the more conservative—read that 'bigoted'—slip holders complained that they were throwing 'fag parties.'"

"But we know they were holding sales meetings."

"Right."

"Where'd you get all that?"

"The yacht broker. I pretended I was interested in buying the *Windsong*. He's probably got the commission spent already. Shit, I feel really guilty about it."

A blue Mercedes was approaching. It went past us, slowed, and turned into the driveway of the white Italianate house we'd been watching. I unbuckled my seat belt and said, "Ease your guilt by telling yourself that if you ever do buy a boat, you'll use that broker."

He ignored me, straightening and watching the car pull into an attached garage. "Daniel Pope?"

"Probably."

"So now what do we do?"

Thoughtfully, I looked him over. My brother is a former bar brawler and can be intimidating to those who don't know him for the pussycat he is. And at the moment, he was in exceptionally good shape.

"We," I said, "are going in there and talk with Pope about somebody called Renny D."

❖ ❖ ❖

Daniel Pope was suffering from a bad case of nerves. His bony, angular body twitched, and a severe tic marred his ruggedly handsome features. When we'd first come to the door, he'd tried to shut it in our faces; now that he was reasonably assured that we weren't going to kill him, he wanted a drink. John and I sat on the edge of a leather sofa in a living room filled with sophisticated sound equipment while he poured three fingers of single-malt Scotch. Then I began questioning him.

"Who's Renny D?"

"Where'd you get that name?"

"Who is he?"

"I don't have to talk about—"

"Look, Pope, we know all about the *Windsong* and your trips to Baja. And about the dealers who come to the yawl in between. The rear cabin is littered with grass and coke; I can have the police there in—"

"Jesus! I thought you were working for Troy's parents."

"I am, but Troy's dead, and they're more interested in finding out who killed him than in covering up your illegal activities."

"Oh, Jesus." He took a big drink of whiskey.

I repeated, "Who's Renny D?"

Silence.

"I'm not going to ask again." I moved my hand toward a phone on the table beside me. John grinned evilly at Pope.

"Don't! Don't do that! Christ, I'll . . . Renny Dominguez is the other big distributor around here. He didn't want Troy and me cutting into his territory."

"And?"

"That's it."

"No, it's not." I moved my hand again. John did a fair imitation of a villain's leer. Maybe, I thought, he should have taken up acting.

"Okay, all right, it's not. I'll tell you, just leave the phone alone. At first, Troy and I tried to work something out with Renny D. Split the territory, cooperate, you know. He wasn't having any of that. Things've been getting pretty intense over the last few months: there was a fire at my store; somebody shot at Troy in front of his house; we both had phone threats."

"And then?"

"All of a sudden, Renny D decides he want to make nice with us. So we meet with him at this bar where he hangs out in National City, and he proposes we work together, kick the business into really high gear. But now it's Troy who isn't having any of that."

"Why not?"

"Because Troy's convinced himself that Renny D is small-time and kind of stupid. He thinks we should kick *our* business into high gear and take over Renny's turf. I took him aside, tried to tell him that what he saw as small-time stupidity was only a matter of different styles. I mean just because Renny D doesn't wear Reeboks or computerize his customer list doesn't mean he's an idiot. I tried to tell Troy that those people were dangerous, that you at least had to try to humor them. But did Troy listen? No way. He went back to the table and make Renny look bad in front of his *compadres*, and that's bad shit, man."

"So then what happened?"

"More threats. Another drive-by. And that only made Troy more convinced that Renny and his pals were stupid, because they couldn't pick him off at twenty feet. Well, this kind of stuff goes on until it's getting ridiculous, and finally Renny issues a challenge: the two of them'll meet down in TJ near the bullring and settle it one-on-one, like honorable men."

"And Troy fell for that?"

"Sure. Like I said, he'd convinced himself Renny D was stupid, so he had me set it up with Renny's number two man, Jimmy. It was supposed to be just the four of us, and only Renny and Troy would fight."

"You didn't try to talk him out of it?"

"All the way down there, I did. But Troy—stubborn should've been his middle name."

"And what happened when you got there?"

"It was just the four of us, like Jimmy said. But what he didn't say was that he and Renny would have knives. The two of them moved damn fast, and before I knew what was happening, they'd stabbed Troy."

"What did you do?"

Pope looked away. Went to get himself another three fingers of scotch.

"What did you do, Daniel?"

"I froze. And then I ran. Left Troy's damned car there, ran off, and spent half the night wandering, the other half hiding behind an auto body shop near the port of entry. The next morning, I walked back over the border like any innocent tourist."

"And now you think Renny and his friends'll come after you."

"I was a witness, it's only a matter of time."

That was what Troy's girlfriend had said, too. "Are you willing to tell your story to the police?"

Silence.

"Daniel?"

He ran his tongue over dry lips. After a moment, he said, "Shit, what've I got to lose? Look at me." He held out a shaky hand. "I'm a wreck, and it's all Troy's fault. He had fair warning of what was gonna go down. When I think of the way he ignored it, I want to kill him all over again."

"What fair warning?"

"Some message Renny D left on his answering machine. Troy thought it was funny. He said it was so melodramatic, it proved Renny was brain-damaged."

"Did he tell you what the message was?"

Daniel Pope shook his head. "He was gonna play it for me when we got back from TJ. He said you had to hear it to believe it."

The message was in a weird Spanish-accented falsetto, accompanied by cackling laughter: "Knives at midnight, Winslip. Knives at midnight."

I popped the tape from Troy's answering machine and turned

to John. "Why the hell would he go down to TJ after hearing that? Did he think Renny D was joking?"

"Maybe. Or maybe he took along his own knife, but Renny and Jimmy were quicker. Remember, he thought they were stupid." He shook his head. "Troy was a dumb middle-class kid who got in over his head and let his own high opinion of himself warp his judgment. But he still sure as hell didn't deserve to die in a parking lot of seventeen stab wounds."

"No, he didn't." I turned the tape over in my hands. "Why do you suppose Renny D left the message? You'd think he'd have wanted the element of surprise on his side."

John shrugged. "To throw Troy off balance, make him nervous? Some twisted code of drug dealers' honor? Who knows?"

"This tape isn't the best of evidence, you know. There's no proof that it was Renny D who called."

"Isn't there?" He motioned at another machine that looked like a small video display terminal.

"What's that?"

"A little piece of new technology that allows you to see what number an incoming call was dialed from. It has a memory, keeps a record." He pressed a button, and a listing of numbers, dates, and times appeared. After scrolling through it, he pointed to one with a 295 prefix. "That matches the time and date stamp on the answering machine tape."

I lifted the receiver and dialed the number. A machine picked up on the third ring: "This is Renny D. Speak."

I hung up. "Now we've got proof."

"So do we go see Gary Viner?"

"Not just yet. First I think we'd better report to Mari and Bryce, ask them if they really want all of this to come out."

"I talked with them earlier; they were going to make the funeral arrangements and then have dinner with relatives. Maybe we shouldn't intrude."

"Probably not. Besides, there's something I want to do first."

"What?"

"Get a good look at this Renny D."

❖ ❖ ❖

An old friend named Luis Abrego frequented the Tradewinds tavern in National City, halfway between San Diego and the border. The first time I'd gone there two years before, John had insisted on accompanying me for protection; tonight he insisted again. I didn't protest, since I knew he and Luis were fond of each other.

Fortunately, business was slow when we got there; only half a dozen Hispanic patrons stopped talking and stared when they saw two Anglos walk in. Luis hunched in his usual place at the end of the bar, nursing a beer and watching a basketball game on the fuzzy TV screen. When I spoke his name, he whirled, jumped off his stool, and took both my hands in his. His dark eyes danced with pleasure.

"*Amiga,*" he said, "it's been much too long."

"Yes, it has, *amigo.*"

Luis released me and shook John's hand. He was looking well. His mustache swooped bandit-fashion, and his hair hung free and shiny to his shoulders. From the nearly black shade of his skin, I could tell he'd been working steadily on construction sites these days. Late at night, however, Luis piled a very different and increasingly dangerous trade; "helping my people get where they need to go," was how he described those activities.

We sat down in a booth, and I explained about Renny D and Troy Winslip's murder. Luis nodded gravely. "The young man was a fool to underestimate Dominguez," he said. "I don't know him personally, but I've seen him, and I hear he's one evil *hombre.*"

"Do you know where he hangs out down here?"

"A bar two blocks over, called the Gato Gordo. You're not planning on going up against him, *amiga?*"

"No, nothing like that. I just want to get a look at him. Obviously, I can't go there alone. Will you take me?"

Luis frowned down into his beer. "Why do you feel you have to do this?"

"I like to now who I'm up against. Besides, this is going to be a difficult case to prove; maybe seeing Renny D in the flesh will inspire me to keep at it."

He looked up at my face, studied it for a moment, then nodded. "Okay, I'll do it. But he"—he pointed at John—"waits for us here."

John said, "No way."

"Yes," Luis told him firmly. "Here you're okay; everybody knows you're my friend. But there, a big Anglo like you, we'd be asking for trouble. On the other hand, me and the *chiquita* here, we'll make a damn handsome couple."

❖ ❖ ❖

Reynaldo Dominguez was tall and thin, with razor-sharp features that spoke of *indio* blood. There were tattoos of serpents on his arms and knife scars on his face, and part of one index finger was missing. He sat at a corner table in the Gato Gordo, surrounded by admirers. He leaned back indolently in his chair and laughed and joked and told stories. When Luis and I sat down nearby with our drinks, he glanced contemptuously at us; then he focused on Luis's face and evidently saw something there that warned him off. There was not a lot that Luis Abrego hadn't come up against in his life, and there was nothing and no one he feared. Renny D, I decided, was a good judge of character.

Luis leaned toward me, taking my hand as a lover would and speaking softly. "He is telling them how he single-handedly destroyed the Anglo opposition. He is laughing about the look on Winslip's face when he died, and at the way the other man ran. He is bragging about the cleverness of meeting them in TJ, where he has bribed the authorities and will never be charged with a crime." He paused, listened some more. "He is telling them how he will enjoy stalking and destroying the other man and Winslip's woman —bit by bit, before he finally puts the knife in."

I started to turn to look at Dominguez.

"Don't." Luis tightened his grip on my hand.

I looked anyway. My eyes met Renny D's. His were black, flat, emotionless—devoid of humanity. He stared at me, thin lip curling.

Luis's fingernails bit into my flesh. "Okay, you've had your look at him. Drink up, and we'll go."

I could feel those soulless eyes on my back. I tried to finish my drink, but hatred for the creature behind me welled up and threatened to make me choke. Troy Winslip had in many respects been a useless person, but he'd also been young and naive and hadn't deserved to die. Nor did Daniel Pope or Troy's woman deserve to live, and perhaps die, in terror.

Luis said softly, "Now he is bragging again. He is telling them he is above the law. No one can touch him, he says. Renny D is invincible."

"Maybe not."

"Let's go now, *amiga*."

As we stood, I looked at Dominguez once more. This time, when our eyes met a shadow passed over his. What was that about? I wondered. Not suspicion. Not fear. What?

Of course—Renny D was puzzled. Puzzled because I didn't shy away from his stare. Puzzled and somewhat uneasy.

Well, good.

I said to Luis, "We'll see who's invincible."

❖  ❖  ❖

I'd expected the Winslips to pose an obstacle to bringing Renny D to justice, but they proved to be made of very strong stuff. The important thing, they said, was not to cover up their son's misdeeds but to ensure that a vicious murderer didn't go free to repeat his crime. So, with their blessing, I took my evidence downtown to Gary Viner.

And Gary told me what I'd been fearing all along: "We don't have a case."

"Gary, there's the tape. Dominguez as good as told Winslip he was going to stab him. There's the record of where the call originated. There's the eyewitness testimony of Daniel Pope—"

"There's the fact that the actual crime occurred on Mexican soil. And that Dominguez has the police down there in his hip pocket. No case, McCone."

"So what're you going to do—sit back and wait till he kills Pope and Winslip's woman, or somebody else?"

"We'll keep an eye on Dominguez. That's all I can promise you. Otherwise, my hands're tied."

"Maybe *your* hands are tied."

"What's that supposed to mean? What're you going to do? Don't give me any trouble, McCone—please."

"Don't worry. I'm going to go off and think about this, that's all. When I do give you something, I guarantee it won't be trouble."

When I'm upset or need to concentrate, I often head for water, so I drove north to Torrey Pines State Beach and walked by the surf for an hour. Something was nagging at the back of my mind, but I couldn't bring it forward. Something I'd read or heard somewhere. Something . . .

*Knives at midnight, Winslip. Knives at midnight.*

Renny D's high-pitched, cackling voice in the answering machine tape kept playing and replaying for me.

After a while, I decided to do some research and drove to Adams Avenue to find a used bookshop with a large legal section.

Crimes against the person: homicide. Express and implied malice . . . burden of proving mitigation—no.

Second degree . . . penalty for person previously convicted—no.

Manslaughter committed during operation of a vessel—certainly not.

Death of victim within three years and a day—forget it.

What the hell was I combing the penal code for, anyway?

Mayhem? Hardly. Kidnaping? No, Troy went willingly, even eagerly. Conspiracy? Maybe. No, the situation's too vague. Nothing there for me.

*Knives at midnight, Winslip. Knives at midnight.*

Can't get it out of my head. Keep trying to connect it with something. Melodramatic words, as Troy told Pope. A little old-fashioned, as if Dominguez was challenging him to a—

That's it!

Duels. Duels and challenges. Penal code, 225.

Defined: Combat with deadly weapons, fought between two or more persons, by previous agreement . . .

Punishment when death ensues: state prison for two, three, or four years.

Not much, but better than nothing.

I remember reading this now, one time when I was browsing through statutes that had been on the books for a long time. It's as enforceable today as it was then in 1872. Especially section 231; that's the part I really like.

Gotcha, Renny D.

❖ ❖ ❖

"I'll read it to you again," I said to Gary Viner. He was leaning toward me across his desk, trying to absorb the impact of the dry, formal text from 1872.

" 'Dueling beyond State. Every person who leaves this State with intent to evade any provisions of this chapter, and to commit any act out of the State as is prohibited by this chapter, and who does any act, although out of this State, which would be punishable by such provisions if committed within this State, is punishable in the same manner as he would have been *in case such act had been committed within this State.'*

"And there you have it." I closed the heavy tome with an emphatic thump.

Gary nodded. "And there we have it."

I began ticking off items on my fingers. "A taped challenge to a duel at knifepoint. A probable voiceprint match with the suspect. A record of where the call was made from. An eyewitness who, in order to save his own sorry hide, will swear that it actually *was* a duel. And, finally, a death that resulted from it. Renny D goes away for two, three, or four years in state prison."

"It's not much time. I'm not sure the DA'll think it's worth the trouble of prosecuting him."

"I remember the DA from high school. He'll be happy with anything that'll get a slimeball off the streets for a while. Besides, maybe we'll get lucky and somebody'll challenge Renny D to a duel in prison."

Gary nodded thoughtfully. "I remember our DA from high school, too. Successfully prosecuting a high-profile case like this would provide the kind of limelight he likes—and it's an election year."

✤ ✤ ✤

By the time my return flight to San Francisco left on Saturday, the DA had embraced the 1872 statute on duels and challenges with a missionarylike zeal and planned to take the Winslip case to the grand jury. Daniel Pope would be on hand to give convincing testimony about traveling to Tijuana primed for hand-to-hand combat with Dominguez and his cohort. Renny D was as yet unsuspecting but would soon be behind bars.

And at a Friday-night dinner party, the other half of the "detecting duo" had regaled the San Diego branch of the McCone family with his highly colored version of our exploits.

I accepted a cup of coffee from the flight attendant and settled back in the seat with my beat-up copy of *Standard California Codes*. I had a more current one on the shelf in my office, but somehow I couldn't bring myself to part with this one. Besides, I needed something to read on the hour-and-a-half flight.

Disguised Firearms or Other Deadly Weapons. Interesting.

Lipstick Case Knife. Oh, them deadly dames, as they used to say.

Shobi-zue: a staff, crutch, stick, rod, or pole with a knife enclosed. Well, if I ever break a leg . . .

Writing Pen Knife. That's a good one. Proves the pen can be mightier than the sword.

But wait now, here's one that's *really* fascinating . . .

# THE WALL
## (Rae Kelleher)

I'd been on the Conway case for close to twenty-four hours before I started paying serious attention to Adrian's bedroom wall. A big oversight, considering it was dark purple and covered with a collage of clippings and photographs and junk that looked like it had been dug out of a garbage can. But then I've never been too quick on the uptake on Monday mornings, which was the only other time I'd seen it.

The wall, the missing girl's mother had explained, was a form of therapy, and even though its creation had more or less trashed the room, she—the mother, Donna Conway—considered it well worth the cost. After all, a sixteen-year-old whose father had run off a year and a half ago with a woman of twenty whom she—the daughter, Adrian Conway—insisted on calling "Dad's bimbo" needed *something*, didn't she? And it was cheaper than paying for a shrink.

Or for any more self-help books, I thought, *if* there are any left that you don't already have.

The Conway house made me damn twitchy, and not just because there wasn't a book in it that didn't have the words "relationship" or "self" in its title. It was in San Francisco's Diamond Heights district—a place that looks like some alien hand has picked up an entire suburb and plunked it down on one of our southeastern hills. The streets are cutesily named—Jade, Topaz, Turquoise—and the Conways', Goldmine Drive, was no exception. The house, tucked behind its own garage and further hidden from the street by a high wall, was pretty much like all the other houses and condos and apartments around there: white walls and light carpeting and standard modern kitchen; skylights and picture windows and a balcony with a barbecue that could hardly ever be used because the wind would put icicles on your briquettes up there. The view was nice enough, but it couldn't make up for the worn spots on the carpet and the cracks that showed where the builder had cut corners. When Donna Conway told me—for God knows what reason—that the house was the sum total of her divorce settlement, I started feeling depressed for her. I didn't get much myself when I got divorced, but a VCR and half the good silverware were at least hockable, and from the rust on the FOR SALE sign out front, I gathered that this house was not.

Anyway, Adrian Conway had been missing for two weeks by the time her mother turned for help to the firm where I work, All Souls Legal Cooperative. We're kind of a poor man's McKenzie, Brackman—a motley collection of crusaders and mainstream liberals and people like me who don't function too well in a structured environment, and one of the biggest legal-services plans in northern California. Donna Conway was a medical technician with a hospital that offered membership in the plan as part of their benefits package, so she went to her lawyer when she decided the police weren't doing all they could to find her daughter. Her lawyer handed the case to our chief investigator, Sharon McCone, who passed it on to me, Rae Kelleher.

So on a Monday morning in early November I was sitting in Donna Conway's drafty living room (God, didn't she know about weather stripping?), sipping weak instant coffee and wishing I didn't have to look at her sad, sad eyes. If it weren't for her sadness and the deep lines of discontentment that made parentheses around the corners of her mouth, she would have been a pretty woman —soft shoulder-length dark hair and a heart-shaped face, and a willowy body that about made me green with envy. Her daughter didn't look anything like her, at least not from the picture she gave me. Adrian had curly red-gold hair and a quirky little smile, and her eyes gleamed with mischief that I took to be evidence of an offbeat sense of humor.

Adrian, Donna Conway told me, had never come home two weeks ago Friday from her after-school job as a salesclerk at Left Coast Casuals at the huge Ocean Park Shopping Plaza out near the beach. Turned out she hadn't even shown up for work, and although several of her classmates at nearby McAteer High School had seen her waiting for the bus that would take her to the shopping center, nobody remembered her actually boarding it. Adrian hadn't taken anything with her except the backpack she usually took to school. She hadn't contacted her father; he and his new wife were living in Switzerland now, and the police there had checked them out carefully. She wasn't with friends, her boy-friend, or her favorite relative, Aunt June. And now the police had back burnered her file, labeled it just another of the teenage disap-pearances that happen thousands and thousands of times a year in big cities and suburbs and small towns. But Donna Conway wasn't about to let her daughter become just another statistic—no way! She would pay to have Adrian found, even if it took every cent of the equity she'd built up in the house.

I'd noticed two things about Donna while she was telling me all that: She seemed to harbor the usual amount of malice toward her ex's new wife, and an even larger amount toward Adrian's Aunt June.

On Monday I went by the book: talked with the officer in Missing Persons assigned to Adrian's case; talked with the class-mates who had seen her leaving McAteer that Friday; talked with her supervisor at Left Coast Casuals and the head of security at Ocean Park Plaza. Then I checked out the boyfriend, a few girl-friends, and a couple of teachers at the high school, ran through the usual questions. Did Adrian use drugs or alcohol? Had she been having romantic problems? Could she be pregnant? Had she talked about trouble at home, other than the obvious? No to everything. Adrian Conway was apparently your all-American average, which worked out to a big zero as far as leads were con-cerned. By nightfall I'd decided that it was the old story: gone on purpose, for some reason all her own; a relative innocent who probably hadn't gotten far before becoming somebody's easy victim.

Sad old story, as sad as Donna Conway's eyes.

It was the memory of those eyes that made me go back to take a second look at Adrian's room on Tuesday afternoon—that, and the thought that nobody could be as average as she sounded. I had to find out just who Adrian Conway really was. Maybe then I could locate her.

I started with the collage wall. Dark purple paint that had stained the edges of the white ceiling and splotched on the cream carpet. Over that, pictures cut from glossy magazines—the usual trite stuff that thrills you when you're in your teens. Sunsets and sailboats. Men with chiseled profiles and windblown hair; women in gauzy dresses lazing in flower-strewn meadows. Generic romance with about as much relationship to reality as Mother Goose.

But over all that were the words. They leaped out in bold type: black, white, red and other primary colors. GO FOR IT! HOT. GONE FOREVER. STOLEN MOMENTS. FEAR. YES, NO, MAYBE. LOST. THE RIGHT STUFF. WHAT'S IN/WHAT'S OUT. FLASH, COLOR, CURVES, SPLASH, JUST DO IT! And many more . . .

Words as typical as the pictures, but interesting because they seemed important to a young woman who lived in a house where there wasn't a single book, unless you counted her school texts and her mother's stacks of mostly unread paperbacks on self-improvement.

Now, I'm no intellectual giant. I scraped through Berkeley by the skin of my teeth, and for years afterwards all I could make myself read were shop-and-fucks. I still don't read what passes for literature these days, but I do get mighty uncomfortable in a place where there aren't any old dust-catchers—as my grandmother used to call them—lying around. Apparently Adrian was fond of the written word, too.

Tacked, nailed, and glued to the words—but never completely covering them—was the junk. A false eyelash, like the hairy leg of a sci-fi spider. A lacy red bra, D-cup, with the nipples cut out. A plastic tag like the stores attach to clothing to prevent shoplifting. A lid from a McDonald's carry-out cup, Coke-stained straw still stuck through the opening. Broken gold neck chain, pair of fake plastic handcuffs, card with ink smudges on it that looked like fingerprints. Egret feather, dismembered doll's arm, syringe (unused). Lottery ticket with 7s rubbed off all in a row, $2.00 value unclaimed. And much, much more . . .

Not your standard teenage memory wall. A therapy wall, as Adrian's mom had put it? Maybe. I didn't know anything about therapy walls. The grandmother who raised me would have treated me to two years of stony silence if I'd trashed my room that way.

Donna Conway was standing in the door behind me. She must have felt my disapproval, because she said, "That wall was Adrian's only outlet for her pain. She adored her father. After he left us, she needed a way to begin healing."

So why didn't she hire out to a demolition company? I thought. Then I scowled, annoyed with myself. Next thing you knew, I'd sound just like my boss, Sharon McCone. The generation gap wasn't something I needed to leap yet.

Donna was watching my face, looking confused. I wiped the scowl off and said, "Just thinking. If you don't mind, I'd like to spend some time alone with the wall." Then I started to blush, hearing how truly stupid that sounded.

She didn't seem to notice. Maybe because her daughter had put a private part of herself into the wall, it had become a sort of being to her. Maybe people who were "rediscovering and healing" themselves, as she'd said she was, were either too sensitive or too vulnerable to make fun of other people who expressed sudden desires to commune alone with inanimate objects. Whatever, she just nodded and left, closing the door so the wall and I could have complete privacy.

I sat down on Adrian's brass daybed, kicked off my shoes, and drew my legs up on the ruffly spread. Then I took a good look at the mess on the wall. It had been a long-term project. Adrian started it, Donna had told me, the day the divorce papers were served. "We made an occasion of it," she said. "I had champagne and caviar, Adrian had Coke and a pizza. We painted. I guess it was the champagne that made me paint the edges of the rug and ceiling."

Now I replayed that. She hadn't painted the rug and ceiling because she was drinking champagne; the champagne had made her do it. So perfectly in tune with the philosophies of some of the books I'd glimpsed in passing. This was a household where little responsibility was ever assigned or acknowledged. Not healthy for an adult, and definitely bad for a teenager.

Back to the wall, Rae. You should be able to decipher it—after all, you were a psych major.

First the purple paint. Then the layer of pictures. Idealized, because she was trying to look beyond the bleak now to a better future. Next the layer of words. She was trying to talk about it, but she didn't really know how. So she used single words and phrases because maybe she wasn't ready for whole sentences. Hadn't worked through her feelings enough for whole thoughts.

Finally the layer of junk. Pretty ordinary stuff, very different from the pictures. Her feelings were more concrete, and she was trying to communicate them in concrete form. Unconsciously, of course, because doing it deliberately would be too sophisticated for a kid who'd never been in therapy. Too sophisticated for you, Rae—and you *have* been in therapy. Too bad they didn't encourage you to make a wall like this. Now, that would've given them something to eyeball at All Souls . . .

Back to *this* wall. She's gone through a process of sorts. Has piled concrete things and real words on top of idealized pictures and vague words. And then one day she's through. She walks out of this room and goes . . . where? To do what? Maybe if I knew what the very last thing she added to the wall was . . .

I left the room and found Donna in the kitchen, warming her hands around a cup of tea. "What were the last things Adrian put up on her wall, do you know?" I asked.

For a moment she looked blank. Then she shook her head. "I never looked at the wall before she left. It was her own private thing."

"You never talked about it?"

"No."

"What *did* you talk about?"

"Oh . . ." She stared down into the teacup. "I don't know. About the healing process. About everyone's potential to be."

I waited for her to go on. Then I realized that was it. Great conversational diet for a kid to sink her teeth into: healing process, potential to be.

What happened when Adrian was worried about an exam? When she hurt because her favorite guy didn't ask her to the dance? When she was scared of any one of all the truly scary things kids had to face in this city, in this world? Where did she retreat to lick her wounds?

I was getting mad, and I knew why. Like Adrian, I'd grown up in a home where everything was talked about in abstractions. In my case, shoulds and shouldn'ts, what-will-people-thinks and nice-girls-don'ts. I knew where Adrian Conway retreated: not to a nest of family affection and reassurance, but into a lonely lair within herself, where she could never be sure she was really safe.

I wasn't mad at Donna Conway for her arm's-length treatment of her daughter, though. I was mad at my dead grandmother, who raised me after my parents were killed in a car wreck. Donna Conway, even though she wasn't able to deal with emotion, had said she was willing to spend her last dollar to get Adrian back. Grandma wouldn't have given two cents for me.

I wanted to go back to All Souls and talk the case over with Sharon, but when I got to Bernal Heights, where the co-op has its offices, I made a sidetrip to our annex across the triangular park from our main building. Lillian Chu, one of the paralegals who worked our 800 line, lived in Diamond Heights, and I thought she had a kid at McAteer. Maybe there was something going on with Adrian Conway that the classmates the police and I had questioned couldn't or wouldn't tell.

Lillian was just going off shift. Yes, she said, her son Tom was in Adrian's class, and he was due to pick her up in about five minutes. "We're going shopping for new running shoes," she added. "The way he goes through them, I should have bought stock in Reebok."

"Could I talk with Tom for a few minutes?"

"Sure. I've got to run over to the main building and check about my payroll deductions. If you want, you can wait here and I'll send Tom in."

I sat in Lillian's cubicle, listening to phones ringing and voices murmuring on the 24-hour legal hot line. After a while a shaggy-haired young guy with a friendly face came into the cubicle. "You Rae? Mom says you want to talk to me."

"Yes, I want to ask you about Adrian Conway. Her mom's hired me to find her."

Tom Chu perched on the corner of the desk. His expression was still friendly, but a little guarded now. "What do you want to know?"

"Anything you can tell me."

"You mean like dirt."

"I mean anything that might help me locate her."

Tom looked uncertain.

"This isn't a game," I told him. "Or a case of a mother trying to find out more than her daughter wants her to know. Adrian's been missing for over two weeks now. She could be in serious trouble. She could even be dead."

"Yeah." He sighed heavily. "Okay, I don't really know anything. Not facts, you know? But . . . You talk with her boyfriend, Kirby Dalson?"

"Yes."

"What'd you think of him?"

"What do *you* think of him?"

"Bad news."

"Why?"

Tom drew one of his legs up on the desk and fiddled with the lace of his sneaker; from the looks of the shoe, Lillian *should* have invested in Reebok. "Okay," he said, "Kirby's . . . always into something. Always scamming. You know what I'm saying?"

"Drugs?"

"Maybe, but I don't think they're his main thing."

"What is?"

He shrugged. "Just . . . scams. Like a few times he got his

hands on some test questions beforehand and sold them—for big bucks, too. And for a while he was selling term papers. Scalping sports and concert tickets that you knew had to be stolen. He's always got a lot of cash, drives a sports car that everybody knows his folks didn't buy for him. He tells his parents he's got this parttime job in some garage, but all the time he's just scamming. The only job he ever had was cleaning up the food concession area at Ocean Park Plaza, but that didn't last long. Beneath him, I guess."

"What about Adrian—you think she was in on his scams?"

"She might've been. I mean, this past year she's changed."

"How?"

"Just . . . changed. She's not as friendly anymore. Seems down a lot of the time. And she's always with Kirby."

"Did this start around the time her father left?"

He shook his head. "After that. I mean, her old man left. Too bad, but it happens." His eyes moved to a photograph on Lillian's desk: the two of them and a younger girl, no father. "No," he added, "it was after that. Maybe six months ago."

"Do you remember anything that happened to Adrian around that time that might have caused this change?"

He thought. "No—sorry, I know Adrian okay, but she's not really a good friend or anything like that."

I thanked him and asked him to call me if he thought of anything else. Then I walked across the park to the freshly-painted Victorian where our main offices—-and the attic nest where I live—are.

The set-up at All Souls is kind of strange for a law firm, but then even the location is strange. Bernal Heights, our hillside neighborhood in the southeastern part of the city, is ethnically mixed, architecturally confused, and unsure whether it wants to be urban or semi-rural. At All Souls we're also ethnically mixed; our main building is a combination of offices, communal living space, and employees' separate quarters; and most of us don't know if we're nineties progressives or throwbacks to the sixties. All in all, it adds up to an interesting place to work.

And Sharon McCone's an interesting person to work for. That afternoon I found her behind her desk in the window bay at the front of the second floor—slumped spinelessly in her swivel chair, staring outside with that little frown that says she's giving some problem a workover. She's one of those slim women who seem taller than they are—the bane of my pudgy five-foot-three existence—and manages to look stylish even when she's wearing jeans and a sweater like she had on that day. When I first came to work for her, her dark good looks gave me attacks of inferiority because of my carrot top and freckles and thrift-shop clothes. Then one day I caught her having her own attack—mortified because she'd testified in court wearing a skirt whose hem was still pinned up waiting to be stitched. I told her she'd probably started a new fad and soon all the financial district power-dressers would be wearing straight pins around their hemlines. We had a good laugh over that, and I think that's when we started to be friends.

Anyway, I'd just about decided to stop back later when she turned, frowned some more, and snapped, "What?"

The McCone bark is generally worse than the bite, so I went in and sat in my usual place on her salmon-pink chaise lounge and told her about the Conway case. "I don't know what I should do next," I finished. "I've already talked with this Kirby kid, and if l come back at him so soon—"

"Aunt June."

"What?" I'd only mentioned Adrian's favorite aunt and Donna's apparent dislike of her in passing, and Sharon hadn't even looked like she was listening very hard. She'd been filing her nails the whole time—snick, snick, snick. Someday I'm going to tell her that the sound drives me crazy.

"Go see Aunt June," she said. "She's Adrian's closest relative. Mom disapproves of her. Go see her."

If it didn't save me so much trouble, I'd hate the way she puts things together. I stood up and headed for the door. "Thanks, Shar!"

She waggled the nailfile at me and swiveled back toward the window.

## II

Adrian's aunt's full name was June Simoom—no kidding—and she lived on Tomales Bay in western Marin County. The name alone should have tipped me off that Aunt June was going to be weird.

Tomales Bay is a thin finger of water that extends inland from the Pacific forty-some miles northwest of San Francisco. It's rimmed by small cottages, oyster farms, and salt marsh, and the largest town on its shores—Inverness—has a population of only a few hundred. The bay also has the dubious distinction of being right smack on top of the San Andreas Fault. Most of the time the weather out there is pretty cold and gloomy—broody, I call it—and it's a hefty drive from the city—across the Golden Gate Bridge, then through the close-in suburbs and rolling farmland to the coast.

It was after seven when I found the mailbox that June Simoom had described to me over the phone—black with a silver bird in flight and the word WINGSPREAD stenciled on it, another tipoff—and bounced down an unpaved driveway through a eucalyptus grove to a small cottage and a couple of outbuildings slouching at the water's edge.

My car is a 1964 Rambler American. A couple of years ago when I met my current—well, on again, off again—boyfriend, Willie Whelan, he cracked up at his first sight of it. "You mean you actually *drive* that thing?" he asked. "On the *street*?" No matter. The Ramblin' Wreck and I have gone many miles together, and at the rate I'm saving money, we're going to have to go many more. Barring experiences like Aunt June's driveway, that is.

The cottage was as bad off as my car, but I know something about real-estate values (money is my biggest fascination, because I have too little of it), and this shoreline property, bad weather and all, would have brought opening offers of at least a quarter mil. They'd have to demolish the house and outbuildings, of course, but nature and neglect seemed to already be doing a fine job of that. Everything sagged, including the porch steps, which were propped up by a couple of cement blocks.

The porch light was pee-yellow and plastered with dead bugs.

I groped my way to the door and knocked, setting it rattling in its frame. It took June Simoom a while to answer, and when she did . . . Well, Aunt June was something *else*.

Big hair and big boobs and a big voice. My, she was *big!* Dressed in flowing blue velvet robes that were thrift-shop fancy, not thrift-shop cheap (like my clothes used to be before I learned about credit and joined the millions of Americans who are in debt up to their nose hair). Makeup? Theatrical. Perfume? Gallons. If Marin ever passed the anti-scent ordinance they kept talking about, Aunt June would have to move away.

She swept—no, *tornadoed*—me into the cottage. It was one long room with a kitchen at the near end and a stone fireplace at the far end, all glass overlooking a half-collapsed deck. A fire was going, the only light. Outside I could see moonshine silvering the bay. June seated me—no, forced me down—onto a pile of silk cushions. Rammed a glass of wine into my hand. Flopped grunting on a second cushion pile nearer the hearth.

"You have news of Adrian?" she demanded.

I was struggling to remain upright in the soft nest without spilling the wine. "Umpfh," I said. "Mmmm-r!"

Aunt June regarded me curiously.

I got myself better situated and clung to the wineglass for ballast. "No news yet. Her mother has hired me to find her. I'm hoping you can—"

"Little Donna." She made a sound that might have been a laugh—*hinc, hinc, hinc.*

"You're Donna's sister?" I asked disbelievingly.

"In law. Sister-in-law. Once removed by divorce. Thank God Jeffrey saw the light and grabbed himself the bimbo. No more of those interminable holiday dinners—'Have some more veggies and dip, June.' 'Don't mind if I do, Donna, and by the way, where's the gin?' " Now she really did laugh—a booming sound that threatened to tear the (probably) rotten roof off.

I liked Donna Conway because she was sensitive and gentle and sad, but I couldn't help liking June, too. I laughed a little and sipped some wine.

"You remained close to Adrian after the divorce, though?" I asked.

"Of course." June nodded self-importantly. "My own flesh and blood. A responsibility I take seriously. I tried to take her under my wing, advise her, help her to deal with . . . everything." She flapped her arms, velvet robe billowing, and I thought of the name of the cottage and the bird on her mailbox.

"When was the last time you saw her?"

Now June's expression grew uncertain. She bit her lip and reached for a half-full wineglass that sat on the raised hearth. "Well. It was . . . of course! At the autumnal equinox firing."

"Huh?"

"I am a potter, my dear. Well, more of a sculptor in clay. I teach classes in my studio." She motioned in the direction of the outbuildings I'd seen. "My students and I have ceremonial firings on the beach at the equinox and the solstice. Adrian came to the autumnal firing late in September."

"Did she come alone, or did Donna come, too?"

June shook her head, big hair bobbing. "Donna hasn't spoken to me since Jeffrey left. Blames me for taking his side—the side of joy and loving, the side of the bimbo. And she resents my closeness to Adrian. No, my niece brought her boyfriend, that Kirby." Her nose wrinkled.

"And?"

"And what? They attended the firing, ate, and left."

"Do you know Kirby well?"

"I only met him the one time."

"What did you think of him?"

June leaned toward the fireplace, reaching for the poker. When she stirred the logs, there was a small explosion, and sparks and bits of cinder flew out onto the raised stone. June stirred on, unconcerned.

"Like my name," she murmured.

"What?"

"My name—Simoom. Do you know what that is?"

"No."

"A fierce wind of Africa. Dry. Intensely hot. Relentless. It peppers its victims with grit that burns and pits the skin. That's why I took it—it fits my temperament."

"It's not your real name?"

She scowled impatiently. "One's real name is whatever one feels is right. June Conway was *not*. Simoom is fitting for a woman of the earth, who shelters those who are not as strong as she. You saw the name on my mailbox—Wingspread?"

"Yes."

"Then you understand. What's your last name again?"

"Kelleher."

"Well, what does that mean?"

"I don't know. It's just an Irish name."

"You see my point? You're alienated from who you are."

"I don't feel alienated. I mean, I don't think you have to proclaim who you are with a label. And Kelleher's a perfectly good name, even though I'm not crazy about the Irish."

June scowled again. "You sound just like Adrian used to. For God's sake, what's *wrong* with you young women?"

"What do you mean—about Adrian, that is?"

"Well, there she was, given a wonderful name at birth. A strong name. Adrian, of the Adriatic Sea. The only thing Donna did right by her. But did she appreciate it? No. She wanted to be called Melissa or Kelley or Amanda—just like everyone else of her generation. Honestly, sometimes I despaired."

"You speak of her in the past tense, as if she's dead."

She swung around, face crumpling in dismay. "Oh, no! I speak of her that way because that was before . . . before she began to delight in her differences."

"When was that?"

"Well . . . when she started to get past this terrible thing. As we gain strength, we accept who and what we are. In time we glory in it."

In her way, June was as much into psychobabble as her sister-in-law. I said, "To get back to when you last saw Adrian, tell me about this autumnal equinox firing."

"We dig pits on the beach, as kilns. By the time of the firing, they've been heating for days. Each student brings an offering, a special pot. The gathering is solemn but joyful—a celebration of all we've learned in the preceding season."

"It sounds almost religious."

June smiled wryly. "There's also a great deal of good food and drink. And, of course, when the pots emerge from the earth, we're able to sell them to tourists for very good money."

Now that I could relate to. "What about Adrian? Did she enjoy it?"

"Adrian's been coming to my firings for years. She knows a number of my long-term students well, and she always has a good time."

"And this time was no different?"

"Of course not."

"She didn't mention anything being wrong at home or at school?"

" . . . We spoke privately while preparing the food. I'm sure if there had been problems, she would have mentioned them."

"And what about Kirby? Did he enjoy the firing?"

Wariness touched her face again. "I suppose."

"What did you think of him?"

"He's an adolescent boy. What's to think?"

"I didn't care for him," I said.

"You know him?"

"I've spoken with him. I also spoke with a classmate of his and Adrian's. He said Kirby is always into one scam or another, and that Adrian might have been involved, too."

"That's preposterous!" But June's denial was a shade weak and unconvincing.

"Are you sure Adrian didn't hint at problems when you spoke privately with her at the firing?"

"She's a teenager. Things are never right with teenagers. Adrian took her father's defection very badly, even though he and I tried to explain about one's need for personal growth." June gave her funny laugh again—*hinc, hinc, hinc.* "Even if the growth involves a bimbo," she added.

"June," I said, "since you were so close to Adrian, what do you think happened to her?"

She sobered and her fingers tightened on the shaft of the poker. "I can't tell you. I honestly can't hazard a guess."

Her eyes slipped away from mine, but not before I saw something furtive in them. Suddenly she started stirring the fire, even though it was already roaring like crazy.

I said, "But you have suspicions."

She stirred harder. Aunt June wasn't telling it like it was, and she felt guilty.

"You've heard from her since she disappeared, haven't you?" Sharon taught me that little trick: no matter how wild your hunch is, play it. Chances are fifty-fifty you're right, and then their reactions will tell you plenty.

June stiffened. "Of course not! I would have persuaded her to go home. At the very least, I would have called Donna immediately."

"So you think Adrian's disappearance is voluntary?"

"I . . . I didn't say that."

"Assuming it is, and she called you, would you really have let Donna know? You don't seem to like her at all."

"Still, I have a heart. A mother's anguish—"

"Come off it, June."

June Simoom heaved herself to her feet and faced me, the poker clutched in her hand, her velvet-draped bigness making me feel small and helpless. "I think," she said, "you'd better leave now."

♣ ♣ ♣

When I got back to All Souls, it was well after midnight, but I saw a faint light in Sharon's office and went in there. She was curled up on her chaise longue, boots and socks lying muddy on the floor beside it. Her jeans, legs wet to the knees, were draped over a filing cabinet drawer. She'd wrapped herself in the blanket she keeps on the chaise, but it had ridden up, exposing her bare feet and calves, and I could see goosebumps on them. She was sound asleep. ·

Now what had she gotten herself into? More trouble, for sure.

Was she resting between stakeouts? Waiting for a call from one of her many informants? Or just too tired to go home?

I went down the hall to the room of an attorney who was out of town and borrowed one of his blankets, then carried it back and tucked it around Sharon's legs and feet. She moaned a little and threw up one hand like you do to ward off a blow. I watched her until she settled down again, then turned off the Tiffany lamp—a gift long ago from a client, she'd once told me—and went upstairs to the attic nest that I call home.

Sometimes I'm afraid I'll turn out like Sharon: illusions peeled away, emotional scars turning white and hard, ideals pared to the bone.

Sometimes I'm afraid I won't turn out like her.

We're already alike in some ways. Deep down we know who we are, warts and all, and if we don't always like ourselves, at least we understand what we are and why we do certain things. We often try to fool ourselves, though, making out to be smarter or nobler or braver than we are, but in the end the truth always trips us up. And the truth . . .

We both have this crazy—no, crazy-*making*—need to get at the truth, no matter how bad it may be. I guess that's how we're most alike of all. The withheld fact, the out-and-out lie, the thing that we just plain can't understand—none of them stands a chance with us. For me, I think the need began when my grandmother wouldn't tell me the truth about the car wreck my parents were killed in (they were both drunk). With Sharon, I don't know how the need got started—she's never said.

I didn't used to feel so driven. At first this job was a lark, and I was just playing at being a detective. But things happen and you change—Sharon's living proof of that—and now I'm to the point where I'm afraid that someday I'll be the one who spends a lot of nights sleeping alone in her office because I'm between stakeouts or waiting for a phone call or just too tired to go home.

I'm terribly afraid of that happening. Or not happening. Hell, maybe I'm just afraid—period.

## III

The next morning it was raining—big drops whacking off my sky-lights and waking me up. Hank Zahn, who pretty much holds the budgetary reins at All Souls, had let me install the skylights the spring before, after listening to some well orchestrated whining on my part. At the time they seemed like a good idea; there was only one small window in the part of the attic where my nest is, and I needed more light. But since then I'd realized that on a bad day all I could see was gray and wet and accumulated crud—nothing to lift my spirits. Besides, my brass bed had gotten crushed during the installation, and although the co-op's insurance covered its cost, I'd spent the money on a trip to Tahoe and was still sleeping on a mattress on the floor.

That morning I actually welcomed the bad weather because my rain wear being the disguise it is, it actually furthered my current plan of action. For once the bathroom (one flight down and usually in high demand) was free when I needed it, and in half an hour I was wrapped in my old red slicker with the hood that hides nearly my whole head, my travel cup filled with coffee and ready to go. As I moved one of the tags on the mailboxes that tell Ted Smalley, our office manager, whether we're in or out, I glanced at Sharon's. Her tag was missing—she's always setting it down someplace it doesn't belong or wandering off and completely losing it—and Ted would have quite a few things to say to her about that. Ted is the most efficient person I know, and it puzzles him that Sharon can't get the hang of a simple procedure like keeping track of her tag.

The Ramblin' Wreck didn't want to start, and I had to coax it some. Then I headed for Teresita Boulevard, up on the hill above McAteer High School, where Kirby Dalson lived. I'd already phoned Tom Chu before he left for school and gotten a good description of Kirby's car—a red RX-7 with vanity plates saying KS KAR—and after school started I'd called the attendance office and was told that Kirby hadn't come in that morning. The car sat in the driveway of his parents' beige stucco house, so I u-turned and parked at the curb.

The rain kept whacking down and the windows of the Wreck kept steaming up. I wiped them with a rag I found under the seat and then fiddled with the radio. Static was all I got; the radio's as temperamental as the engine. Kirby's car stayed in the driveway. Maybe he had the flu and was bundled up in bed, where I wished I was. Maybe he just couldn't face the prospect of coming out in this storm.

Stakeouts. God. Nobody ever warned me how boring they are. I used to picture myself slouched in my car, wearing an exotic disguise, alert and primed for some great adventure. Sure. Stakeouts are so boring that I've fallen asleep on a couple and missed absolutely nothing. I finished my coffee, wished I'd brought along one of the stale-looking doughnuts that somebody had left on the chopping block in All Souls's kitchen. Then I started to think fondly of the McDonald's over on Ocean Avenue. I just love junk food.

About eleven o'clock the door of the Dalson house opened. Kirby came out wearing jeans and a down jacket and made for his car. After he'd backed down the driveway and headed toward Portola, the main street up there, I started the Wreck and followed.

Kirby went out Portola and west on Sloat Boulevard, toward the beach. By the time we'd passed the end of Stern Grove, I realized he was headed for Ocean Park Plaza. It's a big multi-story center, over a hundred stores, ranging from small specialty shops to big department stores, with a movie theater, health club, supermarket, and dozens of food concessions. It was built right before the recession hit by a consortium of developers who saw the success that the new Stonestown Galleria and the Serramonte Center in Daly City were enjoying. Trouble is, the area out there isn't big enough or affluent enough to support three such shopping malls, and from what the head of security at Ocean Park, Ben Waterson, had told me when I'd questioned him about Adrian the other day, the plaza was in serious trouble.

Kirby whipped the RX-7 into the eastern end of the parking lot and left it near the rear entrance to the Lucky Store. He ran through the rain while I parked the Wreck a few slots down and hurried after, pulling up the hood on my slicker. By the time I got inside, Kirby was cutting through the produce section. He went out into the mall, skirted the escalators, and halfway to the main entrance veered right toward Left Coast Casuals, where Adrian had worked before she disappeared.

I speeded up, then slowed to the inconspicuous, zombie-like pace of a window shopper, stopping in front of the cookware shop next door. Kirby hadn't gone all the way inside, was standing in the entrance talking with a man I recognized as Ben Waterson. They kept it up for a couple of minutes, and it didn't look like a pleasant conversation. The security man scowled and shook his head, while Kirby went red in the face and gestured angrily at the store. Finally he turned and rushed back my way, nearly bowling over a toddler whose mom wasn't watching her. I did an about-face and started walking toward Lucky.

Kirby brushed past me, his pace fast and jerky. People in the mall and the grocery store gave him a wide berth. By the time I got back to the Wreck, he was already burning rubber. The Wreck picked that minute to go temperamental on me, and I knew I'd lost him.

Well, hell. I decided to run by his house again. No RX-7. I checked the parking lot and streets around McAteer. Nothing. Then the only sensible thing to do was drive over to the McDonald's on Ocean and treat myself to a Quarter Pounder with cheese, large fries, and a Diet Coke. The Diet Coke gave me the illusion I was limiting calories.

I spent most of the afternoon parked on Teresita. I'd brought along one of those little hot apple pies they sell at McDonald's. By the time I finished it, I'd had enough excess for one day.

I'd had enough of stakeouts, too, but I stayed in place until Kirby's car finally pulled up at around quarter to five. I waited until he was inside the house, then went up and rang the bell.

While I was sitting there, I'd tried to figure out what was so off-putting about Kirby Dalson. When he answered the door, I hit on it. He was a good-looking kid—well built and tall, with nice dark hair, even when it was wind-blown and full of bits and pieces of eucalyptus leaves like now, but his facial features were a touch too pointy, his eyes a touch too small and close-set. In short, he looked rodenty—just the kind of shifty-eyed kid you'd expect to be into all kinds of scams. His mother wouldn't notice it, and young girls would adore him, but guys would catch on right away, and you could bet quite a few adults, including most of his teachers, had figured it out.

The shiftiness really shone through when he saw me. Something to hide there, all right, maybe something big. "What do you want?" he asked sullenly.

"Just to check a few things." I stepped through the door even though he hadn't invited me in. You can get away with that with kids, even the most self-assured. Kirby just stood there. Then he shut the door, folded his arms across his chest, and waited.

I said, "Let's sit down," and went into the living room. It was pretty standard—beige and brown with green accents—and had about as much character as a newborn's face. I don't understand how people can live like that, with nothing in their surroundings that says who or what they are. My nest may be cluttered and have no particular decor, but at least it's *me*.

I sat on a chair in a little grouping by the front window. Kirby perched across from me. He'd tracked in wet, sandy grit onto his mother's well-vacuumed carpet—another strike against him, even for a lousy housekeeper like me—and his fingers drummed on his denim-covered thighs.

"Kirby," I began, "why'd you go to see Ben Waterson today?"

"Who?"

"The security head at Ocean Park Plaza."

"Who says I did?"

"I saw you."

His little eyes widened a fraction. "You were following me? Why?"

I ignored the question. "Why'd you go see him?"

For a moment he glanced about the room, as if looking for a way out. "Okay," he finally said. "Money."

"Money? For what?"

"Adrian, you know, disappeared on payday. I thought maybe I could collect some of what she owed me from Left Coast."

"Owed you for what?"

He shook his head.

"For *what*, Kirby?"

"Just for stuff. She borrowed when she was short."

I watched him silently for a minute. He squirmed a little. I said, "You know, I've been hearing that you're into some things that aren't strictly legal."

"I don't get you."

"Scams, Kirby."

His puzzled look proved he'd never make an actor.

"Do I have to spell it out for you?" I asked. "The term-paper racket. Selling test questions when you can get your hands on them."

His fingers stopped their staccato drumming. Damned if the kid didn't seem relieved by what I'd just said.

"What else are you into, Kirby?"

"Where're you getting this stuff, anyway?"

"Answer the question."

Silence.

"What about Adrian? Did you bring her in on any of your scams?"

A car door slammed outside. Kirby wet his lips and glanced at the mantel clock. "Look," he said, "I don't want you talking about this in front of my mother."

"Then talk fast."

"All right, I sold some test questions and term papers. So what? I'm not the first ever who did that."

"What else? That wouldn't have brought in the kind of cash that bought you your fancy car."

"I've got a job—"

"Nobody believes that but your parents."

Footsteps on the front walk. Kirby said, "All right, so I sell a little dope here and there."

"Grass?"

"Uh-huh."

"Coke?  Crack?"

"When I can get them."

"Adrian use drugs?"

"A little grass now and then."

"She sell drugs?"

"Never."

A key turned in the front-door lock.  Kirby looked that way, panicky.  I asked, "What else are you into?"

"Nothing.  I swear."

The door opened.

"What did you get Adrian involved in?"

"I didn't—" A woman in a raincoat stepped into the foyer, furling an umbrella.  Kirby raised a hand to her in greeting, then said in a low voice, "I can't talk about it now."

"When?"

He raised his voice.  "I have to work tonight, I'll be at the garage by seven."

"I'll bring my car in then.  What's the address?"

He got a pad from a nearby telephone table and scribbled on it. I took the slip of paper he held out and glanced at it.  The address was on Naples Street in the Outer Mission—mostly residential neighborhood, middle-class.  Wherever Kirby wanted to meet, it wasn't a garage.

❖ ❖ ❖

By seven the rain was really whacking down, looking like it would keep it up all night.  It was so dark that I had trouble picking out the right address on Naples Street.  Finally I pinpointed it—a shabby brown cottage, wedged between two bigger Victorians.  No light in the windows, no cars in the driveway.  Had Kirby been putting me on?  If he had, by God, I'd stomp right into his house and lay the whole thing out for his parents.  That's one advantage to dealing with kids—you've got all kinds of leverage.

I got out of the Wreck and went up the cottage's front walk.  Its steps were as bad off as the ones at June Simoom's place.  I tripped on a loose board and grabbed the railing; its spindles shook. Where the bell should have been were a couple of exposed wires. I banged on the door, but nobody came. The newspapers and ad sheets that were piled in a sodden mass against the threshold told me that the door hadn't been used for quite a while.

After a minute I went back down the steps and followed the driveway alongside the house. There were a couple of aluminum storage sheds back there, both padlocked. Otherwise the yard was dark and choked with pepper trees. Ruts that looked like they'd been made by tires led under them, and way back in the shadows I saw a low-slung shape. A car. Kirby's, I thought.

I started over there, walking alongside the ruts, mud sucking at my sneakers. It was quiet here, much too quiet. Just the patter of rain in the trees overhead. And then a pinging noise from the car's engine.

It was Kirby's RX-7, all right. The driver's side door was open, but the dome light wasn't on. Now why would he leave the door open in a storm like this?

I moved slower, checking it out, afraid this was some kind of a set-up. Then I saw Kirby sitting in the driver's seat. At least I saw someone's feet on the ground next to the car. And hands hanging loose next to them . . .

I moved even slower now, calling out Kirby's name. No answer. I called again. The figure didn't move. The skin on my shoulders went prickly, and the feeling spread up the back of my neck and head. My other senses kicked into overdrive—hearing sharper, sight keener, smell . . . There was a sweet but metallic odor that some primitive instinct told me was blood.

This was Kirby, all right. As I came closer I identified his jeans and down jacket, caught a glimpse of his profile. He was leaning forward, looking down at his lap. And then I saw the back of his head. God. It was ruined, caved in, and the blood—

I heard somebody moan in protest. Me.

I made myself creep forward, hand out, and touched Kirby's slumped shoulders. Felt something wet that was thicker than rainwater. I pulled my hand back as he slumped all the way over, head touching his knees now. Then I spun around and ran, stumbling through the ruts and the mud. I got as far as the first storage shed and leaned against it, panting.

I'd never seen a dead person before, unless you counted my grandmother, dressed up and in her coffin. I'd never touched one before.

After I got my wind back, I looked at the car again. Maybe he wasn't dead. No, I knew he was. But I went back there anyway and made myself touch his neck. Flesh still warm, but nothing pulsing. Then I turned, wiping my hand on my jeans, and ran all the way down the driveway and straight across the street to a house with a bright porch light. I pounded on the door and shouted for them to call 911, somebody had been murdered.

Afterward the uniformed cops who responded would ask me how I knew it was a murder and not natural causes or an overdose. But that was before they saw Kirby's head.

### IV

I sat at the oak table in All Souls's kitchen, my hands wrapped around a mug of Hank Zahn's super-strength Navy grog. I needed it more for the warmth than anything else. Hank sat next to me, and then there was Ted Smalley, and then Sharon. The men were acting like I was a delicate piece of china. Hank kept refilling my grog mug and trying to smooth down his unsmoothable wiry gray hair. Every now and then he'd take off his hornrimmed glasses and gnaw on the earpiece—something he does when he's upset. Ted, who likes to fuss, had wrapped me in an afghan that he fetched from his own room upstairs. Every few minutes he'd tuck the ends tighter around me, and in between he pulled on his little goatee. Men think women fiddle with our hair a lot, but really, they do more of it than we do.

Sharon wasn't saying much. She watched and listened, her fingers toying with the stem of her wineglass. The men kept glancing reproachfully at her. I guess they thought she was being unsympathetic. I knew differently. She was worried, damned worried, about me. And eventually she'd have something to say.

Finally she sighed and shifted in her chair. Hank and Ted looked expectant, but all she did was ask, "Adah Joslyn was the inspector who came out from Homicide?"

I nodded. "Her and her partner . . . what's his name? Wallace." Joslyn was a friend of Sharon's—a half-black, half-Jewish woman whose appointment to the top-notch squad had put the department in good with any number of civil-rights groups.

"Then you were in good hands."

I waited. So did Ted and Hank, but all Sharon did was sip some wine and look pensive.

I started talking—telling it once more. "He hadn't been dead very long when I got there. For all I know, whoever killed him was still on the scene. Nobody knows whose house it is— neighbors say people come and go but don't seem to live there. What I'm afraid of is that Adrian Conway had something to do with Kirby's murder. If she did, it'll about kill her mother. I guess I can keep looking for her, can't I? I mean, unless they tell me not to?"

Sharon only nodded.

"Then maybe I will. Maybe I ought to take a look at that bedroom wall of hers again. Maybe . . ." I realized I was babbling, so I shut up.

Sharon finished her wine, took the empty glass to the sink, and started for the door. Hank asked, "Where're you going?"

"Upstairs to collect my stuff, and then home. It's been a long day."

Both men frowned and exchanged looks that said they thought she was being callous. I watched her leave. Then I finished my grog and stood up, too.

"Going to bed?" Ted asked.

"Yes."

"If you need anything, just holler."

"I'm upset, not feeble," I snapped.

Ted nodded understandingly. Sometimes he's so goddamn serene I could hit him.

Sharon was still in her office, not collecting anything, just sitting behind her desk, where I knew she'd be. I went in there and sat on the end of the chaise lounge. After a few seconds, I got up again, and began to pace, following the pattern of the Oriental rug.

She said, "I can't tell you anything that'll help."

"I know."

"I'd hoped you'd never have to face this," she added. "Unrealistic of me, I suppose."

"Maybe."

"But maybe not. Most investigators don't, you know. Some of them never leave their computer terminals long enough to get out into the field."

"So what are we—unlucky?"

"I guess." She stood and started putting things into her briefcase. "You're going to keep looking for Adrian?"

"Yes."

"Good."

I stopped by the fireplace and picked up the gorilla mask she keeps on the mantel. It had a patch of hair missing right in the middle of its chin; I'd accidentally pulled it out one day during a fit over something that I couldn't even remember now. "Shar," I said. "it never gets any easier, does it?"

"No."

"But somehow you deal with it?"

"And go on." She put on her jacket, hefted the briefcase.

"Until the next time," I said bitterly.

"If there is one."

"Yeah." I suspected there would be. Look at what Sharon's life has been like. And yet, seeing her standing there—healthy and reasonably sane and looking forward to a good night's sleep—made me feel hopeful.

She came over to me and gave me a one-armed hug. Then she pointed at the gorilla mask and said, "You want to take him to bed with you tonight?"

"No. If I want to sleep with a gorilla, I'll just call Willie."

She grinned and went out, leaving me all alone.

After a while I put the gorilla back on the mantel and lay down on the chaise longue. I dragged the blanket over me and curled up on my side, cradling my head on my arm. The light from the Tiffany lamp was mellow and comforting. It became toasty under the blanket. In a few minutes, I actually felt sleepy.

I'd stay there tonight, I decided. In some weird way, it felt safer than my nest upstairs.

Donna Conway called me at eight-ten the next morning. I'd already gone down to my office—a closet under the stairs that some joker had passed off as a den when All Souls moved into the house years before—and was clutching a cup of the battery acid that Ted calls coffee and trying to get my life back together. When my intercom buzzed, I jerked and grabbed the phone receiver without first asking who it was.

Donna said dully, "The backpack I told you Adrian always took to school with her? They found it where poor Kirby was murdered."

I went to put my cup down, tipped it, and watched coffee soak into my copy of the morning paper. Bad day already. "They—you mean the police?"

"Yes. They just brought it over for me to identify."

"Where was it? In the yard?"

"Inside the house. It'd been there a long time because the yogurt—she always took a cup of yogurt to work to eat on her break—was spoiled."

Not good at all.

"Rae, you don't think it means *she* did that to Kirby, do you?"

"I doubt it." What I thought it meant was that Adrian was dead, maybe had been dead since shortly after she disappeared—but I wasn't going to raise *that* issue yet. "What else was in the pack besides the yogurt?"

A pause. "The usual stuff, I guess. I didn't ask. I was too upset."

I'd get Sharon to check that out with her friend Adah Joslyn.

Donna added, "The police said that Kirby was the one who rented the house, and that there was a girl with him when he first looked at it who matched Adrian's description."

"When?"

"Late last July. I guess . . . well, with teenagers today, you just assume they're sexually active. Adrian and I had a talk about safe sex two years ago. But I don't understand why they thought they needed to rent a place to be together. I'm not home all that much, and neither are Kirby's parents. Besides, they couldn't have spent much time at that house; Adrian worked six days a week, after school and on Saturdays, and she was usually home by her curfew."

I thought about Kirby's "job" at the nonexistent garage. Maybe Adrian's had been a front, too. But, no, that didn't wash—the store's manager, Sue Hanford, and the plaza security man, Ben Waterson, had confirmed her employment both to me and the police.

"Rae?" Donna said. "Will you keep on looking for her?"

"Of course."

"Will you call me if you find out anything? I'll be here all day today. I can't face going to work."

I said I would, but I was afraid that what I'd have to tell her wouldn't be anything she'd want to hear.

❖  ❖  ❖

"Yeah, the little weasel wanted to pick up her pay, in cash." Ben Waterson plopped back in the metal chair behind the front desk in the Ocean Park Plaza security office. Its legs groaned threateningly under his massive weight. On the walls around us were mounted about two dozen TV screens that monitored what was going on in various stores in the center, switching from one to another for spot checking. Waterson glanced at one, looked closer, then shook his head. "In cash, no less, the little weasel said, since he couldn't cash her check. Said she owed him money. Can you imagine?"

I leaned against the counter. There wasn't another chair in the room, and Waterson hadn't offered to find me one. "Why'd he ask you for it, rather than Ms. Hanford? Adrian was paid by Left Coast Casuals, not the plaza, wasn't she?"

"Sue was out and had left me in charge of the store." Waterson scratched at the beer belly that bulged over the waist of his khaki uniform pants. "Can you imagine?" he said again. "Kids today."

He snorted.

Waterson was your basic low-level security guy, although he'd risen higher than most of them ever go. I know, because I worked among them until my then-boss took pity on me and recommended me to Sharon for the job at All Souls. It's a familiar type: not real bright, not too great to look at, and lacking in most of the social graces. About all you need to get in on the ground floor of the business is never to have been arrested or caught molesting the neighbors' dog on the front lawn at high noon. Ben Waterson— well, I doubted he'd been arrested because he didn't look like he had the ambition to commit a crime, but I wasn't too sure about his conduct toward the neighborhood pets.

"So you told Kirby to get lost?" I asked.

"I told him to fuck off, pardon my French. And he got pissed off, pardon it again, and left."

"He say why Adrian owned him money?"

"Nah. Who knows? Probably for a drug buy. Kids today."

"Did Adrian do drugs?"

"They all do."

"But did you ever know *her* to do them?"

"Didn't have to. They all do." He looked accusingly at me. From his fifty-something perspective, I probably was young enough to be classified as one of today's youthful degenerates.

I shifted to a more comfortable position, propping my hip against the counter. Waterson scanned the monitors again, then looked back at me.

"Let me ask you this," I said. "How well did you know Kirby Dalson?"

His eyes narrowed. "What the hell's that supposed to mean?"

I hadn't thought it was a particularly tricky question. "How well did you know him?" I repeated. "What kind of kid was he?"

"Oh. Just a kid. A weasel-faced punk. I had a daughter, I wouldn't let him near her."

"You mentioned drugs. Was Kirby dealing?"

"Probably."

"Why do you say that?"

He rolled his eyes. "I told you—kids today." Then, unself-consciously, he started picking his nose.

I didn't need any more of this, so I headed downstairs to Sue Hartford's office at Left Coast Casuals.

Hanlord was a sleek blonde around my age, in her late twenties. One of those women who is moving up in the business world in spite of a limited education, relying on her toughness and brains. On Monday she'd told me she started in an after school job like Adrian's at the Redwood City branch of the clothing chain and had managed two of their other stores before being selected for the plum position at the then-new plaza. When she saw me standing in her office door, Hanford motioned for me to come in and sit down. She continued working at her computer for a minute. Then she swiveled toward me, face arranged in formally solemn lines.

"I read in the paper about the Conway girl's boyfriend," she said. "So awful. So young."

I told her about Adrian's backpack being found in the house, and she made perfunctorily horrified noises.

"This doesn't mean Adrian *killed* Kirby, does it?" she asked.

"Doubtful. It looked as if the pack's been there since right after she disappeared."

For a moment her features went very still. "Then Kirby might have killed . . ."

"Yes."

"But where is the . . . ?"

"Body? Well, not at the house, I'm sure the cops would have found it by now."

"Or else she . . ."

"She what?"

"I don't know. Maybe she ran away. Maybe he frightened her somehow."

Interesting assumption. "Are you saying Adrian was afraid of Kirby?"

Quickly she shook her head. "No. Well, maybe. It was more like . . . he dominated her. One look from him was all she needed, and she'd do whatever he wanted her to."

"Give me an example."

"Well, one time I saw them at a table near the food concessions in the middle of the mall. He had a burger, she was spooning up her yogurt. All of a sudden, Kirby pointed at his burger, then jerked his chin at the condiment counter. Adrian got up and scurried over there and brought him back some katsup."

"So he pretty much controlled her?"

"I'd say so."

"What else?"

She shrugged. "That's about the best example I can give you. I didn't really see that much of them together. We try to discourage our girls from having their friends come into the store during working hours."

"When I spoke with you earlier this week, you said you doubted Adrian was a drug user. Are you sure of that?"

"Reasonably sure. I observe our girls very carefully. I can't have anything like that going on, especially not on store premises. It would reflect badly on my abilities as a manager." Her eyes lost focus suddenly. "God, what if something has happened to Adrian? I mean, something like what happened to Kirby? That would reflect badly, too. The damage control I'd need to do . . ."

I said wryly, "I don't think that as store manager you can be held responsible for what happens to your employees off-hours."

"You don't understand. It would reflect badly on my abilities to size up a prospective employee." Her eyes refocused on my face. "I can see you think I'm uncaring. Maybe to some degree I am. But I'm running a business here. I'm building a career, and I have to be strong. I have a small daughter to raise, and I'm fiercely protective of her chances to have a good life. I'm sorry Kirby Dalson's dead. If Adrian's also been killed, then I'm sorry about that, too. But, really, neither of them has anything to do with me, with my life."

That's the trouble, I thought. The poet, whoever he was, said no man is an island, but nowadays *every* man and woman is one. A whole goddamn continent, the way some of them act. It's a wonder that they all don't sink to the bottom of the ocean, just like the lost continent of Atlantis is supposed to have done.

## V

I wanted to drive by the house on Naples Street, just to see what it looked like in the daylight. The rain had stopped, but it was still a soppy, gray morning. The house looked shabby and sodden. There was a yellow plastic police line strip across the driveway, and a man in a tan raincoat stood on the front steps, hands in his pockets, staring at nothing in particular.

He didn't look like a cop. He was middle-aged, middle height, a little gray, a little bald. His glasses and the cut of his coat were the kind you used to associate with the movers and shakers of the 1980's financial world, but the coat was rumpled and had a grease stain near its hem, and as I got out of the Wreck and went closer, I saw that one hinge of the glasses frame was wired together. His face pulled down in disappointed lines that looked permanent. Welcome to the nineties, I thought.

The man's eyes focused dully on me. "If you're a reporter," he said, "you'd better speak with the officers in charge of the case." He spoke with a kind of diluted authority, his words turning up in a question, as if he wasn't quite sure who or what he was any longer.

"I'm not a reporter." I took out my i.d. and explained my connection to the case.

The man looked at the i.d., nodded, and shrugged. Then he sighed. "Hell of a thing, isn't it? I wish I'd never rented to them."

"This is your house?"

"My mother's. She's in a nursing home. I can't sell it—she still thinks she's coming back someday. That's all that's keeping her alive. I can't fix it up, either." He motioned at the peeling facade. "My business has been in a flat-out slump for a couple of years now, and the nursing home's expensive. I rented to the first couple who answered my ad. Bad judgment on my part. They were too young, and into God-knows-what." He laughed mirthlessly, then added, "Sorry, I didn't introduce myself. Ron Owens."

I'd inched up the steps toward the open front door until I was standing next to him. I shook his outstretched hand and repeated my name for him.

Owens sighed again and stared glumly at the wet street. "It's a hell of a world," he said. "A hell of a thing when a kid dies like that. Kids are supposed to grow up, have a life. At least outlive their parents." Then he looked at me. "You said the girl's mother hired you?"

"Yes. I haven't come up with any leads, and she's getting frantic. I thought maybe if I could see the house . . ." I motioned at the door.

For a moment Owens hesitated. "What the hell—they said they were done there. Come on in, if you want."

I followed him into a narrow hallway that ran the length of the cottage. "Were you here when they found the girl's backpack?"

"Did that belong to her? Yeah. I came over and let them in as soon as they contacted me. First time I'd been here since the kids rented it. Place is a mess. I'm glad I stored most of my mother's things in the sheds and only left the basic furnishings. They didn't exactly trash it, but they didn't keep it, either."

Mess was the word for it. Dust—both natural and from finger-print powder saturated all the surfaces, and empty glasses and plates stood among empty bottles and cans and full ashtrays in the front room. Owens lead me back past a bathroom draped in crumpled and mildewy-smelling towels and a bedroom where the sheets and blankets were mostly on the floor, to a kitchen. It contained more dirty crockery and glassware. Wrappings from frozen entrees and fast food overflowed the trashcan. A half-full fifth of Jim Beam stood uncapped on the counter. The entire place reeked.

"The cops went through everything?" I asked.

"Yeah. They didn't think anybody had been here for a while. At least not last night. There weren't any muddy footprints inside, and the door was blocked by a few days' worth of newspapers."

"Where did they find the backpack?"

"Front room. I'll show you."

The table where the backpack had been was just inside the

living room door. What was left there was junk mail and ad sheets —the sort of stuff you drag inside with you and dump someplace until you get around to throwing it out. "So," I said, "this was where she'd leave the pack when she arrived. But why not pick it up again when she left?"

Ron Owens made a funny choking sound, and I realized he'd jumped to the obvious conclusion. "No," I said quickly, "the cops would have found evidence if she was killed here. Did you see what was in the pack?"

He shook his head. "One of them said something about there being no money or i.d."

Adrian had been smart, carrying her cash and i.d. someplace else where it wouldn't be snatched if somebody grabbed the pack on the street or on the bus. Smart, too, because if she'd had to run out of this house suddenly—if Kirby had frightened or threatened her, as Sue Hanford had suggested—she'd at least have had the essentials on her.

I'd seen enough here, so I thanked Owens and gave him one of my cards in case he thought of anything else. I was halfway down the front walk when I remembered to ask him if I could see the sheds where he'd stored his mother's things.

For a moment he looked puzzled at the request, then he shrugged and fished a key ring from his pocket. "Actually, it wouldn't hurt to check them."

We ducked under the police line and went up the driveway. The trees dripped on the muddy ground where Kirby's car had been parked. There were deep gouges and tracks where the tow truck had hauled it out. Other than that, you would never have known that anything unusual had happened there. It was just an ordinary backyard that the weeds and blackberry vines were trying to reclaim.

Ron Owens fit a key into the padlock on the first shed. Unfastened it and then the hasp. The door grated as he opened it.

There was nothing inside. Nothing at all except for a little heap of wood scraps.

Owens's face went slack with surprise. Then bright red

splotches blossomed on his cheeks. "They cleaned me out," he said. "Check the other shed."

We hurried back there. Owens opened it. Nothing except for some trash drifted in the corners.

"But how did they . . . ?" He held up his key ring. "I had the only . . . There were no other keys."

I looked closely at the padlock. Cheap brand, more pickable than most. My boyfriend Willie would have had that off of there in five minutes, max—and he's out of practice. Willie's a respectable businessman now, but there are things in his past that are best not discussed.

"You better call the police," I told Owens.

He nodded, shoulders slumping. "I'm glad my mother will never have to find out about this," he said. "Her good china, Grandma's silver, the family pictures—all gone. For the first time I'm glad she's never coming home. There's no home left here anymore."

I watched Owens hurry down the drive to a car with a mobile phone antenna on its trunk. I knew how he felt. For me, the word "home" has a magical aura. Sometimes I can actually *see* it—velvety green like the plants in my nest at All Souls, gold and wine-red like the flames in a good fire. Silly, but that's the way it is for me. Probably for all of us people who've never had a real home of our own.

I turned away and looked back into the empty shed. Adrian had had a real home, but she'd left it. For this shabby little house? I doubted that. But she'd been here shortly after her schoolmates had last seen her, and then she'd probably fled in fear. For where? *Where?*

I decided to consult the therapy wall once more.

## VI

The Conway house was warm for a change, and Donna had closed the drapes to hide the murky city view. Adrian's room, though, was frigid. Donna saving on the heating bill now that Adrian was gone? Or maybe the registers were closed because Adrian was one of those human reptiles who never need much warmth. My ex-husband, Doug, is like that: when other people are bundled in two layers of sweaters, he's apt to be running around in his shirtsleeves.

Before she left me alone, Donna said, "My sister-in-law called and said you'd gone to see her."

"Yes, Tuesday night."

"What'd you think of her?"

"Well, she's unconventional, but I kind of liked her. She seems to have a heart, and she certainly cares about Adrian."

Donna pushed a lock of hair back from her forehead and sighed. She looked depressed and jumpy, dark smudges under her eyes. "I see she's fooled you, too." Then she seemed to relent a little. "Oh, I suppose June's got a good heart, as you say. But she also has an unfortunate tendency to take over a situation and tell everyone what to do. She's the original earth mother and thinks we're all her children. The straw that broke it for me was when she actually advised Jeffrey to leave me. But . . . I don't know. She seems to want to patch it up now, and I suppose for Adrian's sake I should."

The words "for Adrian's sake" hung hollowly in the cold room. Donna shivered and added, "I'll leave you alone with the wall now."

Honestly, the way she acted, you'd have thought the wall was my psychiatrist. In a sense that was what it *had* been to her daughter.

I sat on Adrian's bed like the time before and let the images on the wall speak to me. One, then the other, cried out for attention. Bright primary colors, bold black and white. Words, pictures, then more words. And things—incongrous things. All adding up to . . . what?

After a while I sat up straighter, seeing objects I hadn't noticed before, seeing others in a new light. What they communicated was a sense of entrapment, but not necessarily by the family situation. *Material relating to her absent father—GONE FOREVER, THE YEAR OF THE BIMBO, a postcard from Switzerland where

Jeffrey Conway now lived—was buried deep under more recent additions. So were the references to Adrian's and her mother's new life—JUST THE TWO OF US, A WOMAN ALONE, NEW DIRECTIONS. But on top of that . . .

Fake plastic handcuffs. Picture of a barred window. NO EXIT sign. SOLD INTO WHITE SLAVERY. Photo of San Quentin. Images of a young woman caught up in something she saw no easy way out of.

I got up and went over to the wall and took a good look at a plastic security tag I'd noticed before. There were similar ones on the higher-priced garments at Left Coast Casuals. Next to it, the word "guilt" was emblazoned in big letters; smaller repetitions of it tailed down like the funnel of a cyclone. My eyes followed them, then were caught hypnotically in the whorls of a thumb-print on a plain white index card.

On top of all these were Adrian's final offerings. Now that I'd discovered a pattern, I could tell which things had been added last. FREEDOM! Broken gold chain. A WAY OUT. Egret feather and silhouette of a soaring bird. She was about to break loose, fly away. I wasn't sure from what, not exactly. But guilt was a major component, and I thought I knew why.

I started searching the room. Nothing under the lingerie or sweaters or socks in the bureau drawers. Nothing pushed to the back of the closet or hidden in the suitcases. Nothing under the mattress or the bed. Nothing but school supplies in the desk.

Damn! I was sure I'd figured out that part of it. I had shameful personal experience to guide me.

The room was so cold that the joints of my fingers ached. I tucked my hands into my armpits to warm them, The heat register was one of those metal jobs set into the floor under a window, and its louvers were closed. I squatted next to it and tried to push the opener. Jammed.

The register lifted easily out of its hole. I peered through the opening in the floor and saw that the sheet metal furnace duct was twisted and pushed aside. A nail had been hammered into the floor joist, and something hung down from it into the crawl space. I reached in and unhooked it—a big cloth laundry bag with a drawstring. I pulled the bag up through the hole and dumped its contents on the carpet.

Costume jewelry—rings, bracelets, earrings, necklaces—with the price tags still attached. Silk scarves. Pantyhose. Gloves, bikini underpants, leather belts, hair ornaments. They were all from Left Coast Casuals.

Although the items were tagged, the tags were not the plastic kind that trip the sensors at the door. Left Coast Casuals reserved the plastic tags for big-ticket items. All of the merchandise was brand new, had never been worn. No individual item was expensive, but taken together, they added up to a hell of a lot of money.

This told me a lot about Adrian, but it didn't explain her disappearance. Or her boyfriend's murder. I replaced the things in the bag, and the bag beneath the flooring. Then I got out of there and went to bounce this one off Sharon.

❖ ❖ ❖

Sharon was all dressed up today, probably either for a meeting with one of our tonier clients or a court appearance. The teal blue suit and silk blouse looked terrific on her, but I could tell she wasn't all that comfortable in them. Sharon's more at home in her jeans and sweaters and sneakers. The only time she really likes getting gussied up is for a fancy party, and then she goes at it with the excitement of a kid putting on her Halloween costume.

She said she had some time on her hands, so I suggested we stop down at the Remedy Lounge, our favorite bar-and-grill on Mission Street, for burgers. She hesitated. They serve a great burger at the Remedy, but for some reason Sharon—who's usually not fastidious when it comes to food—is convinced they're made of all sorts of disgusting animal parts. Finally she gave in, and we wandered down the hill.

The Remedy is a creaky local tavern, owned by the O'Flanagan family for longer than anybody can remember. Brian, the middle son and nighttime bartender, wasn't on yet, so we had to fetch our own food and drinks. Brian's my buddy, and when he's working,

I get table service—something that drives everybody else from All Souls crazy because they can't figure out how I manage that. I just let them keep guessing. Truth is, I remind Brian of his favorite sister, who died back in '76. Would you refuse table service to a family member?

While we waited for the burgers, I laid out the Adrian Conway situation for Sharon. When I was done, she went and got our food, then looked critically at her burger, taking off the top half of the bun and poking suspiciously at the meat patty. Finally she shrugged, bit into it, and looked relieved at finding it tasted like burger instead of entrail of monkey—or whatever she thinks they make them from. She swallowed and asked, "All the stuff was lifted from Left Coast Casuals?"

"Uh-huh."

"Employee pilferage." She shook her head. "Do you know that over forty-three percent of shrinkage is due to insiders?"

I didn't, but Sharon's a former department-store security guard and she keeps up on statistics. I just nodded.

"A lot of it's the employers' fault," she added. "They don't treat their people well, so they don't have a real commitment to the company. The clerks see it as a way of getting even for low wages and skimpy benefits."

"Well, whatever Adrian's reasons were," I said, "she dealt with the loot in the usual way. Once she got it home, it wasn't any good to her. Her mother would notice if she wore a lot of new things and ask where she got the money to buy them. Plus she felt guilty. So she hid the loot away were Donna wouldn't find it and—more important—where she couldn't see it and be reminded of what she'd done. Out of sight, out of mind. Only it doesn't work that way. She was probably aware of that bag of stuff hanging between the floor joists every minute she was in that room. She probably even dreamed about it."

My voice had risen as I spoke, and I couldn't keep an emotional quaver out of it. When I finished, Sharon didn't say anything, just watched me with her little analytical frown. I ate some of my burger. It tasted like cardboard. I drank some Coke. My hand shook when I set the glass down.

"Anyway," I said, "Adrian being a shoplifter doesn't explain the important things. Did you ask Adah Joslyn what was in the backpack, like I asked you to?"

"I've got a call in to her."

She was still watching me. After a moment I gave it up. "All right," I said, "I used to shoplift."

"I suspected as much."

"Thanks a lot!"

"Well, you did get pretty worked up for a moment there. You want to tell me about it?"

"No! Well, maybe." I took a deep breath, wishing I'd ordered a beer instead of a Coke. "Okay, it started one day when I was trying to buy some nail polish. The clerk was off yapping with one of the other clerks and wouldn't stop long enough to notice me. So I got pissed, stuck the bottle in my purse, and walked out. Nobody even looked at me. I couldn't believe I'd gotten away with it. It was like . . . a high. The best high I'd ever felt. And I told myself the clerk had goaded me into it, that it was a one-shot thing and would never happen again."

"But of course it did."

"The second time it was a scarf, an expensive scarf. I had a job interview and I wanted to look nice, but I couldn't afford to because I didn't have a job—the old vicious circle. I felt deprived, really angry. So I took the scarf. But what I didn't count on was the guilt. By the day of the interview, I knew I couldn't wear the scarf—then or ever. I just tucked it away where I wouldn't have to see it and be reminded of what I'd done. And where my husband wouldn't find it."

"But you kept stealing."

"Yeah. I never deliberately set out to do it, never left the apartment thinking, today I'm going to rip some store off. But . . . the high. It was something else." Even now, years after the fact, I could feel aftershocks from it—my blood coursing faster, my heart pounding a little. "I was careful, I only took little things, always went to different stores. And then, just when I thought I was untouchable, I got caught."

Sharon nodded. She'd heard it all before, working in retail security.

I looked down at my half-eaten burger. Shame washed over me, negating the memory of the high. My cheeks went hot, just thinking about that day. "God, it was awful! The security guy nabbed me on the sidewalk, made me go back inside to the store office. What I'd taken was another scarf. I'd stuffed it into a bag with some underpants I'd bought at K-Mart. He dragged it out of there. It was still tagged, and of course I didn't have any receipt."

"So he threatened you."

"Scared the hell out of me. I felt like . . . you know those old crime movies where they're sweating a confession out of some guy in a back room? Well, it wasn't like that at all, he was very careful not to do or say anything that might provoke a lawsuit. But I still felt like some sleazy criminal. Or maybe that was what I thought I deserved to feel like. Anyway, he threatened to call my employer." I laughed—a hollow sound. "That would really have torn it. My employer was another security firm!"

"So what'd you do—sign a confession?"

"Yes, and promised never to set foot in their store again. And I've never stolen so much as a stick of gum since. Hell, I can't even bring myself to take the free matchbooks from restaurants!"

Sharon grinned. "I bet one of the most embarrassing things about that whole period in your life is that you were such a textbook case."

I nodded. "Woman's crime. Nonsensical theft. Doesn't stem from a real need, but from anger or the idea you're somehow entitled to things you can't afford. You get addicted to the high, but you're also overcome by the guilt, so you can't get any benefit from what you've stolen. Pretty stupid, huh?"

"We're all pretty stupid at times—shoplifters haven't cornered the market on that."

"Yeah. You know what scared me the most, though? Even more than the security guy calling my employer? That Doug would find out. For a perpetual student who leaned on me for everything from financial support to typing his papers, he could be miserably self-righteous and superior. He'd never even have tried to understand that I was stealing to make up for everything that was missing in our marriage. And he'd *never* have let me forget what I did."

"Well, both the stealing and Doug are history now." Sharon patted my hand. "Don't look so hangdog."

"Can't help it. I feel like such a . . . I bet you've never done anything like that in your life."

Sharon's eyes clouded and her mouth pulled down. All she said was, "Don't count on it." Then she scrubbed her fingers briskly on her napkin and pushed her empty plate away. "Finish your lunch," she ordered. "And let's get back to your case. What you're telling me is that Adrian was shoplifting and saw a way to break free of it?"

"A way to break free of something, but I'm not convinced it was the shoplifting. It may have been related, but then again, it may not." My head was starting to ache. There was too damn big a gap between the bag of loot under the floor of Adrian's room in Diamond Heights and the abandoned backpack in the living room of the house on Naples Street. I'd hoped Sharon would provide a connection, but all she'd done was listen to me confess to the absolutely worst sin of my life.

She looked at her watch. "Well, I'll try to find out what you need to know from Adah later this afternoon, but right now I've got to go. I'm giving a deposition at an upscale Montgomery Street law firm at three." Her nose wrinkled when she said "upscale."

I waved away the money she held out and told her I'd pick up the tab. It was the least I could do. Even though she hadn't helped me with the case, she'd helped me with my life. Again.

I've always felt like something of a fraud—pretending to be this nice little person when inside I'm seething with all sorts of resentments and peculiarities and secrets. But since I've been with All Souls, where people are mostly open and nonjudgmental, I've realized I'm not that unusual. Lately the two me's—the outside nice one and the inside nasty one—are coming closer together.

Today's conversation with Sharon was just one more step in the right direction.

## VII

I'd come up with a plan, an experiment I wanted to try out, and while it probably wouldn't work, I had a lot of time on my hands and nothing to lose. So after I finished my burger, I went back up the hill to our annex and got Lillian Chu to call her son Tom at McAteer and command his presence at my office as soon as school let out. When Tom arrived, he'd traded his friendly smile for a pout. To make up for my high-handedness, I took him to the kitchen and treated him to a Coke.

Tom perched on one of the counter tops and stared around at the ancient sink and wheezy appliances. "Man," he said, "this is really retro. I mean, how can you people *live* like this?"

"We're products of a more primitive era. You're probably wondering why I—"

"Pulled this authority shit. Yeah. You didn't have to get my mom to order me to come here."

"I wasn't sure you would, otherwise. Besides, the people at McAteer wouldn't have called you to the phone for me. I'm sorry, but I really need your help. You heard about Kirby, of course."

The anger in his eyes melted. He shook his head, bit his lip. "Oh, man. What an awful . . . You know, I didn't like the dude, but for him to be *murdered* . . ."

"Did you hear that Adrian's backpack was found in the house whose backyard he was killed in?"

"No." For a few seconds it didn't seem to compute. Then he said, "Wait, you don't think *Adrian* . . . ?"

"Of course not, but I'm afraid for her. If she's alive, it's possible Kirby's killer is after her, too. I need to find her before anyone else does."

Tom sat up straighter. "I get you. Okay, what can I do to help?"

"You have a group of friends you hang out with, right? People you can trust, who aren't into anything—"

"Like Kirby was."

"Right."

"Well, sure I do."

"Can you get some of them together this afternoon? Bring them here?"

He frowned, thinking. "Today's Thursday, right?"

"Uh-huh."

"Okay, football practice'll be over in about an hour, so I can get hold of Harry. Cat and Jenny don't work today, so they should be around. Del—he's just hanging out these days. The others . . . probably. But it'll be getting close to suppertime before I can round them all up."

"I'll spring for some pizzas."

Tom grinned. "That'll help. At least it'll get Del and Harry here."

I realized why when I met Del and Harry—they each weighed around two hundred pounds. Harry's were all football player's muscle, but Del's were pure flab. Both waded into Mama Mia's Special like they hadn't eaten in a week. Even the girls—Anna, Cat, Jenny, and Lee—had appetites that would put a linebacker to shame.

They perched around the kitchen on top of the counters and table and chopping block, making me wonder why teenagers always feel more at home on surfaces where they have no right to plant their fannies. Each had some comment on the vintage of the appliances, ranging from "really raunchy" to "awesome." The staff couldn't resist poking their noses through the door to check out my young guests, but when Tom Chu, who knew full well who Hank Zahn was, pointed to him and called, "Hey, Rae, who's the geezer?" I put a stop to that and got the meeting underway. After shutting the swinging door and shouting for them to get serious, I perched on the counter next to Tom. Seven tomato sauce-smudged faces turned toward me.

I asked, "Do all of you know what brainstorming is?"

Seven heads nodded.

"What we're going to do," I went on, "is to share information about Kirby and Adrian. I'll ask questions, throw out some ideas, you say whatever comes into your heads. Anything, no matter how trivial it may seem to you, because you never know what might be important in an investigation."

The kids exchanged excited glances. I supposed they thought this was just like *Pros and Cons*.

"Okay," I began, "here's one idea—shoplifting."

Total silence. A couple of furtive looks.

"No takers? Come on, I'm not talking about any of you. I could care less. But think of Adrian and Kirby."

The angelic-looking blonde—Cat—said, "Well, Adrian took stuff from the place where she worked sometimes. We all suspected that."

"I didn't," Harry protested.

"Well, she *did*. At first she thought it was a giggle, but then . . ." Cat shrugged. "She just stopped talking about it. She'd get real snotty if you mentioned it."

"When was this?" I asked.

"Sometime last spring. Right about the time things started getting very heavy between her and Kirby."

"When she started sleeping with him," Del added.

"Okay," I said, "tell me about Kirby's scams."

Beside me, Tom muttered, "Dope."

"Test questions." Anna, a pretty Filipina, nodded knowingly.

Cat said, "He sold stuff."

"Like L.L. Bean without the catalog." The one sitting cross legged on the shopping block was Jenny.

I waited, letting them go with it.

Harry said, "Kirby'd get you stuff wholesale. He sold me the new Guns 'n Roses CD for half price."

"You wanted something," Anna added, "you'd give him an order. Kirby filled it."

"A real en-tree-preneur," Del said, and the others laughed. All of them, that is, except Lee, a tiny girl who looked Eurasian. She sat on the far side of the oak table and had said nothing. When I looked at her, she avoided my eyes.

Jenny said, "It's not funny, Del. Kirby was *so* into money. It was like if he got enough of it, he'd really be somebody. Only he wouldn't've been because there was no one there. You know what I mean? He had nothing inside of him—"

"Except money hunger," Tom finished.

"Yeah, but don't forget about his power trip," Cat said. She looked at me and added, "Kirb had a real thing about power. He liked pushing people round, and I think he figured having money would mean he could push all he wanted. He really was a control freak, and the person he controlled best was Adrian."

"Jump, Adrian," Harry said. "How high, Kirby?"

Anna shook her head. "She was getting out from under that, though. Around week before she disappeared, we were talking and she said she'd about had it with Kirby, she was going to blow the whistle and the game would be over. And I said something like, 'Sure you are, Adrian,' and she goes, 'No, I've worked it all out and I've got somebody to take my side.' And I go, 'You mean you got another guy on the line who's going to stand up to Kirb?' And she goes, 'Yes, I've got somebody to protect me, somebody strong and fierce, who isn't going to take any shit off of anybody.' "

"Did you tell the cops about that when they came around?" Del asked. Anna tossed her long hair. "Why should I? If Adrian took off with some guy, it's her business."

I caught a movement to one side, and turned in time to see Lee, the silent one, slip off the table and through the swinging door to the hall. "Lee?" I called.

There was no answer but her footsteps running toward the front of the house. I was off the counter top and out the door in seconds. "Help yourself to more Cokes," I called over my shoulder.

By the time I spotted her, Lee was on the sidewalk heading downhill toward Mission. As I ran after her I realized what truly lousy shape I'd let myself get into these past few months, what with the caseload I'd been carrying and spending too much time with

Willie. There's only one kind of exercise that Willie likes, and while it's totally diverting, it doesn't do the same thing for you as aerobics.

Lee heard my feet slapping on the pavement, looked back, and then cut to the left and started running back uphill through the little wedge-shaped park that divides the street in front of All Souls. I groaned and reversed, panting.

At the tip of the park two streets came together, and two cars were also about to come together in a great blast of horns and a shout from one of the drivers that laid a blue streak on the air. Lee had to stop, I put on some speed, and next thing I knew I had hold of her arm. Thank God she didn't struggle—I had absolutely no wind left.

Lee's short black hair was damp with sweat, plastered close to her finely fashioned skull, and her almond-shaped eyes had gone flat and shiny with fear. She looked around desperately, then hung her head and whispered, "Please leave me alone."

I got my breathing under control—sort of. "Can't. You know something, and we have to talk. Come on back to the house."

"I don't want to face the rest of them. I don't want any of them to know what I've done."

"Then we'll talk out here." There was a makeshift bench a few yards away—a resting place one of the retired neighborhood handymen had thrown together for the old ladies who had to tote parcels uphill from the stores on Mission. Hell, I thought as I led Lee over there, he'd probably watched me trying to jog around the park before I totally lost it in the fitness department, and built the thing figuring I'd need it one of these days. Eventually I'd keel over during one of my workouts and then they'd put a plaque on the seat: *Rae Kelleher Memorial Bench—Let This Be a Warning to All Other Sloths.*

I gave Lee a moment to compose herself—and me a moment to catch my breath—and looked around at the commuters trudging up from the bus stop. The day had stayed gray and misty until about three, then cleared some, but new storm clouds threatened out by the coast. Lee fumbled through her pockets and came up with a crumpled Kleenex, blew her nose and sighed.

I said, "It can't be all that bad."

"You don't know. It's the worst thing I've ever done. When my father finds out, he'll *kill* me."

I tried not to smile, thinking of all the kids down through the ages who had been positively convinced that they would be killed on the spot if they were ever caught doing something wrong. I myself was in college before it occurred to me that parents—normal, sane parents, that is—don't kill their offspring because kids are too damned expensive and troublesome to acquire and raise. Why waste all that money and effort, plus deprive yourself of the pleasure of becoming a burden to them in your old age?

"Maybe," I said to Lee, "he won't have to find out."

She shook her head. "No way, not this."

"Tell me about it, and then we'll see."

Another tremulous sigh. "I guess I better tell somebody, now that Kirby's been murdered and Adrian . . . but I'm afraid I'll go to jail."

Big stuff, then. "In that case, it's better to come forward, rather than be found out later."

Lee bit her lip. "Okay," she said after a moment. "Okay. I didn't know Kirby very well, just to say hi when I'd see him around, you know? But then one day last August he came to my house with these pictures while my parents were at work."

"What pictures?"

"Of me taking stuff from where I work. You know that stationery and gift shop at Ocean Park Plaza—Paper Fantasy? Well, I worked there full time last summer and now I go in three days a week after school. I kind of got into taking things—pen-and-pencil sets, jewelry, other gift items. I didn't even want them very much. I mean, the stuff they sell is expensive but pretty tacky. But it made me not feel so bad about having this crummy job . . . Anyway, that's what Kirby's pictures showed, me taking jewelry from the case and stuffing it under my sweater." Lee's words were spilling out fast now; I was probably the only person she'd ever told about this.

"There was no way you could mistake what I was doing," she went on. "The pictures showed it clear as could be. Kirby said he was going to go to my boss unless I did what he wanted. At first I thought he meant, you know, sex, and I could have died, but it turned out what he wanted was for me to steal stuff and give it to him. I said I would. I would have done anything to keep from being found out. And that's what I've been doing."

"So Kirby got the merchandise he was selling by blackmailing people into shoplifting for him. I wonder if that's the hold he had over Adrian?"

"It might have been. When they were first going together, they were, you know, like a normal couple. But then she changed, dropped all her friends and other activities, and started spending every minute with Kirby. I guess he used her shoplifting to get control of her."

"What about the other kids? Do you know anybody else who was stealing for Kirby?"

"Nobody who'll talk about it. But there's a rumor about a couple of the guys, that they take orders and just go out and rip off stuff. And a lot of the things he has for sale come from stores where I know other kids from school work."

Kirby had had quite a scam going—a full-blown racket, actually. And Lee was right: There was no way this could be kept from her father. She might even go to juvenile hall.

"The pictures," I said, "did Kirby say how he took them?"

"No, but he had to've been inside the store. They were kind of fuzzy, like he might've used a telephoto."

"From where?"

"Well, they were face on, a little bit above and to the left of the jewelry counter."

"Did you ever see Kirby in the store with a camera?"

"No, but I wouldn't've noticed him if we were busy."

"Would you have taken something while the store was busy?"

"Sure. That's the best time." Lee seemed to hear her own words, because she hung her head, cheeks coloring. "God, those pictures! I looked like a *criminal*!"

Which, of course, she was. I thought about Kirby and his corps of teenaged thieves. What if he'd tried to hit on the wrong person? Homicides committed by teenagers, like all other categories, were on the upswing . . .

"Lee," I said, "you're going to have to tell the cops investigating Kirby's murder about this."

She nodded numbly, hands clenching.

The phrase "shit hitting the fan" isn't a favorite of mine, but that was exactly what was about to happen, and a lot of perfectly nice parents were going to be splattered, to say nothing of their foolish but otherwise nice children. Parents like Donna Conway. Children like Adrian.

I pictured the pretty redhead in the photo Donna had given me—her quirky smile and the gleam in her eyes that told of a zest for living and an offbeat sense of humor. I pictured her quiet, concerned, sad mother—a lonely woman clinging to her stacks of self-help books for cold comfort. Maybe I could still find Adrian, reunite the two so they could lean on each other in the tough times ahead. If Adrian was still alive, there had to be a way.

And if she was dead? I didn't want to think about that.

## VIII

Lee and I went back to All Souls, where the rest of the kids were standing around the foyer wondering what to do next, and while she escaped to my office to call her father, I thanked them and showed them out. Tom Chu hung back, looking worried and throwing glances at my office door. Since he was the one who had put this together for me, I filled him in on some of what Lee had told me, after first swearing him to secrecy.

Tom didn't look too surprised. "I kind of suspected Lee was in trouble," he said. "And you know what? I think Del might've been mixed up with Kirby, too. He got real quiet when Lee ran out on us, and he left in a hurry right afterwards."

"Those're pretty shaky grounds to accuse him on."

"Maybe, but Del . . . I told you he's basically just hanging out this fall? Well, where he's hanging out is Ocean Park Plaza."

Ocean Park Plaza—the focus of the whole case. I thanked Tom and gently chased him out the door so Lee wouldn't have to deal with him when she finished calling her dad.

Her father arrived some fifteen minutes later, all upset but full of comforting words, and agreed to take Lee down to the Hall of Justice to talk to Adah Joslyn. I called Joslyn to let her know a witness was on her way. "Adah," I added, "did Sharon ask you what was in Adrian Conway's backpack?"

"Yeah. I've got the property list right here." There was a rustling noise. "Some raunchy-smelling yogurt, makeup, a Golden Gate Transit schedule, couple of paperbacks—romance variety—and an envelope with the phone number of the Ocean Park Plaza's security office scribbled on it."

"Security office? You check with them?"

"Talked to a man named Waterson. He said she'd lost her i.d. badge the week before she disappeared and called in about getting it replaced. What is this—you trying to work my homicide, Kelleher?"

"Just trying to find a missing girl. I'll turn over anything relevant."

When I got off the phone, Lee and her father were sitting on the lumpy old couch in the front room, his arm protectively around her narrow shoulders. He didn't look like much of a teenager-killer to me; in fact, his main concern was that she hadn't come to him and admitted about the shoplifting as soon as "that little bastard"—meaning Kirby—had started hassling her. "I'd've put his ass in a sling," he kept saying. I offered to go down to the Hall with them, but he said he thought it would be better if they went alone. As soon as they left, I decided to head over to Ocean Park Plaza, check out a couple of things, then talk with Ben Waterson again.

❖ ❖ ❖

The mall wasn't very crowded that night, but it was only Thursday, and the merchants were still gearing up for a big weekend sales push designed to lure in all those consumers who weren't suffering too much from the recession—getting started early on the Christmas season by urging everybody to spend, spend, spend in order to stimulate the economy. The sale banners were red, white, and blue and, really, they were making it sound like it was our patriotic duty to blow every last dime on frivolous things that—by God!—had better be American-made if Americans made them at all. Even I, much as I love to max out my credit cards, am getting totally sick of the misguided economists' notion that excess is not only good for the individual but for the nation. Anyway, the appeals from the politicians and the business community probably wouldn't meet with any more success with patrons of the Ocean Park Plaza this coming weekend than they had with downtown shoppers the previous one, and tonight they were having no affect at all.

When I got to Paper Fantasy I found I was the only browser—a decided disadvantage for checking out the possible angles from which Kirby might have taken the photographs of Lee. I checked anyway, under the suspicious eyes of the lone clerk. Over there was the counter where Lee had been standing when she'd five-fingered the jewelry, and from the way she'd described the pictures, Kirby would have had to be standing not only in front of it, but some three feet in the air. Impossible, unless . . .

Ahah! There it was—a surveillance camera mounted on the wall above and to the left of the counter. One look at that and I recalled the banks of screens in the security office upstairs, closed-circuit TV that allowed you to video tape and photograph.

I hurried out of Paper Fantasy—possibly provoking a call to security by the clerk—and headed for Left Coast Casuals.

Only two salesclerks manned the store, and there were no customers. I wandered up and down the aisles, scanning for the cameras. There were four, with a range that covered the entire sales floor. While stealing jewelry, Adrian would have had to stand around here, in plain sight of that one. For lingerie, camera number two would have done the observing. Stupid. How could the kids *be* so stupid?

Of course I knew the answer to that—anybody who's ever

shoplifted does. The cameras are there, sure, but you just assume they're not recording your particular store at the time, or being monitored. And you're certain that you're being oh-so-subtle when actually you're about as discreet as a moose picking its way through a bed of pansies. And then there's that urge that just washes over you—ooh, that irresistible impulse, that heady pulse-quickening temptation to commit the act that will bring on that delicious soaring high.

Yeah, the kids were stupid. Like I'd been stupid. Like a drug addict, an alcoholic, a binge-eater is stupid.

"Ms. Kelleher?" The voice was Sue Hanford's. "Can I help you?"

I swung around. She'd come out of the stock room and stood a few feet away from me, near the fake angora sweaters. "I was just looking the store over once more, before going up to see Ben Waterson."

Her face became pinched, two white spots appearing at the corners of her mouth. "You won't find him in the office. I know, because I just called up there. I'll tell you, I've about had it with him not being available when I need him."

"This happens a lot?"

"Well, yesterday morning around eleven-thirty. He said he'd come and talk about the problem I've been having with a gang of girls who are creating disturbances outside and intimidating my customers, but then he never showed up. I called and called, but he'd taken off without saying why. He didn't come back until six."

But yesterday morning at around eleven-thirty I'd seen him just outside the store, arguing with Kirby Dalson. Waterson had claimed Sue Hanford was the one who was away, leaving him in charge. "Were you in the store all day yesterday?" I asked.

She nodded. "I worked a fourteen-hour shift."

"And today?" I asked. "Waterson wasn't available again?"

"Yes. He took off about half an hour ago, when he's supposed to be on shift till nine-thirty."

"I see."

"Ms. Kelleher? If you do go up there and find Ben has come

back, will you ask him to come down here?"

"Sure," I said distractedly. Then I left the store.

A taco, I thought. There was a taco stand down in the food concession area. Maybe a taco and a Coke would help me think this one through.

❖ ❖ ❖

Okay, I thought, reaching for Gordito's Beef Supreme taco— piled high with extra salsa, guacamole, and sour cream—somebody in the security office here has been getting the goods on the kids who are shoplifting and turning the evidence over to Kirby so he could blackmail them into working for him. If I wasn't trained not to jump to conclusions I'd say Ben Waterson, because his behavior has been anything but on the up-and-up lately. Okay, I'll say it anyway—Ben Waterson. Kirby was a good contact man for Waterson —he knew the kids, knew their weak spots, and after they ripped off the stuff he would wholesale some of it at school, keeping Waterson out of the transaction. Kind of a penny-ante scheme, though, if you think about it. Would hardly have brought in enough to keep Kirby, much less Waterson, in ready cash. And there had to be something in it for Waterson. But then there were the other kids—like Del—who didn't work here but ripped things off for Kirby, maybe big-ticket items, here and at other malls as well. And there was the rented house on Naples Street.

Those storage sheds in the backyard—sheds full of Ron Owens's mother's things, that Owens claims were worth quite a bit—I'll bet all of that got fenced, and then they filled up the sheds with new merchandise while they tried to find a buyer for it. Not hard to find one, too, not in this town. Neighbors said a lot of people came and went at Naples Street, so it could have been a pretty substantial fencing operation.

I know a fair amount about fencing, courtesy of Willie Whelan, who in recent years, thank God, has "gone legit," as he puts it. So far the scenario made sense to me.

The taco was all gone. Funny—I'd barely tasted it. I looked longingly at Gordito's, then balled up the wrappings and turned my attention back to the case.

Where does Adrian fit into all this? Last spring she starts to change, according to her school friends. She's been taking her five-finger employee discount for a while, oblivious to what Kirby and Waterson are up to. Then Kirby comes to her with pictures, and suddenly he's got the upper hand in the relationship. Adrian's still pretty demoralized—the father leaving, the mother who's always spouting phrases like "potential to be"—so she lets Kirby control her. Did she steal for him? Help him with the fencing? Had to have, given that she was familiar enough with the Naples Street house to walk in and plunk her backpack down in the living room. I'm pretty sure she slept with him—even the other kids know that.

Okay, suppose Adrian does all of that. Maybe she even glamorizes the situation as young women will do in order to face themselves in the morning. But fetching the condiments for the hamburgers of a young man who can damned well get them himself grows old real fast, and after a while she starts to chafe at what her therapy wall calls "white slavery." So, as she tells her friend Anna, she's decided to "blow the whistle and the game would be over." How? By going to the cops? Or by going to the head of mall security, Ben Waterson?

I got up, tossed my cup and the taco wrappings in a trash bin, and headed for the security office.

Waterson wasn't there. Had left around six after a phone call, destination unknown, the woman on the desk told me. I persuaded her to check their log to see if Adrian Conway had reported losing her i.d. badge about a week before she disappeared, as Waterson had told Adah Joslyn. No record of it, and there would have been had it really happened.

Caught you in another lie, Ben!

Back down to the concession area. This time I settled for coffee and a Mrs. Fields cookie.

So Adrian probably went to Waterson, since she had the phone number of the security office scribbled on an envelope in her backpack. And he . . . what? Lured her away from the mall and killed her? Hid her body? Then why was her backpack at Naples

Street? Waterson would have left it with the body or gotten rid of it. And would Waterson have gone to such lengths, anyway?

Well, Kirby was murdered, wasn't he?

But would Kirby have kept quiet if he thought Waterson had murdered his girlfriend? The kid was a cold one, but . . . Maybe I just didn't want to believe that anybody that young could be that cold. And that was poor reasoning—if you don't believe me, just check out the morning paper most days.

Another thing—who was this person Adrian had talked about, who would take her side and not take any shit off of anybody? Maybe Waterson had played it subtle with her, pretended to be her protector, then spirited her off somewhere and—

The prospects for her survival weren't any better with that scenario.

I was so distracted that I bit clear through the cookie into my tongue. Swore loud enough to earn glares from two old ladies at the next table.

Back to Ben Waterson. Kirby came to the mall the other day and argued with him—not about getting hold of Adrian's back pay, as they both claimed, because Waterson lied about Sue Hanford leaving him in charge at Left Coast Casuals. And right after the argument, Kirby stormed out of the mall and drove off burning rubber. Waterson took off around that time, too. And tonight Waterson left again, after a phone call around six—about the time the kids, Del preceding them, left All Souls. Did Del or another of them warn him that everything was about to unravel? Is Waterson running, or did he leave for purposes of what Sue Hanford calls damage control?

Damage control. I suppose you could call Kirby's murder damage control . . .

I got up, threw my trash in the bin, and began walking the mall—burning off excess energy, trying to work it out. If only I knew what Kirby and Waterson had argued about. And where they'd each gone Wednesday afternoon. And why Kirby had asked me to meet him at the Naples Street house. Had Waterson found out about the meeting, gotten there early? Killed Kirby before he could talk with me? And what about Adrian? If she was dead, where was her body? And if she was alive—

And then I saw something. It wasn't related to my case at all, was just one of those little nudges you get when you have all the information you need and are primed for something to come along and help you put it all together. I'm sure I'd have figured it out eventually, even if it hadn't been for the poster of the African veldt in the window of a travel agency—a poster that made the land look so parched and windswept and basically unpleasant that you wondered why they thought it would sell tours. But as it was, it happened then, and I was damned glad of it.

## IX

The Wreck and I sped through the night, under a black sky that quickly started leaking rain, then just plain let go in a deluge. The windshield wipers scraped and screeched, smearing the glass instead of clearing it. Dammit, I thought, why can't I get it together to buy a new car—or at least some new wiper blades? No, a whole car's in order, because this defroster isn't worth the powder to blow it to hell, and I'm so sick of being at the mercy of third-rate transportation.

Then I started wondering about the tread on the Wreck's tires. When was the last time I'd checked it? It had looked bad, whenever, and I'd promised myself new tires in a few hundred more miles, but that had to be several thousand ago. What if I got a flat, was stranded, and didn't reach Adrian in time? She was probably safe; I didn't know for sure that Waterson had figured it out. Hell, *I'd* barely done that. Could anybody manage, without knowing Adrian the way I did from her therapy wall?

The rain whacked down harder and the wind blew the Wreck all over the road. My shoulders got tense, and my hands actually hurt from clinging to the wheel. Lights ahead now—the little town of Olema where this road met the shoreline highway. Right turn, slow a little, then put the accelerator to the floor on the home stretch to Aunt June's.

She lied to me—-that much was obvious at the time—but I hadn't suspected it was such a big lie. How could I guess that Adrian was with her—right there on the premises, probably in June's studio—and had been with her since shortly after her disappearance? Maybe I should have picked up on the fact that June didn't seem all that worried about her niece, but otherwise I'd had no clues. Not then.

Now I did, though. The Golden Gate Transit schedule in Adrian's backpack, for one. Golden Gate was the one bus line that ran from the city to Marin County, and she would only have needed it if she planned a trip north. There had been no one with a Marin address other than June Simoom on the list of people who were close to Adrian that the police had checked out. And then there was the graphic evidence on the therapy wall—the soaring bird so like the symbol of June's place, Wingspread, next to one broken gold chain and the word FREEDOM. But most of all it was Adrian's own words that had finally tipped me: "somebody to protect me, somebody strong and fierce." That was June's way of describing herself, and Adrian had probably heard it enough to believe it. After all, her aunt had taken the name of a fierce, relentless African wind; she had called her home Wingspread, a place of refuge.

But there was another side to June—the possessive, controlling side that Donna Conway had described. Frying pan to fire, that's where Adrian had gone. From one controlling person to another —and in this case, a control freak who probably delighted in keeping the niece from the hated sister-in-law. June hadn't called Donna after my visit to make peace; she'd probably been fishing to find out if I'd relayed any suspicions to her.

I slowed to a crawl, peering through the smears on the wind- shield and the rain soaked blackness for the mailbox with the soaring bird. That stand of eucalyptus looked about right, and the deeper shadows beyond it must hide Tomales Bay. Hadn't the road curved like this just before the turnoff to the rutted driveway? Wasn't it right about here . . . ?

Yes! I wrenched the wheel to the left, and the Wreck skidded onto the gravel shoulder.

What I could see of the driveway looked impassable. Deep tire gouges cut into the ground, but they were filling with muck and water. Better not chance it. I turned off the engine—it coughed and heaved several times, not a good sign, Willie had recently told me—and then I got out and started for the cottage on foot.

The wind blew even stronger now, whipping the branches of the trees and sending big curls of brittle bark spiraling through the air. The rain pelted me, stinging as it hit my face, and the hood of my slicker blew off my head. I grabbed at it, but I couldn't make it stay up, and soon my hair was a sodden mess plastered to my skull.

Adrian, I thought, you'd better be worth all this.

I couldn't see any lights in the cottage, although there was a truck pulled in under the trees. That didn't mean anything—the other night June had relied on the fire for both heat and light, and there was no reason she would have turned on the porch lamp unless she was expecting company. But what kind of a life was this for Adrian, spending her entire evenings in darkness in that crumbling shack? And what about her days—how could she fill the long hours when she should have been in school or working or doing things with her friends? If her mother hadn't hired me and I hadn't figured out where she was, how long would she have hidden here until reality set in and she began to want to have a life again?

My slicker was an ancient one, left over from my college days, and its waterproofing must have given out, because I was soaked to my skin now. Freezing, too. Please have a fire going, June, because I'm already very annoyed with you, and the lack of a fire will make me truly pissed off—

Movement up ahead, the door of the cottage opening. A dark figure coming out, big and barrel-shaped, bigger than June and certainly bigger than Adrian . . . Ben Waterson.

He came down the steps, hesitated, then angled off toward the left, through the trees. Going where? To the studio or the other outbuilding?

I began creeping closer to the cottage, testing the ground ahead of me before I took each step. Foot-grabber of a hole there, ankle-turner of a tree root here. At least the wind's shrieking like a scalded cat so he can't possibly hear me.

The cottage loomed ahead. I tripped on the bottom step, went up the rest of them on my hands and knees, and pushed the door open. Keeping low, I slithered inside on a splintery plank floor. There was some light at the far end of the room, but not much; the fire was burning low, just embers mainly.

What's that smell?

A gun had been fired in there, and not too long ago. I opened my mouth, tried to call to June, but a croak came out instead. The room was quiet, the wind howling outside. I crept toward the glowing embers . . .

There June was, reclining on her pile of pillows, glass of wine beside her on the raised hearth. So like the other night, but something was wrong here, something to do with the way she was lying, as if she'd been thrown there, and why was the fireplace poker in her hand— Oh God June no!

I reeled around, smashing my fist into the wall beside me. My eyes were shut but I could still see her crumpled there on the gaudy silk pillows, velvet robes disarrayed, hand clutching the poker. Why was she still holding it? Something to do with going into spasm at the moment of death.

Disconnected sounds roared in my ears, blocking the wind. Then I heard my voice saying bitterly to Sharon, "Until the next time," meaning until the next death. And Sharon saying to me, "If there is one."

Well, Shar, this is the next time, and I wish you were here to tell me what to do because what I'm about to do is go to pieces and there's a killer somewhere outside and a helpless young woman who I promised to bring back to her mother—

*Go to the phone, Rae, and call the sheriff.*

It wasn't Sharon's voice, of course, but my own—a cool, professional voice that I'd never known I had. It interrupted the hysterical thoughts that were whirling and tumbling in my brain, calmed me and restored my balance. I dredged up memories of the other night, pictured an old-fashioned rotary-dial phone sitting on the kitchen counter. I felt my way until I touched it, and picked up the receiver. No dial tone.

Maybe the storm, maybe something Waterson had done. Whatever, there wasn't going to be any car full of Marin County Sheriff's deputies riding to my rescue.

*You'll just have to save yourself—and Adrian.*

With what? He's armed. I don't even have a flashlight.

Kitchen drawer. I felt along the edge of the warped linoleum counter, then down to a knob. Pulled on it. Nothing in there but cloth, dishtowels, maybe. Another knob, another drawer. Knives. I took one out, tested its sharpness. Another drawer, and there was a flashlight, plus some long, pointed barbecue skewers. I stuck them and the knife in the slash pocket of my slicker.

And then I went outside to face a man with a gun.

The wind was really whipping around now, and it tore the cottage's door from my grip and slammed it back against the wall. I yanked it closed, went down the slick, rickety steps, and made for the eucalyptus trees. As I ran I felt the flashlight fall from my slash pocket, but I didn't stop to find it. Silly to have taken it, anyway —if I turned it on, I'd be a target for Waterson.

Under the trees I stopped and leaned against a ragged trunk, panting and feeling in my pocket for the knife and the skewers. They were still there—not that they were much of a match against a gun. But there was no point in stewing over the odds now. I had to pinpoint those outbuildings. If I remembered correctly, they were closer to the shore and to the left of this grove.

I slipped through the trees, peering into the surrounding blackness. Now I could make out the shoreline, the water wind-tossed and frothy, and then I picked out the shapes of the buildings—two of them, the larger one probably the studio. Roofs as swaybacked as the cottage's, no lights in either. Windows? I couldn't tell. They sat across a clearing from me, a bad way to approach if there were windows and if Waterson was inside and looking out. A bad way if he was outside and looking in this direction.

How else to get over to them, then? Along the shore? Maybe. June had said something about a beach . . .

I went back through the trees, their branches swaying overhead, ran for the cottage again, then slipped along its side and ducked under the half-collapsed deck. The ground took a sudden slope, and I went down on my butt and slid toward the water. Waves sloshed over my tennis shoes—icy waves.

Dammit! I thought. What the hell am I doing out here risking pneumonia—to say nothing of my life—for a thieving teenager I've never even set eyes on?

I pulled myself up on one of the rotten deck supports—nearly pulling it down on my head—and started moving again. Then I stopped, realizing there was no beach here now, just jumbled and jagged rocks before the spot where the sand should begin. The beach was completely submerged by the high storm-tide.

Stupid, Rae. Very stupid. You should have realized it would be this way and not wasted precious time. You should have gotten back into the Wreck as soon as you found June's body and driven to the nearest phone, called the sheriff's department and let them handle it.

No time for recriminations now. Besides, the nearest phone was miles away, and even if I had driven there immediately, the deputies wouldn't have gotten here fast enough to save Adrian. I wasn't sure *I'd* gotten here fast enough to save her.

I crawled back up the incline and looked around, trying to measure the distance I'd have to run exposed to get to the shelter of the outbuildings. From here it was twenty, maybe twenty-five yards. Not that far—I'd go for it.

I hunched over, made myself as small as I could, and started running—not much of a run, but still the longest, scariest of *my* life. I kept expecting the whine of a bullet—that's what you hear, Sharon's told me, before you hear the actual report, and she ought to know. You hear the whine, that is, if the bullet doesn't kill you first.

But all I heard was the howl of the wind and the banging of a door someplace and the roaring of my own blood in my ears. Then I was at the first outbuilding, crouching against its rough wood wall and panting hard.

The banging was louder here. When my breathing had calmed, I crept around the building's corner and looked. Door, half off its hinges, and no sound or light coming from inside. I crept a little closer. Empty shed, falling down, certainly not June's studio.

I moved along until I could see the larger building. The space between the two was narrow, dark. I ran again, to a windowless wall and flattened against it, putting my ear to the boards and trying to hear if anyone was inside.

A banging noise, then a crash—something breaking. Then an angry voice—male, Waterson's. "Where the hell is it?"

Sobbing now, and a young woman saying, "I *told* you I don't know what you're talking about. Where's Aunt June? I want—"

"Shut up!" It sounded like he hit her. She screamed, and my hand went into my pocket, grasping the knife.

More sobbing. Waterson said, "I want those pictures and the negatives, Adrian."

"*What* pictures? What negatives? I don't know anything about them!"

"Don't give me that. Kirby said you were holding them for him. Just tell me where they are and I'll let you go."

Sure he would. He'd shoot her just like he had June, and hope that this would go down as a couple of those random killings that happen a lot in remote rural areas where weirdos break into what look like empty houses for stuff to steal and sell for drug money.

"I wouldn't hold *anything* for Kirby!" Adrian said through her sobs. "I'm scared of him!"

"Then why did he come out here yesterday after he tried to hit me up for money? Coming to get his evidence to prove to me that I'd better pay up, that's why. And don't lie to me about it—I followed him."

"No! I didn't even see him! He figured out where I was and wanted to talk me into going back to the city. I hid from him, and Aunt June ran him off."

So this was where Kirby had gone when I'd lost him. I remembered the eucalyptus leaves in his hair, the sand on his shoes when I'd talked with him at his parents' house—probably picked up while he was skulking around outside here, looking for Adrian after June had told him he couldn't see her. Waterson had not only followed Kirby here, but later to the Naples Street house, where he'd killed him.

There was a silence inside the studio, then Adrian screamed and cried some more. He'd hit her again, I guessed. Then he said, "I'm not going to ask you again, Adrian. Where're the pictures?"

"There *aren't* any! Look, Kirby's always bullshitting. He had me fooled. I was going to go to you about what he was doing at the plaza, until I saw you at the house with him, making a deal with that fence."

That was what had made her run out of the Naples Street place so fast she'd left her backpack—made her run straight to Aunt June, the only person she'd told about the trouble she was in, the person who'd offered to take her side and shelter her. Well, June had tried. Now it was up to me.

I started moving around the building, duck-walking like my high-school phys ed teacher had made us do when we goofed off in gym. Inside, I heard Waterson say, "You never knew about a hidden camera at that place in the Outer Mission?"

"No."

"Kirby never asked you to take pictures of me doing deals with the fences?"

"Neither of us took any pictures. This story is just more of Kirby's bullshit."

Waterson laughed—an ugly sound. "Well," he said, "it was Kirby's last shovelful of bullshit. He's dead."

"What . . . ?" Adrian's question rose up into a shriek.

I stopped listening, concentrated on getting to the corner of the building. Then I peeked around it. On this side—the one facing the water—there was a window and a door. I duckwalked on, thanking God that I still had some muscles left in my thighs. At the window I poked my head up a little, but all saw were shadows—a big barrel-shaped one that had to be Waterson, and some warped, twisted ones that were downright weird. The light shivered and flickered—probably from a candle or oil lamp.

The door was closed, but the wind was rattling it in its frame. It made me think of how the wind had torn the cottage door from my grasp. I stopped, pressed against the wall, and studied this door. From the placement of its hinges, I could tell it opened out. I scuttled around to the hinged side, paused and listened. Adrian was screaming and sobbing again. Christ, what was he *doing* to her?

Well, the sound would hide what I was about to do.

I stood, pressed flat as could be against the wall, then reached across the door to its knob and gave it a quick twist. The door opened, then slammed shut again.

"What the hell?" Waterson said.

Heavy footsteps came toward the door. I tensed, knife out and ready.

*Don't think about how it'll be when you use it, Rae. Just do it—two lives are at stake here, and one's your own.*

The door opened. All I could see was a wide path of wavery light. Waterson said, "Fuckin' wind," and shut the door again. Well, hell.

I waited a few seconds until his footsteps went away, reached for the knob again, and really yanked on it this time. The wind caught the door, slammed it back, and it smashed into me, smacking my nose. I bit my lip to keep from yelling, felt tears spring to my eyes. I wiped them away with my left hand, gripped the knife till my right hand hurt.

The footsteps came back again, quicker now, and I grasped the knife with both hands—ready, not thinking about it, just ready to do it because I had to. When he stepped outside, I shoved the door as hard as I could with my whole body, slamming him against the frame. He shouted, staggered, reeled back inside.

I went after him, saw him stumbling among a bunch of weird, twisted shapes that were some sort of pottery sculptures—the things that had made the strange shadows I'd glimpsed through the window. Some were as tall as he was, others were shorter or stood on pedestals. He grabbed at one and brought it down as he tried to keep his balance and raise his gun.

The gun went off. The roar was deafening, but I hadn't heard any whine, so his shot must have gone wide of me. Waterson stumbled back into a pedestal, flailing. I lunged at him, knife out in front of me. We both went down together. I heard the gun drop on the floor as I slashed out with the knife.

Waterson had hold of my arm now, slammed it against the floor. Pain shot up to my shoulder, my fingers went all prickly, and I dropped the knife. He pushed me away and started scrambling for the gun. I got up on my knees, grabbed at the base of the nearest sculpture, pushed. It hit his back and knocked him flat.

Waterson howled. I saw the gun about a foot from his hand and kicked out, sending it sliding across the floor. Then I stood all the way up, grabbed a strange many-spouted vase from a pedestal. And slammed it down on his head.

Waterson grunted and lay still.

I slumped against the pedestal, but only for a moment before I went to pick up the gun. The room was very quiet all of a sudden, except for sobbing coming from one corner. Adrian was trussed up there, dangling like a marionette from one of the support beams, her feet barely touching the plank floor.

She had the beginnings of a black eye and tears sheened her face, and she was jerking at her ropes like she was having some kind of attack. I located the knife, made what I hoped were reassuring noises as I went over there, and cut her down. She stumbled toward a mattress that lay under the window and curled up fetus-like, pulling the heavy blanket around her. I went over to Waterson and used the longer pieces of the rope to truss *him* up.

Then I went back to Adrian. She was shivering violently, eyes unfocused, fingers gripping the edge of the blanket. I sat down on the mattress beside her, gently loosened her fingers, and cradled her like a baby.

"Sssh," I said. "It's over now, all over."

X

I was lolling around All Souls' living room on Friday night, waiting for Willie and planning how I'd relate my triumph in solving the Conway-Dalson case to him, when the call came from Inspector Adah Joslyn,

"I just got back from Marin County," she told me. "Waterson's finally confessed to the Simoom murder, but he denies killing Kirby Dalson."

"Well, of course he would. Dalson was obviously premeditated, while the poker in Simoom's hand could be taken to mean self-defense."

"He'll have to hire one hell of a lawyer to mount a defense like that, given what he did to the niece. But that's not my problem. What is is that he's got a verifiable alibi for the time of Dalson's death."

"*What?*"

"Uh-huh. Dalson didn't leave his parents' house until six-twenty that night. Six to seven, Waterson was in a meeting with several of the Ocean Park Plaza merchants, including Adrian Conway's former boss."

I remembered Sue Hanford saying Waterson had taken off the morning before Kirby was killed and hadn't come back until six. I hadn't thought to ask her how she knew that or if he'd stayed around afterwards. Damn! Maybe I wasn't the hotshot I thought I was.

Adah asked, "You got any ideas on this?"

Unwilling to admit I didn't, I said, "Maybe. Let me get back to you." I hung up the phone on Ted's desk. then took the stairs two at a time and went to Sharon's office.

She wasn't there. Most of the time the woman practically lived in her office, but now when I needed her, she was gone. I went back downstairs and looked for her mailbox tag. Missing. There was one resting on the corner of the desk, like she might have been talking with Ted and absentmindedly set it down there. I hurried along the hall to the kitchen, where five people hadn't yet given up on the Friday happy hour, but Sharon wasn't one of them. Our resident health freak, who was mixing up a batch of cranberry-juice-and-cider cocktails, said she'd gone home an hour ago.

I said, "If Willie shows up before I get back, will you ask him to wait for me?" and trotted out the door.

Sharon doesn't live far from All Souls—in Glen Park, a district that's been undergoing what they call gentrification. I suppose you could say her brown-shingled cottage—one of a few thousand built as temporary housing after the '06 quake that have survived far better than most of the grand mansions of that era—has been gentrified, since she's remodeled it and added a room and a deck, but to me it's just nice and homey, not fancy at all. Besides, things are always going wrong with it—tonight it was the porch light, shorting out from rain that had dripped into it because the gutters were overflowing. I rang the bell, hoping it wouldn't also short out and electrocute me.

Sharon answered wearing her long white terry robe and furlined slippers and looking like she was coming down with a cold—probably from the soaking she'd gotten Tuesday night, which meant I would be the next one in line to get sick, from the soaking I'd gotten last night. She looked concerned when she saw me on the steps.

Last night, after I'd dealt with the Marin authorities and driven home feeling rocky and ready to fly apart at the slightest sound or movement, she'd come over to the co-op—Ted had called her at home, I guess—and we'd sat quietly in my nest for a while. Neither of us had said much—there was nothing to say, and we didn't need to, anyway. This second horror in a week of unpleasantness had changed me somehow, maybe forced me to grow up. I wasn't looking to Sharon for wisdom or even comfort, just for understanding and fellowship. And fellows we were—members of a select group to which election was neither an honor nor a pleasure.

Tonight I could tell that she was afraid I was suffering delayed repercussions from the violent events of the week, so quickly I said, "I need to run some facts by you. Got a few minutes?"

She nodded, looking relieved, and waved me inside. We went to the sitting room off her kitchen, where she had a fire going, and she offered me some mulled wine. While she was getting it, her yellow cat, Ralph, jumped into my lap. Ralph is okay as cats go, but really, I'm more of a dog person. He knows that, too—it's why he always makes a beeline for me when I come over. The little sadist looked at me with knowing eyes, then curled into a ball on my lap. His calico sister Alice, who was grooming herself in the middle of the floor, looked up, and damned if she didn't wink!

Sharon came back with the wine, wrapped herself in her afghan on the couch, and said, "So run it by me."

I did, concluding, "Adrian couldn't have killed Kirby. Her hysterics when Waterson told her he was dead were genuine."

"Mmmm." Sharon seemed to be evaluating that. Then she said, "Maybe one of the other kids Kirby was blackmailing?"

"I thought of that, too, but it doesn't wash. Adrian talked a little while we were driving to Point Reyes to call the sheriff. She said none of the kids knew about the house on Naples—Kirby insisted it be kept a secret."

"What about one of the fences he dealt with? Maybe he'd crossed one of them."

"I tend to doubt it. Fences don't operate that way."

"Well, you should know. Willie . . ."

"Yeah." I sipped wine, feeling gloomy and frustrated.

Sharon asked, "Who else besides Adrian knew about that house?"

"Well, Waterson, but his alibi is firm. And Aunt June. Adrian called her from a pay phone at a store on the corner the day she walked in on Kirby and Waterson making a deal with a fence, and June drove over to the city and picked her up. Adrian had told June about the trouble she was in when she and Kirby went to Tomales for the autumnal equinox firing in late September, and June'd offered to take her in after she went to security about what was going on. I don't know how June thought Adrian could escape prosecution for her part in the scam, but then, she didn't strike me as a terribly realistic person."

"Caring, though," Sharon said. "Caring and controlling."

I nodded. "June, the fierce protectress. Who died with a fireplace poker in her hand. Waterson had a gun, and she still tried to go up against him."

"And Kirby had come out to her place. Had scared Adrian."

"Yes," I said.

Sharon got up, took our glasses, and went to the kitchen for refills. I stared moodily into the fire. When I'd taken this job, I'd assumed I'd be running skip traces and interviewing witnesses for lawsuits. Now I'd found two dead bodies, almost killed a man, almost gotten killed myself—all in the course of a few days. Add to that an ethical dilemma . . .

When Sharon came back I said, "If I suggest this to the police, and June really was innocent, I'll be smearing the memory of a basically good woman."

She was silent, framing her reply. "If June was innocent, the police won't find any evidence. If she was guilty, they may find a weapon with blood and hair samples that match Kirby's somewhere on the premises at Tomales, and be able to close the file."

"But what will that do to Adrian?"

"From what you tell me, she's a survivor. And you've got to think of Kirby's parents. You've got to think of justice."

Leave it to Sharon to bring up the J-word. She thinks about things like that all the time, but to me they're just abstractions.

"And you've got to think about the truth," she added.

Not fair—she knows how I feel about the truth. "All right," I finally said. "I'll call Adah back later."

"Good. By the way, how are Adrian and her mother doing?"

"Well, all of this has been tough on them. Will be tough for a while. But they'll make it. Adrian is a survivor, and Donna—maybe this will help her realize her 'potential to be.' "

We both smiled wryly. Sharon said, "Here's to our potential to be," and we toasted.

After a while I went into her home office and called Adah. Then I called All Souls and spoke with Willie, who was regaling the folks in the kitchen with stories about the days when he was on the wrong side of the law, and told him I'd be there soon.

"So," Sharon said as I was putting on my slicker. "How're *you* holding up?"

"I'm still rocky, but that'll pass."

"Nightmares?"

"Yeah. But tonight they won't bother me. I plan to scare them off by sleeping with my favorite gorilla."

Sharon grinned and toasted me again, but damned if she didn't look a little melancholy.

Maybe she *still* knew something that I didn't.

# RECYCLE
## (Hy Ripinsky)

On their fortieth birthdays, most women want a little romance, right? Be taken out to dinner, given a present, maybe some flowers. Not McCone, though. She's one of a kind. On *her* fortieth, she wanted me to go with her to the dump.

Sure, I know we're supposed to call it a refuse disposal site, but politically correct doesn't always cut it with me. A dump's a dump, and the proof of that's in the smell.

The dump we're talking about was in Sonoma County, some 45 miles north of the Golden Gate, out in the middle of farmland near the town of Los Alegres. A long blacktop road led uphill from the highway; at its top earthmovers worked on the edge of the landfill and seagulls perched on a mountain of recycled yard waste.

"Nasty little scavengers flew twenty miles inland to feast at this fancy establishment," I commented.

McCone gave me a look that said she wasn't impressed with the gulls' navigational talents, and then slammed on the brakes inches short of the bumper of a van crammed with plastic garbage bags—the last in a line of vehicles that were stopped at the gate waiting to pay the entrance fee.

"I know, Ripinsky, I know," she muttered, even though I hadn't said anything. "Eyes front." Then she steered her MG around the van and took a side road toward the recycling sheds—a row of board shacks surrounded by busted furniture and rusted appliances, where a hand lettered sign advertised:

RECYCLED MERCHANDISE!
LOW PRICES!
HOUSEWARES, BOOKS, CLOTHING, AND MORE!

Books?  The morning was looking better.  Maybe while she did her business I'd lay hand to an old western for my collection.

We'd come north from San Francisco on a lead one of McCone's operatives had turned up, to hunt for a man calling himself Nick Galway.  Not his real name; she had good reason to believe he was really the well known sculptor, Glenn Farrell.  Ten years ago Farrell had disappeared from his farm in Vermont, leaving behind his wife and child and taking with him the gold for three pieces of sculpture commissioned by a wealthy client who invested in precious metals and wanted some of his holdings put to aesthetic use.  Recently a friend of the client had spotted Farrell in northern California, and the client hired McCone to find him and either take back the gold or turn Farrell over to the authorities.

It was odds even that Galway/Farrell still had the gold.  At least if you took into account the condition of the caretaker's cottage he rented on a small ranch west of Los Alegres, where we'd stopped earlier.  It was sagging and in bad repair, overgrown by ivy and surrounded by weeds and a collection of junk—not the sort of place anybody with the wherewithal to live the good life would've chosen.  When nobody came to the door, we drove up to the main house and McCone spoke with the landlady, who identified Glenn Farrell's photo as her tenant.  She said he was probably scavenging at the dump, as he did most mornings.

Now as we got out of McCone's MG, a dark-haired woman with a weatherbeaten face and a grimy t-shirt came from the first of the sheds, carrying something that looked like part of a plane's prop.  She saw us, did an about-face, and tossed the thing into a refuse barrel.  Then she came over and asked, "Help you?"

McCone said, "I'm looking for Nick Galway.  His landlady told me he'd probably be here."

She gave us an odd look, as if she couldn't imagine anybody wanting Galway.  "Haven't seen him today.  You a friend of his?"

"A friend of a friend asked me to look him up."

"Why?  The lunatic owe him money or something?"

"Lunatic?"

"Well, what else would you call a guy spends half his life

scrounging for dirt-cheap stuff?"

"What kind of stuff?"

"Anything. Everything. So long's it's cheap."

"What does he do with it?"

"Claims he's a sculptor. Says he used to be famous under another name. Made expensive art for rich folks, but now his art's in his junk. Weird way of putting it, huh?"

"Well, artists . . ."

"Yeah, artists. Comes around nearly every day, yaps at me the whole time. Nonsense about runnin' away from crass commercialism and middle-class values. Guess he's lonely and tryin' to impress me, but he talks so crazy I mostly don't listen."

"Well, if he comes in today, will you give me a call?" The woman nodded and McCone wrote her cell phone number on a scrap of paper, wrapped a twenty around it. "But don't tell him somebody's looking for him, okay?"

The dump lady grinned at the twenty. "He comes in, you'll hear from me."

❖ ❖ ❖

In case Galway had turned up at home, McCone decided to check the ranch again, but nobody answered her knocks at the door of the cottage. She was just trying the knob—and finding it unlocked—when an old sedan pulled up next to where I was sitting in the MG, and I recognized white-haired Mrs. Mallory, the landlady. She leaned out her window and asked me, "You didn't find Nick at the dump?"

"No, ma'am." I glanced at McCone. She'd turned away from the door, had her hands clasped innocently behind her. "The woman who runs the recycle shop says he hasn't been there today."

"Strange." She shut off her engine and got out of the car, spry and slim in her work shirt, jeans, and mud-splattered boots—the kind of tough old bird that a lifetime of ranching breeds. She reminded me of my dead mother.

Shaking her key ring, she isolated one and called to McCone, "We better check inside. Nick never stays away this long unless he's at the dump or—"

"The door's not locked," McCone said, and stepped inside.

I got out of the MG and followed at a distance. The case was McCone's, and I knew from long and sometimes hellacious experience to maintain a hands-off attitude.

The cottage was pretty dingy inside: matted pea-green shag carpet, dark scarred paneling, furniture that belonged at the dump—and had probably come from there. Mrs. Mallory went through the place calling out for Galway, while McCone followed close on her heels and I cooled mine in the front room. They came back, Mrs. Mallory shaking her head. "Not here. Worries me."

McCone asked, "Can you think of anyplace else he might've gone?"

"Did you check his studio?"

"I didn't know he had one. Where is it?"

"The barn. It's not used any more, so I let him have it."

"So he's still sculpting?"

"Well, I wouldn't call it that. Don't know what I *would* call it. Maybe putting together atrocities. Huge, horrible things that're a mishmash of what he drags home from the dump. Let's see if he's there."

✤ ✤ ✤

I wouldn't've let that barn stand two minutes on my ranch in Mono County. Of course, one good windstorm, and it probably wouldn't be standing here much longer. The door was open, hanging crooked on weak hinges, and a rust-spotted pickup was nosed inside.

"Galway's?" McCone asked Mrs. Mallory.

The landlady nodded and called out to him. There was no answer. Quiet there. Only the rustle of a eucalyptus windbreak and flies buzzing under the eaves. And a feeling of wrongness. I felt the hair on my neck bristle, looked at McCone and saw she was getting the same warning signs. Together we moved through the door and stopped by the truck.

The clotted shadow was broken by shafts of light from holes in the high roof. They filtered down on a couple of eight-foot towers shaped like oil derricks made of metal, wood, glass, and plastic.

Their components were all different pieces of junk: beercans, chair legs, bottles, parts of a baby stroller; an automobile bumper, fence rails, barbed wire, a window pane, a refrigerator drawer.

"My God," McCone said. She didn't mean it reverently.

My eyes had adjusted to the gloom now, and I saw other towers that were toppled and broken, lying on their sides and canted across one another as if an earthquake had hit the oil field. The one at the top of the heap was crowned by the blades from a small windmill.

"Stay here," McCone said to Mrs. Mallory. Then she started moving through the wreckage.

I followed, because I'd spotted what she had—a pair of blue-jeaned legs sticking out from under the bottommost tower. Blue-jeaned legs and feet in shabby cowboy boots. McCone squatted down and shoved at the debris while I lifted. Together we cleared enough room so we could see the man's face.

Glenn Farrell, aka Nick Galway.

His neck was bent at an unnatural angle, the back of his head caved in and bloody. McCone felt for a pulse, shook her head, pulled her hand away quickly.

"He's cold," she said.

I heard a noise behind us, swiveled, and looked up at Mrs. Mallory. Her eyes moved from the body to us, shocked but unflinching. Yeah, a tough old bird like Ma.

"How did this happen?" she said.

I shook my head and stood up. Like he'd told the dump lady, Farrell's art was junk—or in his junk—and now his lifeblood mingled with it.

I glanced at McCone, who had stood up too. Her expression was as unflinching as Mrs. Mallory's, but I knew what was going on behind those steady dark eyes. She's seen a lot of death, my woman, but she's never grown indifferent to it, any more than I have. By all rights we should both be pretty callous: In her years as an investigator she's had more than her share of nasty experiences, and my own past still gives me nightmares. But inside we've got that essential spark of humanity—which was why we drew closer together now as we stared around at the wreckage.

Broken lamp globes.  A vacuum cleaner bag and part of a rusted wheelbarrow.  Curved chromium chair arms.  A 1973 Colorado license plate.  Mason jars—shattered.  Broken mirror—bad luck proven.  Chipped head of a grinning garden gnome and some paperback romance novels with holes drilled through them.  A toaster's innards.  Moth eaten stuffed deer head.  Busted axe.  The top of the windmill, one blade missing . . .

Behind us Mrs. Mallory asked again, "How did this happen?"

Hands-off attitude be damned!  I said, "I know how.  Let's call 911."

❖ ❖ ❖

"It was an accident!  An *accident!*" Mary Delmar, the dump lady, told the sheriff's deputy.  "I snuck over there late last night to get his gold, and the crazy bastard must've seen my flashlight because he came runnin' out to the barn and attacked me.  I was *defending* myself when those towers started fallin' on us.  I'm lucky I didn't end up like Nick!"

The deputy, whose name was Evans, rolled his eyes at McCone and me.

"Why the hell couldn't he just've stayed in bed?" Delmar added.  "I'd already found the windmill blade.  Why'd he have to come out there?"

Evans said, "Where is the windmill blade?"

Delmar collapsed on a bent lawn chair and put her hands over her eyes.  "Why do things like this always happen to *me?*"

McCone tapped the deputy's arm, motioned at the refuse bin where we'd seen Delmar toss the thing that at first glance looked like part of a plane's prop.  He went to check, came back shaking his head.  "Ms. Delmar, where is it?"

"Oh hell!  All right!  It's in there." She moved her shoulder at the shed behind us.  "I had to paw through all that junk, scraping paint off everything till I found it.  For all I know, it'll never clean up right."

Evans sighed.  "I'll have to read you your rights now."

"My rights?  Why?  I already told you it was an accident.  His fault anyway, runnin' out there and attackin' me."

Evans gave up, motioned to his partner, who was standing by their car, to take over. Right off Delmar started yowling about calling a lawyer.

Evans took McCone and me aside, muttering, "Galway—Farrell—is dead, but *she's* the injured party."

McCone said, "Nowadays, it's always the other guy's fault."

"One thing bothers me: This woman's not very bright, and she doesn't strike me as an art expert. What tipped her to who Farrell was?"

"He told her he used to be a famous sculptor under another name."

"But did he tell her what name?"

McCone hesitated, frowning. "I don't know. Maybe. But he certainly wouldn't've told her about the gold." She looked at me, raising her eyebrows.

I shrugged, then spotted the sign advertising recycled merchandise at low prices. "Well," I said, "maybe she's a reader."

"Oh?" From both of them.

"Come on." I headed for the shed where the books were. Maybe I'd come across an old western or two while I was hunting.

❖ ❖ ❖

Plenty of romances, best sellers, self-help, and cookbooks, but no old westerns. On the back wall, though, there was a pictorial set: *Popular Twentieth-Century Artists.* The fourth volume was missing, and when I checked the introductory volume, I found that number 4 was on sculptors. A glance through number 1 showed that each article was accompanied by a photo of the individual.

I found the index and flipped to "Farrell, Glenn." There were several notations, but the most interesting was "theft and disappearance." I showed it to McCone and Evans.

"So," she said, "Mary Delmar *is* a reader—at least when she smells a potential profit."

"Yeah, she is. She spotted this set, decided to see if she could find out who Galway actually was. Read about the stolen gold, and figure out what he meant about his art being in his junk."

To my astonishment, McCone hugged me. "Ripinsky, what an

absolutely fabulous birthday present!"

I leered down at, her. "You like that one, wait till you see what else I've got for you."

She narrowed her eyes at me, then flicked them toward Evans. She's a very private woman, one of the many reasons I love her. And now I'd gone and said something that would make her all prickly.

"McCone and I are both pilots," I said to Evans, who was looking quite interested. To her I said, "Think airport. Think the Citabria fueled and ready to go. Think terrific destination."

"Oh?"

"Terrific—and surprising." I nodded.

Now, if I could only come up with a terrific, surprising flight plan by the time we got back to the Bay Area . . .

# SOLO
## (Sharon McCone)

"That's where it happened."

Hy put the Citabria into a gliding turn and we spiraled down to a few hundred feet above Tufa Lake. Its water looked teal blue today; the small islands and gnarled towers of calcified vegetation stood out in gray and taupe relief. A wind from the east riffled the lake's surface. Except for a blackened area on the south side of Plover Island, I saw no sign that a light plane had crashed and burned there.

I turned my head from the window and looked into the forward part of the cockpit; Hy Ripinsky, my best friend and longtime lover, still stared at the scene below, his craggy face set in grim lines. After a few seconds he shook his head and turned his attention back to the controls, putting on full throttle and pulling back on the stick. The small plane rose and angled in for the airport on the lake's northwest shore.

Through our dual headsets Hy said, "Dammit, McCone, I'm a good flight instructor, and Scott Oakley was a good student. There's no reason he should've strayed from the pattern and crashed on his first solo flight."

We were entering that same pattern, on the downwind leg for runway two-seven. I waited till Hy had announced our position to other traffic on the unicom, then said, "No reason, except for the one you've already speculated on: that he deliberately strayed and put the plane into a dive in order to kill himself."

"Looked that way to me. To the NTSB investigators, too."

I was silent as he turned onto final approach, allowing him to concentrate on landing in the strong crosswind. He didn't speak again till we were turning off the runway.

"Ninety percent of flying's mental and emotional—you know

that," he said. "And ninety percent of the instructor's job is figuring out where the student's head is at, adapting your teaching methods to the individual. I like to think I've got good instincts along that line, and I noticed absolutely nothing about Scott Oakley that indicated he'd kill himself."

"Tell me about him."

"He was a nice kid, in his early twenties. From this area originally, but went up to Reno to attend the University of Nevada. Things didn't go well for him academically, so he dropped out, went to work as a dealer at one of the casinos. Met a woman, fell in love, got engaged."

He maneuvered the plane between its tie-down chains, shut it down, and got out, then helped me climb from the cramped backseat. Together we secured the chains and began walking toward the small terminal building where his Land Rover and my MG were parked.

"If Oakley lived in Reno, why was he taking flying lessons down here?" I asked. Tufa Lake was a good seventy miles south, in the rugged mountains of California.

"About six, eight months ago his father got sick—inoperable cancer. Scott came home to help his mother care for him. While he was here he figured he'd use the money he was saving on rent to take up flying. There isn't much future in dealing at a casino, and he wanted to get into aviation, build up enough hours to be hired by an airline."

"And other than being a nice kid, he was . . . ?"

"Quiet, serious, very dedicated and purposeful. Set a fast learning pace for himself, even though he couldn't fly as much as he'd've liked, owing to his responsibilities at home. A month ago his father died; he offered to stay on with his mother for a while, but she wouldn't hear of it. Said she knew the separation from his girlfriend had been difficult and she didn't want to prolong it. But he came back down for a lesson each week, and on that last day he'd done three excellent takeoffs and landings. I had full confidence that I could get out of the plane."

"And you noticed nothing emotionally different about him

beforehand?"

"Nothing whatsoever. He was quiet and serious, just like always."

We reached the place where our vehicles were parked, and I perched on the rear of the MG. Hy faced me, leaning against his Rover, arms folded across his chest. His eyes were deeply troubled, and lines of discouragement bracketed his mouth.

I knew what he was feeling: He took on few students, as he didn't need the money and his work for the international security firm in which he held a partnership often took him away from his ranch here in the high desert country for weeks at a time. But when he did take someone on, it was because he recognized great potential in the individual—both as a pilot and as a person who would come to love flying as much as he himself did. Scott Oakley's crash—in his full sight as he stood on the tarmac at the airport awaiting his return—had been devastating to him. And it had also aroused a great deal of self-doubt.

I said, "I assume you want me to look into the reason Oakley killed himself."

"If it's something you feel you can take on."

"Of course I can."

"I'll pay you well."

"For God's sake, you don't have to do that!"

"Look, McCone, you don't ask your dentist friend to drill for free. I'm not going to ask you to investigate for free, either."

"Oh, don't worry, Ripinsky. Nothing in life's free. We'll come up with some suitable way for you to compensate me for my labors."

❖ ❖ ❖

My obvious starting place was Scott Oakley's mother. I called to ask if I could stop by, and set off for her home in Vernon, the small town that hugged the lake's north shore.

It was autumn, the same time of year as when I'd first journeyed here and met Hy. The aspens glowed golden in the hollows of the surrounding hills and above them the sky was a deep blue streaked with high cirrus clouds. In the years that I'd been coming to Tufa

Lake, its water level had slowly risen and was gradually beginning to reclaim the dusty alkali plain that surrounded it—the result of a successful campaign by environmental organizations to stop diversions of its feeder streams to southern California. Avocets, gulls, and other shorebirds had returned to nest on its small islands and feed on the now plentiful brine shrimp.

Strange that Scott Oakley had chosen a place of such burgeoning vitality to end his own life.

❖ ❖ ❖

Jan Oakley was young to have lost a husband, much less outlived her son—perhaps in her early forties. She had the appearance of a once-active woman whose energy had been sapped by sadness and loss, and small wonder: It had been only two weeks since Scott's crash. As we sat in the living room of her neat white prefab house, she handed me a high-school graduation picture of him; he had been blond, blue-eyed, and freckle-faced, with an endearingly serious expression.

"What do you want to ask me about Scott, Ms. McCone?"

"I'm interested in what kind of a person he was. What his state of mind was before the accident."

"You said on the phone that you're a private investigator and a friend of Hy Ripinsky. Is he trying to prove that Scott committed suicide? Because he didn't, you know. I don't care what Hy or the National Transportation Safety Board people think."

"He doesn't want to prove anything. But Hy needs answers—much as I'm sure you do."

"Answers so he can get himself off the hook as far as responsibility for Scott's death is concerned?"

I remained silent. She was hurting, and entitled to her anger.

After a moment Jan Oakley sighed. "All right, that was unfair. Scott admired Hy; he wouldn't want me to blame him. Ask your questions, Ms. McCone."

I asked much the same things as I had of Hy and received much the same answers, as well as Scott's Reno address and the name of his fiancee. "I never even met her," Mrs. Oakley said regretfully, "and I couldn't reach her to tell her about the accident. She knows

192 McCONE AND FRIENDS

by now, of course, but she never even bothered to call."

I'd about written the interview off at that point, but I decided to probe some more on the issue of Scott's state of mind immediately before he left for what was to be his last flying lesson. After my first question, Mrs. Oakley failed to meet my eyes, clearly disturbed.

"I'm sorry to make you relive that day," I said, "but how Scott was feeling is important."

"Yes, I know." For a moment it seemed that she might cry, then she sighed again, more heavily. "He wasn't . . . He was upset when he arrived late the night before."

"Over what?"

"He wouldn't say."

Sometimes instinct warns you when someone isn't telling the whole truth; this was one of those times. "What about the next morning? Did he say then?"

She looked at me, startled. "How did . . . ? All right, yes, he told me. Now I realize I should have stopped him, but he wanted so badly to solo. I thought, One time—what will it matter? All he wanted was to take that little Cessna around the pattern alone one time before he had to give it all up."

"Give up flying? Why?"

"Scott had a physical checkup in Reno the day before. He was diagnosed as having narcolepsy."

❖ ❖ ❖

"Narcolepsy," Hy said. "That's the condition when you fall asleep without any warning?"

"Yes. One of my friends suffers from it. She'll get very sleepy, drop off in the middle of a conversation. One time we were flying down to southern California together; the plane was landing, and she just stopped talking, closed her eyes, and slept till we were on the ground."

"Jesus, can't they treat it?"

"Yes, with ephedrine or amphetamine, but it's not always successful."

"And neither the drugs nor the condition would be acceptable to an FAA medical examiner."

"No. Besides, there's an even more potentially dangerous side to it: A high percentage of the people who have narcolepsy also suffer from a condition called cataplexy in which their body muscles become briefly paralyzed in stressful or emotional situations."

"Such as one would experience on a first solo flight." Hy grimaced and signaled for another round of drinks. We were sitting at the bar at Zelda's, the lakeside tavern at the tip of the peninsula on which Vernon was located. The owner, Bob Zelda, gave him a thumbs-up gesture and quickly slid a beer toward him, a white wine toward me.

"You know, McCone, it doesn't compute. How'd Scott pass his student pilot's medical?"

"The condition was only diagnosed the day before you soloed him. And remember, those medicals aren't a complete workup. They check your history and the obvious—blood pressure, sight, hearing. They're not looking for something that may be developing."

"Still doesn't compute. Scott was a good, responsible kid. Went strictly by the letter as far as the regulations were concerned. I can't believe he'd risk soloing when he knew he could nod off at any time."

"Well, he wanted it very badly."

"Christ, why didn't he level with me? I'd've soloed him without getting out of the plane. He could've flown the pattern with absolutely no input from me, but I'd've been there in case. Doesn't count for getting the license, of course, but his mother told you he'd already decided to give it up."

We drank silently for a minute. I watched Hy's face in the mirrored backbar. He was right: It didn't compute. He needed answers and, now, so did I.

I said, "I'll drive up to Reno tomorrow."

Scott's former apartment was in a newish complex in the hills on the northeast side of Reno, high above the false glitter of the gambling casinos and the tawdry hustle of the Strip. I parked in a windswept graveled area behind it and went knocking on the doors of its immediate neighbors. Only one person was home, and she was house-sitting for the tenant and had never heard of Scott Oakley.

When I started back to my car, a dark-haired man in his mid twenties was getting out of a beat-up Mazda. He started across to the next cluster of apartments, and I followed.

"Help you with something?" he asked, setting down his grocery bag in front of the door to the ground floor unit and fumbling in his pocket for keys.

"The son of a friend of mine lives here—Scott Oakley. Do you know him?"

"Oh God. You haven't heard?"

"Heard what?" I asked, and proceeded to listen to what I already knew. "That's awful," I said when he finished. "How's Christy holding up?"

"Christy?'

"His fiancee."

"Oh, that must be the redhead."

"She and Scott were engaged; I guess I just assumed they lived together."

"No, the apartment's a studio, too small for more than one person. Actually, I didn't know Scott very well, just to say hello to. But one of the other tenants, his downstairs neighbor, did say that Scott told him he wouldn't be living here long, because he planned to marry some woman who worked at the Lucky Strike down on the Strip."

❖ ❖ ❖

The Lucky Strike had pretensions to a gold-rush motif, but basically it wasn't very different from all the other small Nevada casinos: Electronic games and slots beeped, and whooped; bored dealers sent cards sailing over green felt to giddy tourists; waitresses who were supposed to be camp followers, clad in skimpy costumes that no self-respecting camp follower would ever have worn, strolled about serving free watery drinks. The bars, where keno numbers continually flashed on lighted screens, bore such names as The Shaft, Pick 'n Shovel, and The Assay Office.

I located the personnel office and learned that Christy Hertz no longer worked at the casino; she'd failed to show up for her evening cocktail-waitressing shift on the day of Scott Oakley's death and had not so much as called in since. The manager wasn't concerned; on the Strip, he said, women change jobs without notice as often as they do their hair color. But once I explained about Scott's death and my concern for Christy, he softened some. He remembered Scott Oakley from when he'd dealt blackjack there, had thought him a fine young man who would someday do better. The manager's sympathy earned me not only Christy's last known address, but the name of one of her friends who would be on duty that evening in The Shaft, as well as the name of a good friend of Scott who was the night bartender in The Assay Office.

As I started out, the manager called after me, "If you see Christy, toll her her job's waiting."

Christy Hertz's address was in a mobile home park in nearby Sparks. I've always thought of such enclaves as depressing places where older people retreat from the world, but this one was different. There were lots of big trees and planter boxes full of fall marigolds; near the manager's office, a little footbridge led over a man-made stream to a pond where ducks floated. I followed the maze of lanes to Christy's trailer, but no one answered her door. None of the neighbors were around, and the manager's office was closed.

Dead end for now, and the friends didn't come on duty at the Lucky Strike for several hours. So what else could I do here? One thing.

Find a doctor.

Years before, I'd discovered that the key to getting information from anyone was to present myself as a person in a position of authority—and that it was easy to do so without lying. Most people, unless they're paranoid or have something to hide, will cooperate with officials; their motives may range from respect to fear, but the result is the same. I tailored my approach to the situation by first driving to the public library and photocopying the Yellow Pages listings for physicians. Then, in a quiet corner of the stacks there, I went to work with my cell phone.

"My name is Sharon McCone. I'm an investigator looking into the cause of a fatal aviation accident that occurred two weeks ago near Tufa Tower Airport, Mono County, California. The victim was a student pilot who reportedly had been diagnosed with narcolepsy; the diagnosis wasn't noted on FAA form eight-four-two-zero-dash-two, so we assume it was made by a person other than a designated examiner. Would you please check your records to see if Scott Oakley was a patient?"

Only five people asked if I was with the Federal Aviation Agency or the National Transportation Safety Board. When l admitted to being a private investigator working for the victim's mother, two cut me off, citing confidentiality of patient records, but the remainder made searches. All the searches came up negative.

Maybe Clark Morris, Scott's friend who tended bar at The Assay Office, could steer me toward the right doctor.

❖ ❖ ❖

Evening on the Strip: The sun was sinking over the Sierras and the light was golden, vying with the garish neon and coming up a winner. The sidewalks were crowded with people out for a Saturday-night good time—or looking for trouble. A drunken guy in cowboy garb bumped into a middle-aged couple and yelled an obscenity. They stared him down until he slunk off, muttering. I spotted three drug deals going down, two of them to minors. A trio of young Native Americans, probably fresh off one of the nearby reservations, paid an older, cynical-eyed man to buy them a sixpack. Hookers strolled, lonely men's gazes homing in on them like airplanes to radar transmitters. And on the curb a raggedly dressed girl of perhaps thirteen hunched, retching between her pulled-up knees.

I thought of Hy's ranch house, the stone fireplace, the shelves of western novels and Americana to either side of it.  Of the easy chairs where we should now be seated, wineglasses to hand.  Of quiet conversation, a good dinner, and bed . . .

❖   ❖   ❖

"Scott's doctor?" Clark Morris said.  "I don't think he had one."

"He must've gone to somebody for his student pilot's medical exam."

"Excuse me a minute."  The moustached bartender moved to a couple who had just pulled up stools, served them Bud lights, and returned to me.  "You were asking about the medical exam.  I think he got it in Sparks—and only because he had to.  Scott hated doctors; I remember him and Christy having a big blowup once because he wouldn't get a yearly physical."

The cocktail waitress signaled that she needed an order filled.  Morris complied, poured me another glass of wine when he came back.

"Thanks.  The reason I'm asking about the doctor is that Scott saw one the day before he died—"

"No way.  He took Christy on a picnic that day, out at Pyramid Lake, one of their favorite places.  They left real early."

"Well, maybe his mother got it wrong.  It could've been the day before that."

"I don't think so.  Scott was working construction in Sparks all that week."

"Oh?  He wasn't dealing cards anymore?"

"That too—at Harrah's.  He needed the money because he wanted to get married.  He was going to talk to Christy about setting the date while they were on their picnic.  He really loved that woman, said he had to marry her before it was too late."

"Too late for what?"

Morris frowned, then spread his hands.  "Damned if I know."

❖   ❖   ❖

Lynda Collins, Christy Hertz's friend, wore one of the camp follower costumes and looked exhausted.  When the time came for her break from her duties in The Shaft, she sank into the chair opposite me and kicked off her high-heeled shoes, running her stockinged toes through the thick carpet.

"So who hired you?" she asked. "It couldn't've been that no-good bastard of a stepfather of Christy's, trying to find out where she's living now. I know—poor, wimpy Scott."

"You haven't heard about Scott?"

"Heard what?"

"He's dead." I explained the circumstances, watching the shock register in Collins's eyes.

"That's awful!" she said. "I wonder why Christy didn't let me know? I wonder if she knows?"

"I take it you didn't like Scott."

"Oh, he was all right, but he couldn't just let go and have a good time, and he was stifling Christy. The flying was the one real thing he ever did—and look how that turned out."

"I understand he and Christy went on a picnic at Pyramid Lake the day before he died."

"They did? Oh, right, now I remember. Funny that I haven't heard from her since then. I wonder how Scott took it?"

"Took what?"

"Christy was going to break it off with him when they were up there. She met somebody else while Scott was living down at his mom's place—a guy from Sacramento, with big bucks and political connections. Since Scott got back, she couldn't get up the nerve to tell him, but she had to pretty soon because she and this guy are getting married next month. God, I hope she let Scott down easy."

✣ ✣ ✣

Again there was no answer at Christy Hertz's mobile home, but lights shone next door. I went over, knocked, and asked the woman who responded if she'd seen Hertz recently.

"Oh no, honey, it's been at least two weeks. She's probably on vacation, planning her wedding. At least that's what she told me she planned to do."

"When was the last time you saw her?"

"It was . . . Yes, two weeks ago last Thursday. She was leaving with that good-looking blond-haired boy. I guess he's the lucky fellow."

"Did she take any luggage?"

"She must have, but all I saw was a picnic hamper."

The park office was closed. I stood on its steps, debating what could be a foolhardy move, then doubled back to Hertz's. The lights still shone next door, but to the other side all the trailers were dark. I went that way and checked Hertz's windows till I found one that was open a crack, then removed the screen, slid the glass aside, and entered.

Inside I stood listening. The mobile home had the feel of a place that is unoccupied and has been for some time. I took my flashlight from my purse and shone it around, shielding the beam with my hand. Neat stacks of magazines and paperbacks, dishes in a drainer by the sink, a well-scrubbed stove top and counters. My impression of Hertz as a tidy housekeeper was contradicted, however, by a bowl of rotting fruit on the dining table and milk and vegetables spoiling in the fridge.

A tiny hallway led to a single bedroom and bath. The bed was made and clothing hung neatly in the closet. In the bathroom I found cosmetics and a toothbrush in the holder and a round compact containing birth control pills. The date above the last empty space was that of the day before the picnic at Pyramid Lake.

On my way out I spotted the glowing message light on the answering machine. "Christy, this is Dale. Just checking to see how it went. I love you."

"Christy, are you there? If you are, pick up. Okay, call me when you get this message."

"Christy, where the hell are you? For God's sake, call me!"

"Okay, let me guess: You patched it up with Scott. The least you could do is tell me. But then you couldn't tell him about me, now could you?"

"I'm giving you one more chance to explain. If you don't return this call within twenty-four hours, that's it for us!"

Christy Hertz hadn't been too wise in her choice of either man.

I'd never been to Pyramid Lake before, but as I stood on a boat launching ramp on its western shore, I felt as if I'd come home. Like Tufa Lake, it was ancient and surreal, the monolith from which it had taken its name looming darkly; on the far shore clustered domes and pinnacles very like the tufa towers. A high, milky overcast turned the still water to silver; a few boats drifted silently in the distance; above, the migratory waterfowl wheeled, swooping low in their quest for food.

The lake was some thirty miles north of Reno, surrounded by a Paiute Indian reservation. Upon my arrival I'd driven along the shore to Sutcliffe, a village whose prefab homes and trailer parks and small commercial establishments seemed to have been scattered beside the water by some gigantic and indiscriminate hand. There I'd shown the picture Scott Oakley's mother had given me to clerks in grocery stores and boat rental and bait shops—anywhere a couple on a picnic might have stopped—but to no avail. At the offices of the Pyramid Lake Tribal Enterprises—whose function seemed to be to sell fishing licenses—I was advised to try Saltby's Bait and Tackle, some ten minutes north. But Saltby's was closed, and I was fresh out of options.

A sound made me turn away from the water. A rusted-out white pickup, coming this way. It pulled up next to the little store, and an old man got out; he unlocked the door, went inside, and turned the Closed sign over to Open. I hurried up the boat ramp.

The man had longish gray hair and a nut-brown complexion weathered by years of harsh elements, and the reception he gave me was as one of his own. My great-grandmother was a full blooded Shoshone, and my looks reflect her part of the family gene pool; sometimes that's a hindrance, but it can also be a help.

I showed him Scott's picture. "Two weeks ago Thursday, did you see this man? He would've been with a redheaded woman—"

"Yes. They've come here many times. They always rent one of my motorboats and take a picnic to the east shore."

"And you're sure about the date?" He nodded. "What time did they get here?" He reached under the counter and produced a rental log, ran a gnarled finger down the listings. "Ten in the morning. They brought the boat back at four—a long time for them."

"When they brought it back, who returned the keys and paid?"

"The young man."

"Did you see the woman?"

He considered. "No. No, I didn't."

The only other thing I needed to ask him was how to find the office of the tribal police.

The tribal police located what was left of Christy Hertz's body at a little after three that afternoon. It was concealed in a small cavern fashioned by the elements out of a dome on the east shore, and beside it lay a bloodstained rock. Her skull had been crushed.

I could imagine the scenario: Scott pressing her to set a wedding date; Christy telling him she already had, but with someone else. And Scott—the good kid who took life so seriously, who worked hard at doing the right thing and now couldn't understand what he'd done wrong—striking out at her. Striking out in blind anger, because everything he cared about was being taken from him.

After he hid the body, he went through the motions—returning the boat, driving down to Vernon as scheduled. When he was unable to conceal his distress from his mother, he'd come up with a lie that would make his suicide look to be an accident. And then he'd taken the Cessna trainer around the pattern at Tufa Tower— three times, perfectly, so Hy could get out of the plane. Perfectly, so he could end his own life.

The next afternoon I was at the controls of the Citabria, and Hy rode in the backs eat. I put it into a steep-banked turn, keeping the tip of the left wing on Plover Island, where Scott had crashed and burned.

Through our linked headsets, Hy said, "A decent kid is pushed too far, kills somebody he loves, and then kills himself. He was so intent on dying and such a good actor that I hadn't a clue."

"And now his mother will have to live with what happened."

"At least she's got the comfort of knowing he tried to spare her."

"Small comfort."

"Dammit, McCone, why don't suicides think of the people they'll be leaving behind?"

For a moment I didn't speak, concentrating on fighting the winds aloft, trying to keep the wingtip centered on the island. It's an exercise in directional control you learn during flight training, and normally I enjoy it. Not today, though, not in these winds.

I gave up on it and headed south, to check out the obsidian domes at the volcanic field. "Ripinsky," I said, " suicidal people are very self-involved, we all know that. And a lot of them, like Scott, just plain don't want to take responsibility for their own lives."

"So they crap up everybody else's life too."

I put on full throttle and pulled back on the stick; instead of flying over the domes, I'd take it way up, practice some aerobatic maneuvers. Nothing amused Hy more than being along for the ride when I managed to turn a simple loop into something that resembled a corkscrew. And he badly needed to be cheered up right now.

"You know," I said, "it occurs to me that a life lived well is a lot like a solo flight. You accept responsibility, do the best you can, and go on from there."

I glanced back at him; he nodded.

"And that's enough philosophizing for today," I added.

I leveled off, pulled back on the stick, and pushed the throttle in all the way. The plane shot upward on the vertical. In ten seconds, I had him laughing.

## McCONE AND FRIENDS

*McCone and Friends* by Marcia Muller is printed on 60-pound Glatfelter Supple-Opaque recycled paper from 12-point Garamond. The cover painting is by Carol Heyer and the design by Deborah Miller. The first edition comprises three hundred and fifty copies sewn in Roxite-B cloth, signed and numbered by the author, and approximately two thousand copies in trade softcover. Each of the clothbound copies includes a separate pamphlet, *The Time of the Wolves* by Marcia Muller. The book was printed and bound by Thomson-Shore, Inc., Dexter, Michigan, and published in January 2000 by Crippen & Landru Publishers, Norfolk, Virginia.

# CRIPPEN & LANDRU, PUBLISHERS

P. O. Box 9315
Norfolk, VA 23505
E-mail: CrippenL@Pilot.Infi.Net

Crippen & Landru publishes first edition short-story collections by important detective and mystery writers. Most books are issued in two editions: trade softcover, and signed, limited clothbound with either a typescript page from the author's files or an additional story in a separate pamphlet. The following books have been published:

*Speak of the Devil* by John Dickson Carr. 1994. Eight-part impossible crime mystery broadcast on BBC radio in 1941. Introduction by Tony Medawar; cover design by Deborah Miller. Published only in softcover.
Out of Print

*The McCone Files* by Marcia Muller. 1995. Fifteen Sharon McCone short stories by the creator of the modern female private eye, including two written especially for the collection. Winner of the Anthony Award for Best Short Story collection. Introduction by the author; cover painting by Carol Heyer. Signed, limited edition, Out of Print
Softcover, fourth printing, $15.00

*The Darings of the Red Rose* by Margery Allingham. 1995. Eight crook stories about a female Robin Hood, written in 1930 by the creator of the classic sleuth, Albert Campion. Introduction by B. A. Pike; cover design by Deborah Miller. Published only in softcover.
Out of Print

*Diagnosis: Impossible, The Problems of Dr. Sam Hawthorne* by Edward D. Hoch. 1996. Twelve stories about the country doctor who solves "miracle problems," written by the greatest current expert on the challenge-to-the-reader story. Introduction by the author; Sam Hawthorne chronology by Marvin Lachman; cover painting by Carol Heyer.
Signed, limited edition, Out of Print
Softcover, Out of Stock; due Spring 2000

*Spadework: A Collection of "Nameless Detective" Stories* by Bill Pronzini. 1996. Fifteen stories, including two written for the collection, by a Grandmaster of the Private Eye tale. Introduction by Marcia Muller; afterword by the author; cover painting by Carol Heyer.
Signed, limited edition, Out of Print
Softcover, $16.00

*Who Killed Father Christmas? And Other Unseasonable Demises* by Patricia Moyes. 1996. Twenty-one stories ranging from holiday homicides to village villainies to Caribbean crimes. Introduction by the author; cover design by Deborah Miller.          Signed, limited edition, $40.00
Softcover, $16.00

*My Mother, The Detective: The Complete "Mom" Short Stories*, by James Yaffe. 1997. Eight stories about the Bronx armchair maven who solves crimes between the chicken soup and the *schnecken*. Introduction by the author; cover painting by Carol Heyer.          Signed, limited edition, Out of Print
Softcover, $15.00

*In Kensington Gardens Once...* by H.R.F. Keating. 1997. Ten crime and mystery stories taking place in London's famous park, including two written for this collection, by the recipient of the Cartier Diamond Dagger for Lifetime Achievement. Illustrations and cover by Gwen Mandley.
Signed, limited edition, $35.00
Softcover, $12.00

*Shoveling Smoke: Selected Mystery Stories* by Margaret Maron. 1997. Twenty-two stories by the Edgar-award winning author, including all the short cases of Sigrid Harald and Deborah Knott (with a new Judge Knott story). Introduction and prefaces to each story by the author; cover painting by Victoria Russell.          Signed, limited edition, Out of Print
Softcover, third printing, $16.00

*The Man Who Hated Banks and Other Mysteries* by Michael Gilbert. 1997. Eighteen stories by the recipient of the Mystery Writers of America's Grandmaster Award, including mysteries featuring Inspectors Petrella and Hazlerigg, rogue cop Bill Mercer, and solicitor Henry Bohun. Introduction by the author; cover painting by Deborah Miller.
Signed, limited edition, Out of Print
Softcover, second printing, $16.00

*The Ripper of Storyville and Other Ben Snow Tales* by Edward D. Hoch. 1997. The first fourteen historical detective stories about Ben Snow, the wandering gunslinger who is often confused with Billy the Kid. Introduction by the author; Ben Snow chronology by Marvin Lachman; cover painting by Barbara Mitchell.          Signed, limited edition, Out of Print
Softcover, $16.00

*Do Not Exceed the Stated Dose* by Peter Lovesey. 1998. Fifteen crime and mystery stories, including two featuring Peter Diamond and two with Bertie, Prince of Wales. Preface by the author; cover painting by Carol Heyer. Signed, limited edition, Out of Print
Softcover, $16.00

*Renowned Be Thy Grave; Or, The Murderous Miss Mooney* by P. M. Carlson. 1998. Ten stories about Bridget Mooney, the Victorian actress who becomes criminously involved in important historical events. Introduction by the author; cover design by Deborah Miller. Signed, limited edition, $40.00
Softcover, $16.00

*Carpenter and Quincannon, Professional Detective Services* by Bill Pronzini. 1998. Nine detective stories, including one written for this volume, set in San Francisco during the 1890's. Introduction by the author; cover painting by Carol Heyer. Signed, limited edition, Out of Print
Softcover, second printing, $16.00

*Not Safe After Dark and Other Stories* by Peter Robinson. 1998. Thirteen stories about Inspector Banks and others, including one written for this volume. Introduction and prefaces to each story by the author; cover painting by Victoria Russell. Signed, limited edition, Out of Print
Softcover, second printing, $16.00

*The Concise Cuddy, A Collection of John Francis Cuddy Stories* by Jeremiah Healy. 1998. Seventeen stories about the Boston private eye by the Shamus Award winner. Introduction by the author; cover painting by Carol Heyer. Signed, limited edition, Out of Print
Softcover, $17.00

*One Night Stands* by Lawrence Block. 1999. Twenty-four early tough crime tales by a Grandmaster of the Mystery Writers of America. Introduction by the author; cover painting by Deborah Miller. Published only in a signed, limited edition. Out of Print

*All Creatures Dark and Dangerous* by Doug Allyn. 1999. Seven long stories about the veterinarian detective Dr. David Westbrook by the Edgar and Ellery Queen Readers Award winner. Introduction by the author; cover painting by Barbara Mitchell. Signed, limited edition, Out of Print
Softcover, $16.00

*Famous Blue Raincoat: Mystery Stories* by Ed Gorman. 1999. Twelve detective and crime stories by the author described as "great, possibly one of *the* greats" by the British mystery journal *Shots*. "If George Orwell had written thrillers, he might have written them this way; never a word too many, never a word too few, never a word that doesn't come from the heart." Introduction by the author; cover design by Gail Cross.

Signed, limited edition, $42.00

Softcover, $17.00

*The Tragedy of Errors and Others* by Ellery Queen. 1999. Published to celebrate the seventieth anniversary of the first Ellery Queen novel, this book contains the lengthy plot outline of the final, never published EQ novel, six previously uncollected stories, and essays, tributes, and reminiscences of EQ by family members, friends, and some of the finest current mystery writers. Limited edition, Out of Print

Softcover, $16.00

*McCone and Friends* by Marcia Muller. 2000. Seven of Muller's recent mystery stories—three told by Sharon McCone and four by her colleagues, Rae Kelleher (including a novella), Mick Savage, Ted Smalley, and Hy Ripinsky. Introduction by the author; cover painting by Carol Heyer.

Signed, limited edition, $40.00

Softcover, $16.00

## Pamphlets Published by Crippen & Landru

Many of our limited editions include a separately printed pamphlet: *The Problem of the Emperor's Mushrooms* (to accompany James Yaffe's *My Mother, The Detective*), *Walking in Kensington Gardens* (to accompany H.R.F. Keating's *In Kensington Gardens Once . . .*), *Five Rings in Reno* (to accompany Edward D. Hoch's *The Ripper of Storyville*), *Murder by Christmas Tree* (to accompany Peter Lovesey's *Do Not Exceed the Stated Dose*), *Farewell the Plumed Troop* (to accompany P.M. Carlson's *Renowned Be Thy Grave*), *City Life* (to accompany Jeremiah Healy's *The Concise Cuddy*), *Make a Prison* (to accompany Lawrence Block's *One Night Stands*), *Saint Margaret's Kitten* (to accompany Doug Allyn's *All Creatures Dark and Dangerous*), *Mom and Dad at Home* (to accompany Ed Gorman's *Famous Blue Raincoat*), *Selected Facsimile Pages of a Draft of The Tragedy of Errors* (to accompany Ellery Queen's *The Tragedy of Errors*), and *The Time of the Wolves* (to accompany Marcia Muller's *McCone and Friends*). These pamphlets are not available separately but are listed here for completeness.

Crippen & Landru also published pamphlets to acknowledge two of the "Ghosts of Honor" at Malice Domestic conventions. Each one contains previously unpublished or uncollected material. The pamphlets were given to each person in attendance as well as to our Standing Order Subscribers; copies are no longer available from the publisher.

*The Adventure of the Scarecrow and the Snowman, A Radio Mystery* by Ellery Queen. 1998.
*The Detective in Fiction and Harem-Scarem* by John Dickson Carr. 1999.

Published as a Christmas gift to Standing Order Subscribers (and not for sale) was:

*Room to Let, A Radio-Play* by Margery Allingham. 1999.

## Forthcoming Short-Story Collections

*Challenge the Widow Maker and Other Stories of People in Peril* by Clark Howard.
*The Velvet Touch* by Edward D. Hoch.
*Stakeout on Page Street and Other DKA Files* by Joe Gores.
*Fortune's Fortunes: Dan Fortune's Casebook* by Michael Collins.
*Tales Out of School* by Carolyn Wheat.
*Strangers in Town: Three Newly Discovered Stories* by Ross Macdonald.
*The Spotted Cat and Other Mysteries: The Casebook of Inspector Cockrill* by Christianna Brand.
*Adam and Eve on a Raft: Mystery Stories* by Ron Goulart.
*Kisses of Death: Nate Heller Stories* by Max Allan Collins.
*The Reluctant Detective and Other Stories* by Michael Z. Lewin.
*Nine Sons and Other Mysteries* by Wendy Hornsby.
*The Dark Snow and Other Stories* by Brendan DuBois.
*The Adventure of the Murdered Moths and Other Radio Mysteries* by Ellery Queen.
*Solving Problems* by Bill Pronzini and Barry N. Malzberg.

Crippen & Landru offers discounts to individuals and institutions who place Standing Order Subscriptions for its forthcoming publications. Please write or e-mail for details.